Murder in a Lavender Daze

Kensington Books by Daryl Wood Gerber:

The Aroma Wellness Mystery series

Essence of Foul Play

Murder in a Lavender Daze

The Literary Dining Mystery series

Murder on the Page

Murder by the Millions

The Fairy Garden Mystery series

A Sprinkling of Murder

A Glimmer of a Clue

A Hint of Mischief

A Flicker of a Doubt

A Twinkle of Trouble

Murder in a Lavender Daze

Daryl Wood Gerber

Kensington Publishing Corp.
kensingtonbooks.com

KENSINGTON BOOKS are published by

Kensington Publishing Corp.
900 Third Avenue
New York, NY 10022

ISBN: 978-1-4967-5152-2
First Trade Paperback Printing: May 2026

ISBN: 978-1-4967-5153-9 (e-book)

10 9 8 7 6 5 4 3 2 1

Printed in the United States of America

The authorized representative in the EU for product safety and compliance
is eucomply OU, Parnu mnt 139b-14, Apt 123
Tallinn, Berlin 11317, hello@eucompliancepartner.com

To all of you who make me want to write and entertain: It is my sole purpose. I don't try to educate. I don't try to illuminate. I want you to feel and empathize and find pleasure in reading mysteries.

"Feelings come and go like clouds in a windy sky.
Conscious breathing is my anchor."
—Thich Nhat Hanh

Cast of Characters

Addison Lacey, née McKay
Brady Cash, owner of Hideaway Café
Cara Guest, Addison's friend
Courtney Kelly, Fairy Garden shop owner
Dottie Summers, Emma's neighbor
Dylan Summers, police detective
Emma Brennan, owner of Aroma Wellness Spa
Everett Brennan, Emma's father
Frederick Gibson, brother of Gianna
Gianna McKay, née Gibson, Addison's mother
Hattie Hopewell, Happy Diggers Garden Club leader
Idha Gibson, wife of Frederick
Kate Brennan, Emma's mother
Lissa Reade, Emma's grandmother
Meryl Kim, manicurist
Mah Kim, Meryl's mother and receptionist at spa
O'Malley McKay, golf course designer
Peyton Pelagatti, Gianna's friend
Riley Rhimes, Addison's friend
Sierra Reade, Emma's cousin
Sophie Reade, Emma's aunt
Tatiana Perez, Addison's friend
Teresa Rodriguez, police officer
Ursula Josipovic, fortune teller
Wyatt Lacey, husband of Addison
Yoly Acebo, employee at Aroma Wellness gift shop
Zane Ashford, tai chi instructor

Fairies and Animals

Dewberry, nurturer fairy
Fiona, righteous fairy
Merryweather Rose of Song, a guardian fairy
Vivi, Emma's cat

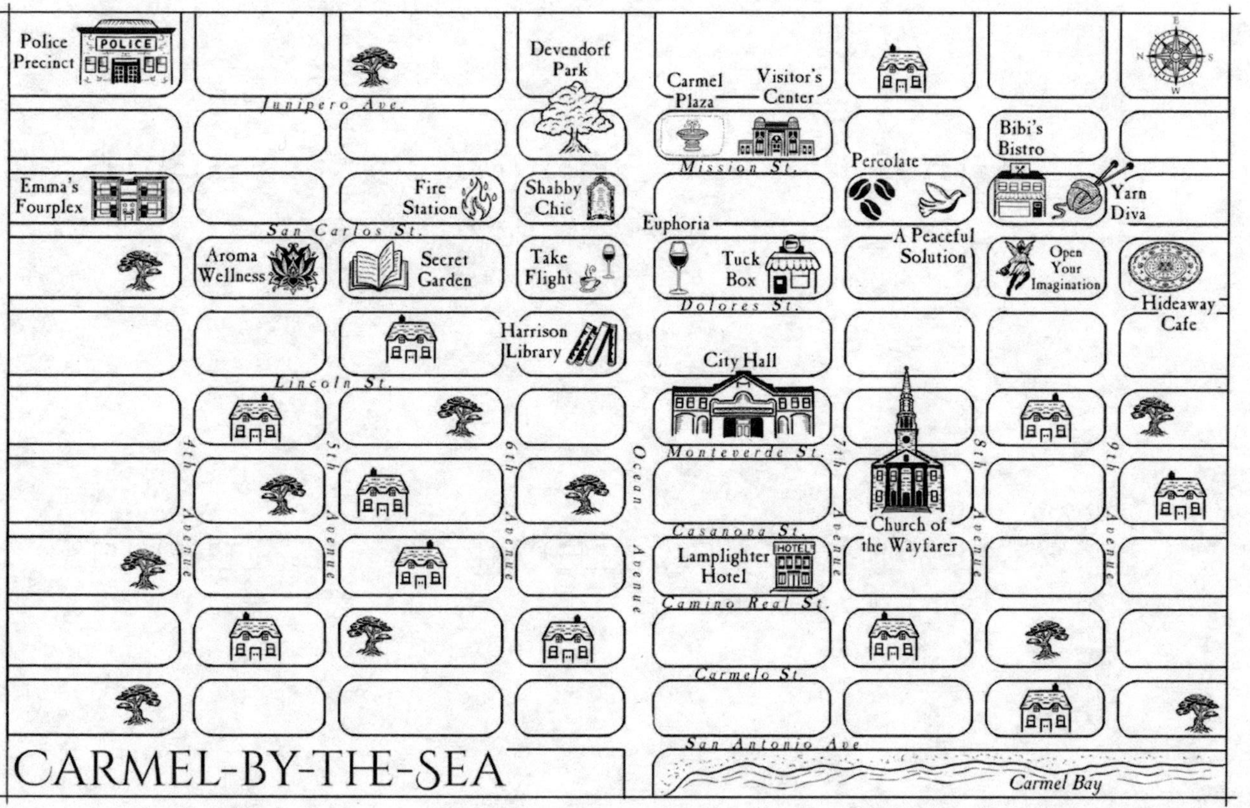
CARMEL-BY-THE-SEA
Police Precinct
POLICE
Devendorf Park
Carmel Plaza
Visitor's Center
Junipero Ave.
Bibi's Bistro
Mission St.
Percolate
Emma's Fourplex
Fire Station
Shabby Chic
Yarn Diva
Euphoria
San Carlos St.
A Peaceful Solution
Aroma Wellness
Secret Garden
Take Flight
Tuck Box
Open Your Imagination
Dolores St.
Hideaway Cafe
Harrison Library
City Hall
Lincoln St.
Monteverde St.
4th Avenue
5th Avenue
6th Avenue
Ocean Avenue
7th Avenue
8th Avenue
9th Avenue
Church of the Wayfarer
Casanova St.
Lamplighter Hotel
HOTEL
Camino Real St.
Carmelo St.
San Antonio Ave
Carmel Bay
N
E
S
W

Chapter 1

I was adjusting the spa menu to reflect the Halloween-themed treatments we would offer during the month of October, like the pumpkin spice facial and apple cider wraps—the latter being great for detoxification—when the silent alarm flashed in big red letters on my computer screen and cell phone. *Alert! Gift Shop! Alert! Gift Shop!* My insides snagged. Although Aroma Wellness Spa, gift shop, and café were located in the aptly named Courtyard of Peace, one of the many charming courtyards in Carmel-by-the-Sea, whatever was going on did not sound in the least serene.

"Sierra!" I rasped.

My cousin, who was in charge of the café, was on her break and pouring a glass of cucumber water from the pitcher by the spa's reception desk. "What's wrong?"

"I don't know. There might be a break-in at the shop."

"Doubtful. I saw Yoly enter earlier and switch off the alarm."

A few months ago, two incidents had occurred that had scared the spit out of me. Within a week, I'd installed security systems at Aroma Wellness, as well as where I lived. Until now, nothing untoward had happened at either location. "Yoly must have triggered the—"

"Mine!" a woman screamed in the courtyard.

"Mine!" a second woman bellowed.

Through the plate-glass window we'd decorated for Halloween with silk spiders and spiderwebs, I caught sight of two women having a tug-of-war with a small pillow. It wasn't a robbery, but it wasn't good. One of the women had pink streaks in her waist-length blond braid. The other and larger of the two had flaming reddish-brown hair.

"Sierra, I think Yoly activated the self-monitored alarm." One that wouldn't alert the security company, only someone at the spa. "Help me!" I raced outside, patting down my tawny hair, which was slightly frizzy from the cooler autumn air. At the same time, I made sure the front of my *Breathe Easy* T-shirt was smooth. Even though I donned comfortable clothing when working, and yoga pants or leggings and colorful tees were the norm, I wanted to present a strong persona to the combatants.

"Mine!" the woman with the braid repeated.

Usually the sound of the burbling fountain soothed my soul, but the scene playing out was making the hackles on my neck rise.

"Mine, mine, mine!" the woman repeated like a ravenous seagull. She was in her early thirties, I guessed, and had lethal-looking teeth, which were visible as she snarled at her rival.

The younger woman, closer to my age—twenty-five—glowered. A dragon couldn't look as fierce. "Let me have it!"

The smallish lavender-infused pillow they were tugging was one of a collection I'd purchased from a talented Etsy designer. Lavender was a delicious scent that could help a person experience a more tranquil and rejuvenating night's sleep. If only the two opponents would drift into slumber.

"Over my dead body!" The younger one grabbed the older woman's braid and yanked.

"Ow!"

I cleared my throat and approached. "Ahem. Hello, I'm Emma Brennan, the owner of Aroma Wellness. Please . . ." I dared to press a hand on each of their shoulders. It was a calming technique I'd learned when studying meditation in Tibet. "Breathe." I inhaled deeply and let it out slowly as an example.

Neither obeyed.

"Breathe," I repeated more firmly. "Let's be civil."

From a safe distance, Sierra clapped her hands. "C'mon, you two, show some decorum." She didn't draw nearer. She was having too much fun watching me attempt to be an enforcer.

A small crowd was gathering in the courtyard. Customers in robes were peeking through the window from inside the spa. A few from the café were catching a glimpse, as well. Dang. I didn't want to lose clientele because of a contentious spat. I had to get this under control.

Yoly Acebo, a delightful Latina woman and coordinator of the gift shop, emerged in the store's doorway, hands on hips. Her brown hair was knotted in a messy bun and her pretty face pinched with exasperation. The women must have started fighting inside the shop and taken their argument outdoors.

I signaled to Yoly I had this. "Ladies, be advised this is a spa, which means it's a noise-free zone. You're supposed to be relaxing and—"

"I preordered this one," Braid Woman whined, shaking off my hand. "I know because it's sage green."

"Well, mine isn't here yet." The younger shimmied to be free of me. "And I'll settle for green. I arrived at the gift shop first."

"But the saleswoman wasn't supposed to show you mine."

"Well, she did."

"And you stole it!" Braid Woman bared her teeth again.

"I paid cash."

"And ran out!"

Their ardent refusal to comply didn't deter me. I was slightly taller than both of them, and thanks to an encounter with a killer a couple of months ago, I had been studying karate and tai chi ever since. I was no expert. A bantamweight wrestler could take me down. But I had some skills, which wouldn't be hampered by my yoga pants. I glared at my cousin to chide her for keeping her distance. Granted, she was pint-size and probably worrying about how effective she might be in a tussle, but I knew firsthand she was fierce. If only she was holding a carving knife.

"Why don't we go inside for a mindful meditation session?" I refocused on the squabblers, mentally urging them to agree. "My treat."

"She stole my pillow," Braid Woman carped.

"Are you deaf?" the other said. "I paid cash."

"Liar."

"Gimme."

"No, you gimme."

The way they were hissing at each other reminded me of crows I'd observed fighting over a snake that had been flattened by a car. Man, how their beaks and talons had worked overtime.

"Breathe, please," I tried again. "We have more pillows coming tomorrow for a party. I'll make sure two green ones are among them." The item they were tangling over was mangled.

"A party?" The younger woman stopped pulling, which sent her adversary sailing backward.

Sierra caught Braid Woman before she pitched headlong into a set of wrought-iron chairs. *Phew*. The spa was up-to-date on its insurance payments, but I didn't know if our plan would cover this kind of fracas.

"We love parties." The younger woman tucked the pillow beneath her arm and brushed a strand of hair coyly behind one ear.

We? Did they know each other? Carmel was such a small community. Were they friends or frenemies? Did it matter?

"May we attend?" she asked, her voice suddenly as sweet as honey.

"Not unless you know the celebrant," I replied.

"Perchance we do," she said.

Appearing equally enthralled, Braid Woman drew near. "Yes, *perchance*. What's she celebrating?"

"Divorce," I said.

The two exchanged a baffled look.

"Yeah." I laughed. "I didn't think you'd want to attend a happily divorced party."

A happily divorced party was exactly what it sounded like. Addison Lacey, née McKay, a regular spa client who was a couple of years older than me, had been married for eight years, but she didn't love her husband any longer, if she ever had. He'd tricked her, she alleged, by convincing her he was Mr. Nice when he turned out to be a duplicitous, controlling young man. She was through, through, through with him. In less than two weeks the divorce would be truly final. California laws could be challenging in that regard. In order to begin the journey of becoming a better version of herself, she wanted to celebrate big-time.

"Only friends and family are invited," I added. "Listen, why don't you come with me to the gift shop and we'll sort out your issue?" I held out a hand for the pillow, but the younger woman seemed reluctant to release her hold on it. "Pretty please? I'll offer you a ten percent discount on whichever color you choose. Good?"

She smiled and handed it over.

Yoly beckoned them. Sierra and I followed as they traipsed across the travertine tile.

Sierra said under her breath, "I'm coming, too. In case."

I threw her the side-eye. "Yeah, you were so helpful back there."

She tittered.

When I reached Yoly, I said, "How are you doing?"

She whispered, "I couldn't . . . they wouldn't . . ."

I patted her arm. "It's fine. Crisis averted. Thanks for triggering the alarm."

"It worked? I didn't hear a thing."

"That's what *silent alert* means," Sierra jibed.

The company I'd hired had suggested the soundless version so, should there be a false warning, it wouldn't scare neighbors or family. An added benefit was intruders rarely knew the police were on their way. I'd protested, saying the noisy kind might be a better way to scare off a burglar, but the sales rep maintained if an intruder intended to steal, they would not run away because of the noise. The rep also suggested installing a panic button under the counter by the cash register.

I stepped inside the shop after Sierra and drew in the heavenly scent of burning cinnamon candles. Yoly had done a bit of decorating for the season, adding natural items like pumpkins, gourds, and autumn leaves, all in muted colors to maintain a relaxing vibe. It looked perfect. "Yoly," I said softly, "I bet you wish you were a masseuse instead of the shop manager right about now. Am I right?"

She was working as manager until she obtained a massage therapist's license. "About my future . . ." She scrunched up her mouth. "I'm having second thoughts. Can we talk about my plans sometime this week? Not now. We have to handle this situation pronto."

"Sure," I said, though sadness cut through me. I had been looking forward to having her work as a masseuse, but if the path wasn't right, it wasn't meant to be. I was skilled at going with the flow. Okay, *almost* skilled. The breakup with my last boyfriend still saddened me.

Heading for the counter, I caught sight of the plaque I'd hung above the register to the right of a starburst mirror. I liked posting inspirational messages in all three of the spa's locations. At home, too. This one read: *A creative project is a moving target. You never end up where you start. ~ Evangeline Lilly*. She was the actress who'd come to fame as one of the leads on the hit TV show *Lost*. As with all the quotes I put up, this one filled me with joy because it evoked a memory of bringing Aroma Wellness to fruition. How desperately I'd wanted to create a spa similar to the one my aunt owned in Sedona—a place where people could relax and find their centers through massage and sound baths. Aunt Sophie was the person who had taught me how to make and employ essential oils. She was a master at crystal divination and held fast to the belief that a crystal reading could offer spiritual insight and clarity as well as energy alignment and healing. I'd grown up in Carmel-by-the-Sea and knew since the moment I turned thirteen the town would be the perfect place for my own spa. With its charming environment, the salty scent of the Pacific Ocean, the lush vegetation and towering cypress trees, ingenuity and calm reigned supreme.

Designing the gift shop had taken some work. I'd wanted it to be soothing yet packed with items that would please customers. The walls were painted a soft mossy green. On the shelves stood dozens of books about how to find bliss. We sold wind chimes and small gongs and Chinese stress-reducing Baoding balls. We also carried geodes and crystals, obelisks and jewelry. Thanks to savvy marketing advice, we'd clustered many of the geodes and larger items like Zen gardens on the glass sales counter to prompt impulse buys. Currently, the gardens, which Yoly had decorated with tiny skulls and bats nestled among the sand, were a fan favorite.

"Ladies"—I addressed the pillow fighters—"we have color choices other than green."

The pillow designer lived fifteen miles north in Monterey. She'd assured me a quick order wouldn't be difficult, seeing as shipping delays would be a nonissue. I'd found her because Addison, the soon-to-be happily-divorced divorcée, had introduced me to her. She was also an Etsy entrepreneur. She designed gorgeous, handmade greeting cards. I'd purchased a few.

"Now I want pink," Braid Woman decided.

Of course she did. To go with the pink swath of hair weaved into her lengthy plait.

"And I want blue," the younger one said. "To go with my eyes."

Sierra said, "I believe your eyes are green."

"They turn blue when I wear blue. They're like chameleons."

"Whatever you desire. Yoly will handle your order," I said. "Thanks for understanding."

Sierra and I exited the shop and almost ran smack-dab into Addison. With her pixie-style black hair, sweet face, and round eyes—she'd coated them with an extra-heavy dose of mascara—she reminded me of Betty Boop, the iconic cartoon character from the 1930s. Her formfitting, polka-dotted dress further cemented the notion. It wasn't a costume. Addison loved to wear quirky fashions.

"Emma, Sierra, hi! I'm ready to finalize plans," she announced. "The fun and all of our treatments start tomorrow. Eek!" Her excitement was contagious. "Here's the guest list." She waggled a tablet of Halloween paper with a list of names. "I'll text it to you, Emma." She referred to her notepad as we crossed the patio and entered the spa.

My cell phone *pinged* in my yoga pants pocket.

Addison turned in a circle. *"Ooh,* I love this spa. It's my happy place."

"Glad to hear it," I said.

I'd put a lot of thought into the spa's design. The check-in desk was brass-and-hardwood and polished to a shine. The beverage cart to the right of the desk held glasses and a pitcher for water, plus an urn for coffee and another for hot water. A tea caddy filled with herbal teas stood at the ready, alongside accoutrements. A pair of giant ferns in soft green ceramic pots flanked the entry. A magazine rack held health and wellness issues that customers could browse before their appointments. Two sea-blue-and-sea-green armchairs invited customers to sit and relax. How relieved I was the pillow fighters hadn't burst into reception and destroyed the tranquility.

"Come with me." I beckoned Addison and my cousin, and turned down the hall.

I pivoted into my office, which was sparse. Sunlight filtered through a window that opened to the alleyway between our courtyard and the neighboring building. A feng shui ceramic water fountain sat on the corner of the white desk and emitted a soothing burble. My spiritually centered aunt told me moving water roused one's life force. I wondered what she'd say about the two-foot-tall haunted house I had placed beside it.

Addison swept into the room, her voice breathy. "The guests include Mother, Daddy, and bridesmaids who told me the marriage would never work out."

"Guess they were right," Sierra quipped.

"Don't tell them so. They will gloat." Addison hiccupped a laugh. "Also on the list are my aunt Peyton, who isn't really my aunt—she's my mother's best friend—and my aunt Idha." She glanced up. "Did I ever tell you Idha's name means intelligence and perception in Hindi?"

"No," I replied. We were friendly but hadn't spent a lot of one-on-one time together.

"Wait until you meet her. She's smart and clever and gorgeous with her lustrous black hair and hazelnut skin. Did I tell you she worked for the CIA, and after she retired, she became an independent editor for spy novels and thrillers?"

I did recall that tidbit.

"She writes, too. Short stories."

"Talented," I said.

"She sure is." Using the fingers of both hands, Addison mimed her head exploding at the concept. "I mean, I graduated college, but I don't have half her brain. She's a good match for my uncle. He's super bright. A bit quirky, but I love him. Now for the menu . . ."

My cell phone *pinged* with more texts from Addison.

"I hope you can make everything, Sierra." Addison peered at my cousin.

"I'm sure I can." Sierra had been working as a sous-chef in a vegan restaurant when I convinced our grandmother, Lissa Reade, the head librarian at Harrison Library, to fund the Aroma Wellness venture and bring on Sierra as partner and chef at the café. Not only did Sierra make deliciously healthy smoothies and treats, but she could compete head-to-head with Michelin star chefs, thanks to her education at a renowned culinary institution in St. Helena, California. Her duck confit was to die for. Her dry cure of salt and herbs and spices was the reason, she boasted.

"We set up appointments for almost everyone tomorrow. Daddy

included." Addison was the apple of her father's eye. "FYI, Mother will want to make sure you don't muss her hair when you give her a facial on Thursday."

"I'll do my best." I'd hired extra masseuses and technicians from spas north and south on the days I needed to accommodate all of Addison's requests.

"At the party a week from Saturday, I'd like a champagne toast."

Aroma Wellness didn't have a liquor license, but for a private party on the patio, we would be allowed to serve it, seeing as Addison was providing the wine and we wouldn't be charging any fees. California had very restrictive regulations, but last month we'd double-checked the rules in order to throw another private event, and we'd been in compliance.

Addison's mobile chimed. She glanced at the readout. "Ugh. Wyatt. Again." Her tone was bitter and dismissive. "He phoned me earlier and asked why I was going through with the divorce. He begged me to reconsider. As if. I told you he has ASPD, didn't I?"

"Yes." Afterward, I'd searched the internet for the diagnosis. People with antisocial personality disorder often sought treatment. Per Addison, Wyatt had not.

"He's not a sociopath," she said in his defense. She'd said the same the first time she'd mentioned his condition. "But he's a liar and insincere, and he had an affair. I mean, c'mon. I'm so done. I actually told him to suck eggs." The way she grinned made her look like a maniacal Betty Boop.

Sierra gasped. "Addison, don't lash out. What if he takes it the wrong way? Someone with his ailment might, you know . . ."

"Nah, don't worry," Addison said. "I've told him to suck eggs on other occasions. He's never been abusive. He's threatened to harm himself, but he won't. It's just his passive-aggressive way to manipulate me. I've been to counseling—a lot of it—and I'm stronger now. Thank you, therapy!" She resumed studying her notepad and muttered, "Where was I? Oh, right!" She reached into her oversize red tote and pulled out a package of handmade cards tied with ribbon. "I made these for my besties." She held them out.

I took the cards, removed the ribbon, and shuffled through them. "They're gorgeous."

The quilling technique she'd employed required using strips of paper that she rolled, looped, or curled to make different shapes and glued together to create decorative designs.

"Look inside one," she said.

Using a stylized font, she'd written, *Divorce is final and sometimes brutal, but you are my guiding light. I am forever grateful. ~ Addison.*

"What a lovely sentiment," I murmured.

"They all say the same thing because, well, I didn't want my friends to compare and contrast. Smart, right? They've been there for me from the outset." She pressed a hand to her heart. "I couldn't have made the decision to leave Wyatt if not for them."

"Addison!" a woman called.

"Oof. It's my mother," she whispered to us.

"Is anything wrong with her being here?" Sierra asked.

"No, of course not, but she can be, um, daunting. Her energy is, like, through the roof."

"Darling." Gianna McKay, a repeat customer at the spa, made quite an entrance. She always did. She was a statuesque woman with chocolate-brown eyes and cheekbones that could cut ice. Her shoulder-length, golden-red hair framed her face perfectly. Prior to marrying her husband, she'd been a fashion model. When her bookings grew slimmer, she turned to selling real estate. When she realized she was bored with all the success, she gave up and decided to play golf, tennis, and canasta. During the first facial I'd ever given her, she'd confided she ought to donate her time to a worthy cause, except she couldn't make up her mind about which one . . . hence, not donating to any yet. I'd suggested Family2Family, a group that assisted impoverished families. The notion hadn't sparked interest.

Over her shoulder, she yelled, "O'Malley, they're in here."

"Shh, Mother," Addison warned. "There are guests getting treatments."

There was little resemblance between the two women other than the length of their hair.

"Sorry." Gianna bussed her daughter on the cheek, leaving a trace of red lipstick.

Addison dutifully wiped it off with her knuckle.

O'Malley McKay tramped through the door and grabbed his daughter in a bear hug. Addison said she took after her father's side of the family, and she was right. Like his daughter, O'Malley had an easy grin, and his pointy right ear gave him an impish appeal. "Hello, Cupcake. Emma. Sierra." Not a hair of his steel-blond flattop style was out of place. If he hadn't become a golf course designer, with his golden voice and gift for gab, I could see him making it in politics or podcasting. "All the details handled?"

"Everything but the payment," I said to them as a group.

"Ahem. On you, dear," O'Malley said to his wife.

He and Gianna had agreed to cover the cost of the happily-divorced party. From what I gathered, neither of them had liked Wyatt, but Addison had been headstrong and determined to marry the guy. Were they now saying *I told you so* in private, or were they taking the high road?

"Twenty percent up front," Gianna said to me.

"Correct."

Sierra said, "Plus the cost of the items needed to make all the appetizers for the soiree." She rattled off a number.

"Yes, of course." Gianna rummaged in her Prada purse. "Drat. I don't have my checkbook."

"Are you kidding?" O'Malley squawked. "After I explicitly reminded you—"

"Don't carp at me. I put it in my purse." She glared at her daughter. "Did you borrow it before you left the house?"

Addison gawked. "Me? Why would I borrow your checkbook?"

"I know you've forged my signature a time or two."

"Solely when you've told me to do so."

"By the way, are you the one who's been eating all the ice cream in the freezer?" Gianna asked. "Straight out of the carton? I've given you the run of our home, and what do I get in return?"

"Gianna!" O'Malley barked. "Cut it out."

"If you're not careful"—Gianna aimed a finger at her daughter—"I'll boot you to the curb."

"Don't guilt me, Mother," Addison snapped. "I'll be moving on in less than ten days." Until she was settled in a place of her own, she had relocated all her personal items and card-making materials to the extra bedroom of her parents' house.

"Don't rely on your trust fund to pay for everything," her mother said.

"I'm not. I won't. I make a good living."

Gianna aimed a finger at Addison. "I'm warning you, young lady—"

"Enough, Gianna!" O'Malley shook his head. "Honestly, woman, you can be petty. We offered the house to our only daughter so she could have our support during this trying time. As for your checkbook, don't take it out on her. You thought you put it in your purse, but I'll bet you left it on the side table in the foyer. End of story." He turned graciously to me and Sierra. "I'll give you a credit card for the twenty percent. My wife will pay you cash for the food items. Won't you, dear?"

She leveled him with a searing look that could start a bonfire.

Chapter 2

Addison's parents stomped out, and Sierra and I let out a wheeze of relief, which prompted Addison to offer apologies for them. To make up for the brouhaha, she invited Sierra and me to dinner tonight at her mother's house and asked us to bring our grandmother. Nana Lissa was friendly with Gianna. Addison assured us it wouldn't be fancy. "However, needless to say, prepare for a few fireworks. As you saw, my mother and father can get pretty intense."

"No kidding," Sierra said. "Intense doesn't cut it. Your mother is passionate to the max."

"Ain't love grand?" I joked. "And it's only Monday. Can you imagine the exchanges they'll be having by Friday? But I knew they'd ignite. I'd steeled myself."

"You did?" Addison raised an eyebrow.

"Sure. Your father has come in for treatments on the same days as your mother. They often spar."

"Why did you say yes to hosting my party then?" Addison asked.

"How could I resist? It's such a novel idea. It'll look great in our advertising." Using my hands, I mimed creating a headline. "AROMA WELLNESS SPA HELPS YOU ON THE PATH TO BECOMING YOUR BETTER SELF." They might have been Addison's words, but I was going to steal them.

"I suppose next we'll offer relationship breakup parties," Sierra said. "EX-FIANCÉ GETS THE BOOT. RATFINK BOYFRIEND IS ERASED FROM MY CONTACTS. There are so many variations on the theme." Laughing, she bid us adieu and returned to the café to prep for the morning brunch and lunch crowd.

Addison kissed my cheek and gave me a firm hug. "Thank you. For everything."

The rest of the day went off without a hitch. No clients canceled appointments at the last minute. The mindful meditation I led at two o'clock was relaxing, not purely for my customer but also for me. I found myself breathing rhythmically and realized I'd been holding my breath when Gianna and O'Malley had gone at it. What would tonight's dinner be like? I refused to ask Gianna for payment with guests around. It could wait until tomorrow.

I went home and threw on a simple silk sweater over black stretch jeans. My cat Vivi, a beautiful Birman with deep blue eyes and contrasting white gloves on each paw, wasn't happy I was leaving so soon. She craved a game of attack-the-laser-beam or chase-the-Ping-Pong-ball. "I'll return soon. Promise," I cooed. I wasn't lying. I didn't like to party hearty on a work night.

She yowled.

"Fine." To appease her, I played a quick round of fetch-the-catnip-mouse, after which I took a moment to rearrange the Jane Austen magnets on my refrigerator—they held postcards from my father in place—and then I fed her.

At six thirty, I stood outside the Spanish-style fourplex where Sierra and I lived. Our grandmother owned the building and leased three units to us. I had two on the lower level because I'd needed a studio where I could make essential oils and other items for the spa. Sierra's was above my second unit. A fortune teller rented the one above me.

There wasn't much traffic on 4th Avenue at this time of night, so I yelled up to the second floor knowing I'd be heard. "Cuz, let's go!"

"Coming!" she responded. Seconds later, she trotted down the stairs in a mini knit dress over a white blouse decorated with black spiders.

"Wow. Darling."

"I just bought it." She twirled. "Good for this time of year, right?"

"Yes."

We climbed into my Land Rover and drove lickety-split to Gianna and O'Malley McKay's house. They lived in a two-story home not far from the ocean. The front yard was beautifully landscaped with succulents and bougainvillea. The aqua-blue door stood out against the pale stucco exterior. On a previous occasion, Addison had informed me her great-grandfather on her mother's side, who'd made his fortune in lumber, had built the house. Like my ancestors, hers traced their roots to the artistic Carmelites who had relocated south after the 1906 earthquake in San Francisco. Apparently, in addition to Gianna's illustrious career and O'Malley's thriving golf-design business, Addison's great-grandfather had been an amateur artist and, posthumously, the family had made a fortune from the sale of his artwork. I wasn't familiar with any of his pieces. My art knowledge was limited to what I saw in museums or galleries, plus my heritage stemmed from intellectuals who preferred to read and write books.

I pulled to the curb and parked. "There's Nana Lissa. Hi, Nana!"

Our hip septuagenarian grandmother didn't look a day over sixty. She was boldly walking among the succulents admiring the Halloween décor. A blow-up dragon with a bright red belly was facing off an inflatable knight in shining armor. She burst out laughing, which made me automatically giggle.

"What's tickling your funny bone?" I asked.

"Look at the headstones."

Everywhere there were fake slabs boasting wickedly funny sayings. I hadn't read any of them until now.

"*'Here lies Charlie; may he rest in pieces,'*" I intoned.

"This one's great." Sierra pointed to *Here lies No Remains.*

"My favorite is this one." Nana Lissa cackled before reading it aloud. "*'Claire Voyant—didn't see this coming.'* So clever."

As always, she had dressed elegantly. Her gray cigarette pants looked expensive, as did her silver satin blouse. Invariably, she wore the sapphire earrings my grandfather had given her on their thirty-fifth wedding anniversary. The outfit was understated for her, but it put me to shame. Her short-cropped silver hair was neat, as always. I'd tamed my hair by sweeping it into a clip, but I could feel baby fine strands already coming loose. Swell. Maintaining a perfect appearance wasn't in my wheelhouse.

"Darling girl." She kissed me *a la bisé*, the French term for air kissing. "You look adorable."

"Ha!" At five-foot-six with what friends termed a warm husky voice, I was far from adorable. I had wide-set eyes that tended to squint whenever I was attempting to be silly. And my lips were often chapped because I chewed them when I was nervous. "However, my cousin does look cuter than a button. Agreed?"

"She does." Nana Lissa greeted Sierra as she had me.

"Cut it out, you two." Sierra raised her fists in mock indignation. "I am an athlete. Athletes are not as cute as buttons."

"Some are," I crooned. "Mary Lou Retton comes to mind." The 1984 Olympic star gymnast had been America's Sweetheart.

Sierra knuckled my arm. "Hey, did I tell you I joined a biking club?"

I gawked at her. "Why? You're a runner. When did you start riding a bike?"

"I've always ridden. Duh. But a friend talked me into getting more involved, and I love it!" she trilled. "It's exhilarating."

We made our way to the porch. Gigantic grinning pumpkins flanked the doorway.

Before we could press the doorbell, the door opened, and Addison appeared. "Come in. So good to see you. We're already on our second glass of wine."

"We're not late, are we, Sierra?" I asked.

My cousin checked her watch and shook her head.

"At Mother's house," Addison said, "everyone starts early. We're all in the kitchen or out in the yard. This way."

She was dressed casually in jeans and a pumpkin-orange sweater, so I breathed easier. Nobody would think I was a complete slob.

As we trailed her through the elaborately decked out living room that boasted a primary-colored area rug, an extra-long pale-blue couch, warm brown-accent chairs, and moss-green floral curtains, I got the sense a designer had enjoyed a field day of mixing and matching. It was striking. The ogival arched doorways, wood-beam ceilings, and tall windows added extra elegance. The abstract paintings, which I guessed were her great-grandfather's, were unique, to say the least. He had clearly been influenced by Pablo Picasso's abstracts. Noses and ears and mouths looked intentionally out of place.

The kitchen was equally gorgeous, with marble counters, high-end appliances, expertly organized glass-faced cabinets, and teardrop lights hanging over the expansive island.

"Welcome!" Gianna looked like a model straight out of a Halloween issue of *Vogue*, dressed in a slinky black sheath and spiky heels, her hair anchored off her face by a pair of rhinestone spider-adorned combs. She greeted us with a wiggle of her fingers. "Drinks are outside. Make yourselves at home. Lissa, I'll get to the library soon."

"You said that the last time we ran into each other," my grandmother replied.

"I promise."

"I'll hold you to it."

"And Emma, I found my checkbook."

Addison cleared her throat.

Gianna smiled. "I mean, my daughter found it. On the floor. Under a table. I can write you a check—"

"Not tonight," I said, sticking to my plan. "Tomorrow or the next day will be fine."

"Ladies, follow me," Addison said.

We strolled through the French doors to the backyard, which was breathtaking. The covered patio provided plenty of shade. More succulents and bougainvillea abounded, and there was a gorgeous bed of autumnal-toned annual flowers. I made a mental note to ask Addison who her parents' landscaper was. Perhaps I could pick his or her brain on what to do with the fourplex's garden. I was in charge of it and wanted it to thrive. I'd been hoping the nurturer fairy named Dewberry that I'd seen a few months earlier would return, but she seemed to have vanished. Of course, I questioned whether I'd really spied her at all. My grandmother assured me I had, saying fairies often got busy.

O'Malley, casual in a Hawaiian shirt and slacks, was tending the bar. "Welcome, guests!"

Chatting with him was a curly-haired young woman.

"Who's that?" I asked Addison.

"Do you mean the zaftig one in the va-va-voom dress?" she proclaimed loudly enough for all to hear.

"Cut it out." The young woman playfully stuck out her tongue at Addison as she approached. "Jersey is clingy. And I'm not zaftig."

"Fine. The skinny, self-deprecating one in the jersey dress ridiculously adorned with seahorses," Addison revised, "is my bestie since forever, Riley Rhimes. She recently got an offer to publish her children's book about, guess what? Seahorses. Hence, the dress. She's a fab illustrator, and she and her high school sweetheart are engaged. How cute, right?"

"White wine, ladies?" O'Malley asked.

My grandmother, Sierra, and I all chimed in, "Please."

He poured each of us a glass of chardonnay, quickly explained the flavors we should expect, and told us to enjoy ourselves.

A winged insect dive-bombed my face. I swatted the air and missed.

"If you need bug spray," O'Malley said, "there's an atomizer over there on the table."

Addison said, "Daddy never gets bitten. He used to all the time. He was a mosquito magnet."

"Until a golfer buddy shared a tip with me," he said, taking over the story. "Now I've got a secret weapon to use against good old Mother Nature. My brother-in-law Frederick happens to be a bug buffet, too, but he refuses to ask me what I do to combat it, the dimwit."

I hadn't met Addison's aunt and uncle, but I knew Idha Gibson instantly by the way Addison had described the color of her skin and her lustrous black hair. She was standing at the far end of the lap pool with a bone-thin man who reminded me of Ichabod Crane, his gangly arms so long the cuffs of his shirtsleeves were two inches too short.

"I recognize your aunt," I said. "Is your uncle beside her?"

"Uh-huh. Like I told you, Uncle Frederick is super smart, but a fashion horse he is not."

"He's a scientist communicator," Riley added, "meaning he makes complex astronomical concepts accessible to the public through books and articles. Cool, isn't it?"

I supposed his challenging career might explain his gawky, professorial look.

"Leave it to Riley to spell it out in long form." Addison elbowed her friend. "Why you create children's books is beyond me."

"If I wrote an adult book, it would wind up over two-hundred-thousand words. A publisher's nightmare." Riley made a goofy face.

I said, "Addison, didn't you tell me your aunt and uncle live near here?"

"Not near here. Near your spa. They work online with their clients, which allows them to reside anywhere in the world."

Gianna swept through the French doors and hailed her brother. "Frederick, come meet our guests."

Idha's expression darkened as if Gianna had snubbed her purposely.

"Uh-oh," Addison whispered. "My aunt hates the way Mom talks to my uncle, like he's her lap dog."

"Keep alert," Riley warned. "Idha is no wallflower. If provoked, she might give Gianna an earful."

"Idha, darling." Peyton Pelagatti, lifelong friend of Gianna, intercepted Idha with arms open wide for a hug. I'd met her on two occasions when she'd come to the spa with Gianna. The embrace looked painful. Peyton suffered from polymyalgia rheumatica, which caused severe osteoporosis. Recently, she'd also been taking a heavy dose of steroids, which made her face super puffy.

"Good old Peyton, coming to the rescue." Addison applauded silently. "She is decorum personified. That's how she runs her real estate business. Everyone feels her love and knows she won't let them down."

Peyton and Gianna had grown up together. At one time, she had been Gianna's modeling agent. When Gianna gave up her career and went into real estate, Peyton joined her. When Gianna decided to retire completely, Peyton bought her out. A few of Peyton's clients were regulars at the spa and raved about her expertise and compassion.

"Come say hi, everyone," Addison prompted, and headed for her aunt and Peyton.

O'Malley, Riley, and my family followed her, and we greeted one another.

Briskly, Peyton tucked her short hair behind both ears, but it didn't stay put. "Idha, how's the anthology selling?"

Addison leaned toward me. "I forgot to tell you, my aunt published an anthology of her short stories last year."

"Self-published." Idha's voice was lyrical, but her smile was tight. She smoothed the seams of her stylish sheath.

"I've read a couple." Addison held up fingers.

"Same." Riley raised her hand.

"I've browsed a few, as well. They're excellent," O'Malley said, and offered a thumbs-up. "Lots of suspense. Any chance you'll write a novel, Idha?"

"Why should she, Dad?" Addison asked. "Her short fiction stories are really good."

"You don't make money writing short stories."

"She doesn't need to," Addison countered. "She earns a decent paycheck."

"And to be honest, O'Malley, long form is not my strength," Idha said modestly.

"Mine either," Riley jibed.

Nana Lissa held out her hand, palm up. "Idha, we should invite you to give a chat at the library on short story fiction."

Idha blushed. "No thank you. I don't . . . I'm not a public speaker."

"We'll make it informal. Nothing big. You and I will talk." My grandmother offered a sly smile. "I'm sure I can convince you."

"Dinner is being served!" Gianna announced. "Everyone, into the dining room."

"Mother hired staff for tonight so she wouldn't have to do dishes," Addison joked.

"Ha!" O'Malley scoffed. "As if she ever does the dishes. She might break a nail."

"Dad, be cool." Addison cut her father a hard look.

"Don't worry, sweetheart." He waved both hands in surrender. "I'll be on my best behavior."

We moseyed into the dining room.

"It's beautiful," I exclaimed before I could stop myself.

Gianna smiled. "Thank you."

The table was custom-made, with a herringbone top and burl accents on the edges. Twelve chairs matched the design. A gorgeous chandelier hung above the table. I could've sworn I'd seen a fixture like it in the movie *The Mask of Zorro*. The place settings were bright red, the white china plates red-rimmed, and the cut-glass wine goblets top-of-the-line.

"All it takes is money," Sierra quipped.

"If you've got it, flaunt it," my grandmother teased.

"You don't show off," I said under my breath.

Nana Lissa lived in a beautiful house with a view of the ocean, but everything about her place was understated and muted, like a home in a Nancy Meyers movie.

"Everyone, find your nameplate and sit," Gianna suggested. "We're having a feast, thanks to our fabulous chef."

She positioned herself at one head of the table and O'Malley took his place at the other. Nana Lissa and Peyton flanked Gianna. Sierra and Addison sat on either side of me. Riley perched on the chair beyond Addison. Frederick folded himself into the seat beside his wife on the opposite side of the table. Idha was still frowning, which didn't do her pretty features any favors.

"You know, Addison," Peyton cooed, "Reginald isn't married yet."

Addison mock-groaned. "Don't start. We aren't right for each other."

"You two were inseparable growing up. He made you laugh."

"He lives in Los Angeles."

"He'll move home for you."

Addison sniffed. "Tell him not to bother. We're total opposites."

"Totes," Riley said, using the slang term for *totally*.

"He wanted to become a comedian." Peyton directed the comment to me.

"*Wanted to* and *becoming* are two different things," Addison retorted.

Peyton's face pinched with annoyance. She forced a neutral expression. "He's an agent for comedians now."

"An assistant to an agent," O'Malley muttered.

"Stop, Peyton!" Gianna ordered. "O'Malley, you too. Enough already. Reginald is not a good fit for Addison. Besides, there should be no talk of fixing her up until she's divorced."

"I will be soon." Addison gleefully lifted her glass of wine.

Riley raised hers and clinked it against her bestie's.

"Not to mention our daughter has to get her act together first," Gianna continued. "Look at her. She's a mess."

"Mother!"

"She is not." Riley patted her friend's hand.

"Gianna, don't," O'Malley cautioned.

"Well, she is," Gianna persisted, unwilling to be submissive. "You are. You're slumping and you've put on weight."

"I . . . I . . ." Addison sputtered.

"Honestly, Gianna, you try my nerves. Cut it out." O'Malley cracked his napkin like a whip.

Addison scooched her chair away from the table with a screech. "You know I look this way, Mother, because I had to stop cycling when I hurt my knee. I'll start up again soon." She said to me and Sierra, "I used to swim and play lacrosse, too."

"She is great at all sports." Riley bobbed her head.

"Was," Addison said. "But Wyatt—" She stopped short and sipped her wine, leaving us hanging.

Wyatt *what*? I mentally begged her to continue.

Addison set down the glass with a clack. "Wyatt demanded I bike and do nothing else. Biking, he said, required complete focus."

"Wyatt has been a loser since day one," Riley said.

Gianna tapped her water glass with a spoon. "Let's table any further discussion of him. Thank you."

Idha nudged her husband, encouraging him to speak.

Frederick started and cleared his throat. "O'Malley, I heard you sold your Corvette."

"Gianna made me."

Gianna frowned. "You had to. You were getting too many speeding tickets. Red is the color the police notice most."

"What are you driving now, O'Malley?" Nana Lissa asked. "It's common knowledge how much you like your toys."

"An Acura TLX."

Frederick snorted. "Really? Why not go with a Mercedes EQE?"

"I test-drove it. I didn't like it."

"Do you get looks from the valets when you show up in a lesser car?" Frederick confided to his wife, "O'Malley always uses the valet. It's a class thing. He says if you park your car yourself, you look cheap."

"It's not a class thing," O'Malley said, a bite in his tone. "Don't be ridiculous. I merely like the convenience. I have appointments to keep. I don't abide tardiness. Plus I avoid the hassle of searching for a parking space in the City."

"The City. How urbane to call San Francisco by its nickname," Frederick said.

"Live with it." O'Malley clipped off his words.

"Boys!" Gianna tapped her wineglass again. "Can we please not talk about cars?"

No talk of Wyatt or cars, I mused. *Which subject will be taboo next?*

Two waiters in black suits and white shirts entered as if summoned. They carried trays filled with plates of salad. Had Gianna triggered a silent bell? Perhaps there was a panic button installed under the table by her seat.

"I hope no one has a shrimp allergy," she said. "I adore a shrimp and butter lettuce salad."

Addison elbowed me and Riley. "Nice of her to ask now, seeing as you're all here."

The waiter was placing a dish in front of me when a slim man clad in a yellow-and-red road cycling jersey and red tights burst into the room. His dark hair was mussed. His eyebrows made him look as ominous as that actor in *Psycho*. For the life of me, I could never remember the actor's name.

"Oh no." Riley gasped.

"Addison!" the cyclist said loudly.

"Wyatt!" Addison exclaimed.

Sierra whispered to me, "I know him. I didn't know his name before now, but he's in the Pedaling Pioneers, the cycling group I joined. He's pretty nice. He's always complimenting me."

I recalled a passage I'd read while researching Wyatt's disease and said, sotto voce, "Someone with antisocial personality disorder might use charm or wit to control others."

"Maybe so, but he doesn't want to control me." Sierra placed a hand on her chest. "Only Addison."

"Point taken."

"What are you doing here?" Addison bumped the table as she struggled to rise. Her wineglass teetered. She steadied it. "You are not welcome."

O'Malley also got to his feet. "Son, leave."

"No." Wyatt stomped his foot. "I have something I need to say."

"Young man!" Gianna shouted. "I'm going to call the police if you don't leave."

"It's your fault, Gianna!" he blurted out. "You drove a wedge between us."

"I did no such thing."

Wyatt turned to Addison. "Don't divorce me. If you do, I'll kill myself."

"No, he won't," Riley assured her.

Addison glowered at him. "Wyatt, stop. Don't lie. You do it to try to manipulate me."

"No I don't. I haven't. Addison, I will love you until the day I die."

"Liar, liar, liar." She aimed a finger at him. "You lie about where you're going. You lie about how much you make. You even lied about cheating on me with another woman."

"I didn't have an affair. How many times do I have to tell you?"

"Yes, you did."

"Own it, bro," Riley quipped.

Addison let out an exasperated sigh. "Why are you wearing yet another ridiculous getup? Have you been out riding again?"

"This is marketing." Like a Home Shopping Network salesman, he flourished a hand along his torso.

"You're obsessed and neurotic and dangerous," Addison sniped. "I've told you before, if you ride at night, a car is going to strike you dead."

"I'm careful."

"Go. We're through." She extended her arm in the direction of the door.

"Please." He dodged O'Malley, reached for Addison, and nabbed her elbow. "Come outside so we can talk."

"Let go of me."

Riley scrambled to her feet.

So did Gianna. "I've had it! I'm calling the police." She stabbed three numbers on her cell phone.

While she explained to the dispatcher that there was an emergency and provided her address, O'Malley pried Wyatt off his daughter and gripped him by the shoulders. "Leave."

"I love her," Wyatt mewled. "I want her to come home. Addison, don't do this."

O'Malley muscled him toward the door. "You need help, son. Therapy. Now go before you're arrested, and do not bother our daughter again or we'll get a restraining order."

"You heard him. A restraining order," Gianna echoed.

After everyone sat down and tucked into their salads, things reverted to normal. Or seminormal. Peyton mentioned a new volunteer effort Gianna might be interested in called Women for Women. Gianna said she'd think about it. O'Malley wisecracked that his wife could never find time in her busy schedule to help others. Gianna glared at him. Nana Lissa tried to calm the waters by turning the conversation to books. Frederick went silent and forked his food passively.

Soon after, dinner arrived.

While the staff served a savory meal of leg of lamb, roasted potatoes, and autumn vegetables seasoned with pink Himalayan salt, O'Malley regaled the table with stories about his newest golf-course design and the multiple meetings he had to attend in the City.

"Freddie Couples is going to love the new track." How easily he dropped the professional golfer's name. "It suits his game. Arnie would've loved it, as well, in his heyday."

"You knew Arnold Palmer?" Nana Lissa propped her chin on one hand attentively.

"Yep. What a hoot he was. Great joke teller. A real man's man." He sipped his wine.

"Who's your favorite golf-course designer?" Peyton asked. "Other than yourself, of course."

"I think Pete Dye influenced the art of golf-course design more than any other designer," O'Malley said. "Sure, the good ones include Nicklaus and Kidd—a Scotsman who conceived Bandon Dunes in Oregon—but Dye would move heaven and earth to create a truly sadistic track." He cackled with malicious glee. "There's nothing like making a golfer work for par."

"Enough about you and your business," Gianna said snippily. "May I remind you, we will be celebrating our wedding anniversary in two weeks, and we have a trip scheduled, so don't book any of your hugely important meetings then."

"Let's see if we make it that long," he joked.

Addison shot him a look. "Tell me, Daddy, how has your marriage lasted this many years?"

"Addison!" Gianna shouted.

She smiled devilishly at her mother, pleased to have gotten a rise out of her. "Daddy, care to answer?"

"Because your mother and I hate each other fifty percent of the time and tolerate each other the other fifty. True love."

Gianna spanked the table. "Stop it, O'Malley. We adore each other."

"Ah, the secrets a family will keep," Frederick mumbled, slurring his words.

Was he drunk? I hadn't seen him imbibing much. Perhaps he'd downed a couple of drinks before coming to his sister's house. Possibly the constant conflict between his wife and his sister added to his discomfort.

"Butt out, Little Brother." Gianna's gaze was venomous. "You don't know squat."

Frederick said, "I happen to know—"

"Don't, darling." Idha put a hand on his arm. "Don't bait her."

"Go on, Freddie. What could you possibly know other than facts and figures?" Gianna's tone was riddled with judgment. "You may be a scientist, but you have no people sense. You are what some people would call a—"

"Stop, Gianna!" Idha yelled. "Just stop. You're such a bully. Why are you so vile to your brother and your husband and your daughter? I . . . I won't stand for it any longer." She slammed her wineglass on the table so fiercely it shattered. Without apologizing, she shot to her feet. "Frederick, we're leaving."

Chapter 3

In my dreams, I replayed the evening's events. Wyatt bursting in. Addison shaking with fury. O'Malley threatening Wyatt. Gianna and O'Malley bickering. Frederick taunting his sister. Idha defending her husband. Glass shattering.

At five a.m. I bolted upright in bed. Not because Idha had smashed a wineglass but because the last thing I remembered dreaming about was a cascade of shards from a glass ceiling raining down around me.

Vivi wasn't happy with me and yowled her displeasure.

"Sorry, little one. I'm a tad tense, I guess." I stroked her under the chin, and she purred and forgave me for interrupting her beauty sleep. Then, without leaving the bed, I texted Aunt Sophie. She was the most centered person I knew. Nothing could upset her. Ever. I asked if she had time for a crystal reading this morning at nine.

Within thirty seconds she responded: **For you, anything.**

After a morning walk to clear my head, I dressed for work, fed my sweet Birman, and swung by the Aroma Wellness café for a protein smoothie. Sierra hadn't done more than post a few black cat decals in the windows, but she had gone all out with providing flavors of the season. Many of the customers, most in Halloween costumes—a few wearing ghoulish masks, so I couldn't tell if they were regulars—wanted a beverage infused with pumpkin spice, cinnamon, or candied nuts. The latter surprised me until I learned the way the café candied the nuts was with honey.

When it was my turn to order, I asked for a clove-laced pumpkin smoothie. Something about the fall season always brought out the spice lover in me. However, Sierra heard my request and hurried out to consult with me. She recommended I try the special blueberry-banana-acai smoothie instead, reminding me how acai helped boost a person's antioxidants and blueberries promoted a strong heart, but I was young and my antioxidants were fine, so I declined. However, my cousin drove home that it was never too soon to start eating healthier, and I bowed to her suggestion. She pumped an arm as if she'd conquered me. She hadn't. I'd chosen to give her the win.

When I entered the spa, Meryl Kim, our manicurist by day and stand-up comedian by night, was at the reception desk. According to her, she was an Asian blend rather than Asian American. She claimed it sounded *trippier*—her word—and made people less likely to label her.

"Morning, Boss." Her voice was husky, as if she'd been screaming for hours.

"Good morning. How're things?"

"My ex is pulling his old tricks again." Meryl had divorced her musician husband years ago and despised him because recently her teenaged son asked to live with him.

"Do you need to see a lawyer?"

"Nah." She loathed giving up too much personal information, though she regularly imparted enough to whet my appetite for more. "It's nothing deep breathing won't cure."

"Where's Mah?"

Meryl's plucky mother had come on board to work the desk after the first receptionist I hired quit to pursue a writing career.

"She needed to use the facilities."

"Oh."

Meryl sniggered and aimed a finger at me. "Wow, did you ever take a face journey."

I happened to know *face journey* was the trendy term for a series of expressions a person made when reacting to new and possibly prickly information.

"What's wrong? Don't you like to talk about potty breaks?" She chuckled again. "Hey, why do people take naps on the toilet? Because it's called the restroom."

I batted the air. "Stop. No jokes this morning."

"*Ooh.* Touchy?"

"I don't want to bust a gut." And I would. Meryl was one of those people who could be funny even when she didn't mean to be. I was smart enough never to ask her to imitate a popular Hollywood star. She could nail every nuance of their voices and routines. The last time she mimicked Margaret Cho, a sociopolitical comedian and one of Meryl's favorites, I spit out the water I was drinking.

"You like my bling?" Meryl did a twirl, using one hand to point out the floral hairpin securing a knot of her blue ombré, mostly black hair. "It looks good with my new"—she made quotation marks around the word *new*—"floral jacket, yeah?"

"Yes, it does." *New* was a stretch. The hem was frayed. The colors had faded. She'd most likely found it at a rummage sale. She was always hunting for bargains.

"Morning, Emma!" Mah Kim joined us. Like her daughter, she had tattoos on her upper extremities and blue-black hair. Also like Meryl, she was a wry comedian. She used to live in Los Angeles, where she steadily booked gigs, but a few months ago, missing Meryl something awful, she moved north. "Here is your schedule for today." She rattled off the names of the customers to whom I'd give facial treatments at ten and eleven. "At twelve, before Addison Lacey and her friends come in, I'll fill you in on the afternoon's plans. Her father and Peyton"—the name came out snidely—"came in already and left."

I arched an eyebrow.

"Sorry for the tone, but she is super agro."

"Aggressive," Meryl translated.

"Got it." I mouthed, *Thank you.*

"We scheduled early treatments for them since they're so busy." Mah dragged out the word *so* with exaggeration. "Also, Addison's mother called. She'll bring you a check by the end of the day."

"Thanks."

The spa phone rang. Mah answered. "Aroma Wellness." Another line jingled. She asked the first caller to hold and answered the second. "Aroma Wellness. I'll be right back. There is one customer ahead of you." She returned to the first one and listened as whoever it was made a request.

Meryl held up a finger. "By the way, Emma, I did the mani-pedi for Mr. McKay."

Mah covered the mouthpiece as she spoke. "Say O'Malley, Daughter. He told us to use his first name, O'Malley."

"Hard to do," Meryl retorted. "I mean, like, he's so much older. It's about respect, you know?"

Mah refocused on the phone call.

"Anyway, he seemed pretty nice," Meryl went on. "Boy, does he like to talk about golf. He professes to be a scratch golfer."

"I think he is," I replied.

"He also said he met Tiger Woods."

"He might have. He's well-connected."

"He dotes on his daughter and dubbed her his little princess." She mimed donning a tiara and tilted her head as if the crown was too heavy.

"Goofball." I grinned.

"Honestly, she can do no wrong."

"Lots of fathers feel the same." I was sure my dad did at times.

He and my mother divorced when he realized his calling was to serve the world, but he and I remained close. Unlike my mother, he had supported my dream of opening Aroma Wellness. We remained in contact by phone calls, texts, and emails.

"Where is he nowadays?" Meryl asked.

"Off the grid in Timbuktu or somewhere equally exotic."

"*Ooh.*"

Dad studied botany in college, which led to a keen interest in worldwide plant diseases. His expertise was raising money for areas struggling with blight and horrible water conditions, but he didn't mind digging into the problem and getting his hands dirty.

"Has he sent you any postcards?"

"I received one last week." I hooked my thumb over my shoulder. "I'm going to call my aunt. She's giving me a crystal reading."

"Do not disturb." Meryl shot a finger into the air. "Got it!"

I retreated to the office, sat at the desk, and FaceTimed Aunt Sophie.

"Darling." She sounded so much like Nana Lissa I couldn't suppress a smile. I wouldn't say she was my grandmother's favorite daughter, but my mother and Nana didn't always see eye to eye and Sophie and Nana did.

Ergo, Sophie was a thorn in my mother's side. Like me, she had always found calm in nature and spirituality. When she migrated to Sedona to open her own spa, my mother was dismissive, calling it a lark and a pipe dream, a business destined to fail. As a girl, I'd desperately wanted to visit my aunt, but my mother refused to take me. Thankfully, my grandmother obliged. Sophie was the one who'd lovingly filled my head with spiritual facts while showing me how to do essential oil extractions and more.

"Your face is pinched, Emma." Sophie adjusted the neckline of her bright pink kimono, centered the crystal amulet hanging at the hollow of her neck, and wriggled on her chair to get comfortable. "What's worrying you?"

"I didn't sleep well. Last night we dined at a friend's house and it was tense." I told her about Wyatt barging in and Gianna nitpicking at Addison and Addison's uncle joking about the secrets a family will keep. "When his wife lost it and smashed a goblet, I was rattled."

"I imagine you were all distressed."

I recapped the dream I'd had of the glass ceiling raining down around me.

"Ahh." Sophie didn't say more. She pushed her fawn-brown loose curls over her shoulders and fixed her otherworldly blue eyes on me. "Breathe."

I obeyed.

"I see the fountain is doing well. Good." She believed the deep aspects of water connected us to intuition, and the flow of water helped interpret how we interacted with the world around us. "I like the haunted house décor, too."

"You do?"

"Halloween is a time to let loose. To think like a child. But right now, let's have you focus on the fountain while I fetch the stones."

I did as instructed and found myself inhaling and exhaling with each burble of the fountain. When my aunt came into view again, I asked the question that had been plaguing me. "Is dreaming about breaking glass a bad omen? I mean, is something horrible going to happen to me or to someone I love?"

"Some say broken mirrors are bad luck, but broken glass, as in a goblet, or even a glass ceiling, can be a sign of release." She motioned with her hands. "A freedom of sorts. It might signify good things coming your way."

I couldn't see how picturing a glass ceiling's destruction could be anything but horrible.

"Remember, glass objects can be recycled and made into new things," Sophie went on. "A rebirth, if you will. Rejuvenation reminds us that life happens in phases."

The way she could put a positive spin on the vision amazed me, but I trusted her, so I tried to absorb all she was saying.

"However, as to your concern, yes, broken glass can also be an indication someone is bottling up emotions, and when a person squelches true feelings, she runs the risk of overflowing the vessel, i.e., the heart. So the lesson for the woman who broke the goblet is that it's time to wear her heart on her sleeve."

I swallowed hard, doubting I could tell Idha, who I barely knew, what I'd learned, but perhaps I could share the message with Addison, and she could reach out to her aunt.

"As for you, you are a visceral person. You identify with others. You experience their pain. It is your gift, but it can feel like a curse. Putting that aside for now, let's focus on the reading."

Sophie turned a velvet bag filled with tumbled crystal stones upside down and released them onto the velvet-lined box she used for sessions. There were twenty in all. The azurite and amethyst clustered together. The celestite tumbled to a corner of its own. The garnet, tiger's-eye, and six others formed a group. Fluorite had partnered up with smoky quartz and so on.

"This arrangement isn't your reading, mind you," she said. "You have to pick—"

"Nine. I know. Then you will shake them in your hands and drop them from three inches onto the mat."

"Sassy," she murmured.

"Did I tell you I'm looking for a crystal reader for the spa?"

"I'm teaching someone online you might know, and she lives in Carmel."

"No way. Who?"

"The fortune teller who lives above you."

"Ursula Josipovic?"

"The very same," Sophie said. "She's quite astute and in tune with nature. Give her a bit of time and she could be the person you seek."

Knock me over with a feather. Ursula hadn't mentioned a thing. She was of Eastern European descent and could be relatively private. Maybe, like Yoly, she didn't want to disappoint me if she stopped taking lessons.

"Choose."

I did, and Sophie rolled the nine I'd picked. By the end of the reading, I was assured my insight, intuition, and courage would be in full force in less than two weeks. Woot!

"Find yourself a tiger's-eye," she coached, "and carry it with you."

"We have some in the gift shop. I'll head there now."

"Excellent. Give Bitty my love."

Sierra was a wee thing when she was born, hence the nickname, which she hated. I thought it was adorable.

For the next two hours, after procuring a tiger's-eye stone and tucking it into my pocket, I provided facials, encouraging each customer—both regulars—what they needed to do for their home regimens. At twelve, Mah updated me on my afternoon schedule.

At one p.m., while I was downing a protein bar at the reception desk, I heard women outside raucously singing "Witchy Woman." I peeked through the plate-glass window but didn't see anyone in the courtyard. I dashed outside to the stairs leading to the street.

By the curb stood a neon-orange, tourist-style party wagon. Addison, Riley, and two other women were perched on stools, propelling bike-style pedals beneath them. The wagon wasn't going anywhere—the driver had put the vehicle in Park—yet the women continued to cycle as if their lives depended on it. Each was wearing a witch's hat. Each was holding a fizzy orange drink.

"Hi, Addison!" I called.

The women stopped singing and peered at me.

"Hello, Emma!" Addison waved. "Everyone, we have arrived. Prepare to be pampered." She set her drink on the wagon's bar, hopped off her stool, and landed on the pavement. In leggings and a thigh-length orange sweater, she reminded me of a pumpkin. A very skinny pumpkin. "Disembark, ladies!" She hoisted her sizable tote over her shoulder.

Her three companions did as told.

How lit were they? I wondered, though it didn't matter. Being relaxed for a treatment was a good thing.

"Emma, you know Riley." Addison motioned to her friend, who was clad in a Little Bo Peep costume, complete with shepherd's crook.

We exchanged greetings.

"The blonde kook with the ski jump nose is Cara Guest."

Cara's outfit of embroidered silk blouse, skimpy leather skirt, and fancy gold sandals screamed money. I wasn't sure if it was a costume. If it was, I couldn't figure out who or what she was supposed to be. Maybe a Kardashian or a rock star. I didn't ask.

"Cara is a trust fund baby," Addison said.

"So are you," countered Cara.

"Not yet I'm not. My mother manages the purse strings."

Riley said, "Addison's grandfather bequeathed a lot of money to Gianna. Being a beneficent mother, she created a revocable living trust for Addison. It's a tidy sum. But Gianna is the co-trustee, meaning she holds the power." She poked Addison and offered an impish grin. "Mothers. Can't live with them. Can't kill them."

Addison continued on her mission of introducing her friends. "Cara is married, with three children already and as happy as ever, which makes all of us gag."

Riley said, "Plus she's a binge reader and finds time to head up the PTA. Gross, right?" She pretended to make a retching sound.

The third woman laughed and offered to shake hands. I obliged.

"Hi," she said. "I'm Tatiana Perez. Devotedly single and never want to be married or have kids." Her long hair was pulled into a tight ponytail, drawing focus to her comely oval face and gorgeous copper-toned skin. She was wearing a 49ers jersey over leggings. I wasn't sure if it was a costume, either. Perhaps she was a fan.

"Tatiana used to be a professional soccer player, but women's soccer doesn't pay much, so she had to work part-time as a bartender." Addison patted her friend on the arm. "Needless to say, she couldn't keep up two jobs, so she finally gave up both and became a full-time high school coach."

That explained Tatiana's athletic physique.

"All three of these wonderful women were my bridesmaids, and they're the ones I told you about. They bet I'd divorce Wyatt within five years. Were they ever wrong."

"Not by much," Riley jibed.

Addison finalized the bill with the party wagon driver and hitched her head to her friends. "Onward!"

I led the way to the spa, checked them in, and introduced them to their masseuses. Each was getting a Swedish massage.

An hour and fifteen minutes later, when they reemerged, they looked refreshed, although their faces were suffering from massage table cradle syndrome.

"How long will this last?" Cara pointed to her cheeks. "I mean, the lines, *gak*!"

Riley chuckled. "Relax. You look fine."

"My husband will freak out."

"It's temporary. At least, I hope so," Addison teased. "Let's have tea and cookies on the patio. By the time we're done, the dents will have vanished."

She'd prearranged with Sierra to serve them at a table by the fountain.

"Join us, Emma." Addison beckoned with one hand. "And bring the gold box I gave you."

This morning, a few minutes before my ten o'clock appointment, she'd popped in to give me the box and cautioned me not to peek inside. Seeing as it wasn't for me, I was able to restrain myself.

I fetched it and informed Mah where I'd be.

"What's in the box?" Cara sat at the table and applauded silently.

The babble of water in the fountain was soothing, and the aroma of the multiple jasmine plants divine. If I didn't own the spa, I could almost imagine myself on holiday.

"Hold your horses. Here comes our tea." Addison raised both hands. "And before I forget, Emma, Riley told me you do tai chi." I'd mentioned it to Riley in passing at the dinner last night. "May I attend a class with you? I'd like to add it to my regimen to become my best new self."

"Sure, it's a beginner's level."

"I've taken a few sessions in the past, but you know how it goes. I got too busy."

"I attend every other Saturday night after work when I can. This is an *on* week."

"Perfect. Now, down to serious business. Sweets." She tittered.

Sierra brought a tray she'd filled with goodies and the fixings for tea. "Addison asked for lavender mint tea." She set it on the table. "It's calming and has wonderful health benefits because it helps balance your immune system and ease anxiety."

Proudly, Addison buffed her fingertips on her sweater. "Who knew I was so smart, right?"

"Cut it out or you'll get a swelled head." Riley flicked her with her index finger.

"What we all need after putting up with your bellyaching for the past few months is a stiff drink," Tatiana joshed.

"Don't tell me you forgot we imbibed on the party wagon?" Cara teased.

Addison sighed. "Argh! I can't wait for this whole thing to be over."

Her friends cooed sympathetically that they felt the same.

Sierra poured the tea into cups and introduced the sweets. "Oatmeal and applesauce cookies. Gluten-free, double-chocolate chip cookies made with coconut oil and flax meal. And soft maple cookies with chopped dried apricots."

"Yum!" Addison snagged a chocolate one and bit into it. "Didn't I tell you Sierra is amazing?"

"What's in the box?" Sierra reset the teapot in the center of the tray.

Cara prodded me. "Open it, Emma."

I regarded Addison, who nodded. I untied the ribbon, removed the box's top, and pulled a thin booklet from inside. In lovely script, the title read, *Party Games for the Recently Divorced*. I stifled a snort.

"What does it say?" Sierra asked.

I uttered the title aloud. "Addison, I suppose you'll tell us what these games are?"

"First, let me give you your party favors. I've already delivered one to my mom and Peyton and my aunt." She reached into her sizable tote and removed the lavender-infused pillows we'd purchased as party favors. Each was a different color.

Her friends *oohed* their approval. None pulled a stunt like the women I'd had to break up yesterday. They each loved the color they received and couldn't wait to use them.

"Favors are a must at a party," Addison said. "But some favors need to be personally selected, so . . ." She opened the Photos app on her cell phone and swiped to a picture. "Which do you want? You can pick one." She displayed the screen to her friends. "A wine bag with the words, 'Pairs well with freshly signed divorce papers.'"

"Me!" Riley shouted. "Mine."

"Wait," Addison cautioned. "Look at all of them before you choose."

Cara, Riley, and Teresa giggled.

Addison displayed a second picture, this one featuring a T-shirt that read: *Divorce Party Support Squad*. "Or a travel mug." On the left-hand side of the mug, there were silhouettes of a couple standing next to each other. On the right, the woman is kicking the man aside.

The girls were laughing hysterically by now.

"Last but not least"—Addison showed them the image of a wineglass—"the perfect beverage holder." Etched on the glass were the words: *Congrats on your divorce. We hated him anyway*.

"I want them all," Tatiana said.

"Me too," Riley chirped.

Meryl exited the spa and strolled to us. "What's so funny? I saw you all laughing."

Addison scrolled through the photos for her.

"You need to have a few breakup songs," Meryl said. "Like 'Better By Myself' or 'Bye Bye Bye.' Or what about Sara Bareilles's 'Gonna Get Over You'?"

"Oh!" Cara raised her hand. "Kelly Clarkson's 'Since U Been Gone.'" She belted out the opening words and danced without rising from her chair.

Riley hooted. "Don't forget Taylor's 'We Are Never Ever Getting Back Together.'"

"We're all Swifties." Addison jiggled both hands, thumbs in the air.

"If marriage is grand," Meryl eyed each of the women, "what is divorce?" She waited for a beat. "A hundred grand."

The women tittered.

Meryl bid us adieu and returned to the spa.

"Games?" I flaunted the booklet at Addison. "What are the games?"

"There's Pin the Tail on the Ex or Who Do Voodoo, where we all make a doll." She howled. "My favorite is coming up with celebrity divorced couples. Ready, Riley? Let's do it now."

"Katie Holmes and Tom Cruise," Riley responded.

"She was too good for him." Addison tattooed the table. "What about Bill and Melinda Gates?"

"Aw." Tatiana fake-sniffed. "Their breakup made me sad."

Addison pointed at Cara.

"Ariana Grande and Dalton Gomez!" Cara cried.

"Not sad about that one." Addison smacked the table. "She had to pay him alimony after a mere three years of marriage. Ugh!"

"She'd have been better off hiring a hit man," Riley teased.

We all gasped.

A silence settled over us until Tatiana broke it. "You know what we could do?" She leaned in conspiratorially. "After the divorce is final, we could have a ring funeral. A friend of mine got divorced last year, and do you know what she did? She invited guests over, and we put the ring inside a tiny casket. Then we lit a bunch of candles, and we drank shots while suggesting why the ex would be better six feet under. Snockered, we went outside and buried the ring and never looked back. Are you willing?"

"I am." Addison applauded, adding she'd been wondering what to do with the darned thing.

I didn't voice my concern, but for some reason the notion of a ring burial gave me the willies.

Chapter 4

At five p.m. I asked Mah if Gianna McKay had brought the deposit check. She said no, so I decided to head home early and call her from there. After all, I'd told her she could pay me today or tomorrow.

A painter with weathered skin was outside the fourplex, finishing for the day. Nana Lissa had warned me the crew was coming to refresh all the woodwork surrounding the windows as well as the railings on the stairs.

"Okay to leave the ladder?" he asked as I was opening the front door of the lower unit with a key. The ladder was resting against the wall beyond the rightmost pot.

"As long as a black cat doesn't walk under it," I joked.

"I don't believe in such gibberish."

"Neither do I," I replied, although saying the words made me wonder if I did. After all, two potted plants adorned with metal black cat garden stakes—the full extent of my seasonal décor—flanked my front door. I unlocked the door, crossed the threshold, and pressed the security code on the pad. An AI voice chirped that I'd disarmed the system, meaning it was safe to enter.

Vivi scampered to me, eager for a game.

"In a sec," I told her, lifting her and nuzzling the top of her head. I carried her to the small but well-appointed kitchen, set her on the faux fur, navy-gray cat pillow nesting on a bistro chair, and fished my mobile from my crossbody purse. I pulled up Gianna McKay's contact and clicked the phone icon.

"Emma," she answered after one ring. She'd probably read my name on her screen. "I'm so sorry. I meant to come by. Will tomorrow morning be soon enough? You could come here first thing if you'd like. I . . . I don't want to be disturbed tonight. I . . ." She sniffed.

Was she crying?

"I . . ." She snuffled again. "I am simply not up to it."

"Are you all right?"

"Ye-es." The word came out jaggedly.

"Is there anything I can do to help?"

"No, dear, honestly. I'm f-fine." She was lying.

"Is your husband there?"

"No, he has a meeting in San Francisco and is staying overnight. Otherwise, I would have him bring you your payment."

"You sound sad, Gianna. I'd like to help."

"I'm . . . I'm okay. Addison will be here shortly. Don't worry about me. See you in the morning." She ended the call abruptly.

But I was fretting because she didn't impress me as the type who would cry easily. Had she and her husband had another fight? Why get married if you're always at each other's throats? My parents had made the right choice to divorce. I hoped I would never need to do the same, when and if I married, but if my past relationship failures were any indication, I'd have to work hard at making a marriage work. Two people don't always see eye to eye.

I dialed Addison. She answered on the first ring. I told her about the distressing chat I'd had with her mother. She informed me she was on her way there and thanked me for the heads-up.

After I set the cell phone and my purse on the white hutch with a blue granite desktop—my home office for lack of more space—I signaled Vivi. She leaped off her perch and brushed her head against my leg. Her tail swished, but I couldn't feel her fur through my yoga pants. For the better. I could be ticklish. Once, when Sierra and I were girls, we had an hour-long tickle fight. By the end of it, my ribs had ached from laughing.

"Hungry?" I asked Vivi.

She offered a yowl, which translated to, *I thought you'd never ask.*

"Let's dine outside." Often in autumn the nights could grow chilly, but a light sweater would keep me warm.

I threw together a quickie meal from weekend leftovers: cold poached salmon, sliced cucumbers in rice wine vinegar, and sprigs of fresh dill from the herb container on the kitchen shelf. I didn't grow a lot of plants—I wasn't a talented cook by any stretch of the imagination—but I really enjoyed the flavors of dill and basil. I dished up Fancy Feast tuna for Vivi, poured a glass of chardonnay into a stemless wineglass for me, and we passed through the small living room to the backyard.

Daylilies and evergreen bushes flourished in the front yard, and there were a number of the same plants doing well in the back, but there were also a plethora of bare spots.

"C'mon, Dewberry, reappear and do your magic," I whispered.

Until my grandmother explained the fairy kingdom to me, I hadn't realized there were four classes of fairies. Sure, as a girl I'd heard about forest fairies and flower fairies, but these classifications were different. There were nurturer, guardian, intuitive, and righteous fairies. A guardian fairy was meant to protect and serve, as well as educate. An intuitive could help humans and other fairies communicate. Nurturers cared for the earth and its environs. A righteous fairy—there was only one in the human world at a time—was destined to help humans solve problems.

I whistled softly, hoping my trill might attract Dewberry, but, alas, no such luck.

"Emma, you lazybones," I chided. "You can't rely on magic to do the work you need to perform yourself."

Vivi agreed with a whine.

I laughed. "Here. Eat." I set down her dish. "And don't share any more opinions, got me? I need a supportive cat who dotes on my every word."

Vivi meowed loudly.

"Uh-uh." I shook a finger. "Don't be judgy."

In the morning I awoke to the sound of birds chirping and peeked out the bedroom window at the backyard. I rubbed my eyes, not believing what I was seeing. Despite the fog and overcast sky—the weatherman was calling for rain in the near future, maybe today, possibly tomorrow—Dewberry was dancing from daylily to daylily, making the flowers perk up as if they were awakened by the tap of her toes and the flutter of her wings. The flower bud she wore upside down on her honey-blond hair as a hat bounced in rhythm. The skirt of the yellow-and-green dress wafted and swirled.

Had she sensed I needed her? Had she heard my whistle? Had she been doing her magic all night long? The Purple de Oro daylilies were more gorgeous than ever.

"Vivi, *psst,* c'mere. Be quiet."

Vivi wasn't used to obeying commands, but she must have sensed the muted excitement in my tone. She joined me and pawed the window.

"You can play with her later. I have to get to work." It was difficult for me to pull my gaze from the wonder, but I did.

I threw on leggings and a long-sleeved black T-shirt adorned with a ghost in a beanie, a grinning pumpkin, and a cauldron of bats. Next, I grabbed my yellow slicker. I wouldn't wear it unless it rained, but I hated umbrellas. They were utter nuisances. I couldn't count how many of mine had whipped inside out in a windstorm.

When I arrived at the Courtyard of Peace, I swung by the café eager to fetch a hot tea with honey and a banana-chocolate protein muffin. Sierra added enough powdered whey protein to pack a punch but not destroy the texture. The place was crowded with early morning customers. Many were admiring the year-round decorative touches. I was pleased with them myself. The white bistro tables and seating in the café were welcoming. Tulip-shaped pendant lights hung over the sit-down counter. On the sage-green accent wall beyond the counter was a huge chalkboard with the day's specialty drinks and treats.

Due to the heavy traffic, I didn't bother my cousin. I simply placed my order and left with a to-go bag in hand. After checking in with Mah, Meryl, and the rest of the staff, I gulped down my breakfast and headed to Gianna's to pick up the check. The business needed a quick infusion of cash. The spa was doing well, but we couldn't float a bunch of unpaid accounts.

I parked my Land Rover in front of the McKays' house, and even before I climbed out I could hear "Monster Mash," a retro, humorous Halloween song, blasting through an opened kitchen casement window. Why weren't the neighbors complaining? Were they all deaf?

I traipsed up the path, my slicker over one arm.

Addison's face appeared in the opened window. "Hi, I'll be right there."

Seconds later, the music vanished—either she'd turned it off or muted it—and she opened the front door.

"Morning, Emma!" Frazzled didn't come close to describing her appearance. The Taylor Swift Eras Tour T-shirt she was wearing over holey sweat pants looked to be two sizes too big. Her feet were stuffed into bunny slippers. And had she styled her pixie-style hair with her knuckles?

"Late night?" I asked.

"I worked until at least two before I crashed. Come in. You can hang your slicker there." She motioned to a hatstand in the foyer to my right and led the way to the kitchen. "Sorry about the ruckus when you arrived. It helps me think. I shouldn't play it so loud, I know, but it blocks out the negative thoughts that try to invade my creative space."

I understood, though playing music at a deafening volume didn't make sense to me. If I wanted to meditate and find my positive center, I required complete quiet or the magical sound of a singing bowl being brought to life by the whisk of a crystal rod.

Addison caught a glimpse of herself in a mirror on the kitchen wall. "*Gak!* I need a facial badly. I look like the bride of Frankenstein." She grimaced. "Not the comparison I should've used. I wonder if there is an almost-divorced woman's bad day comparison?"

"The character Goldie Hawn played in *The First Wives Club* comes pretty close." I'd taken a film class in college and walked away with an easy A and an appreciation of the art of film.

"Yes! Remember how she plumped her lips? Riley and I watched the movie when we were in our teens. It was on a late-night marathon of women-themed flicks. I remember snorting popcorn out my nose because I laughed so hard." She pursed her lips to imitate the hot mess Hawn had portrayed. "I vow never to do cosmetic surgery." She held up a hand to swear. "You?"

"Never, but I understand why some people do."

"Like my mother, but I won't judge." She snickered. "Why are you here so early?"

"Your mother meant to pay me yesterday, but when I called, she said she didn't feel up to coming to the spa and asked me to stop by this morning."

"Aha. I wondered if something was amiss. When I got home last night, she was locked in her bedroom. I yelled through the door, but she replied she wasn't feeling well and didn't want company. I'll go get her." She veered down the hall and knocked on a door. "Mom?"

The primary bedroom must be on the main floor, I reasoned. Unusual, but not unheard of.

"Mother! Yoo-hoo. Wake up! Emma's here." She pounded this time. "Mom!"

I poked my head out of the kitchen. "Everything okay?"

"I don't know. The door's locked. She's not answering." She smacked the door with her palm. "Mom!"

"Maybe she's in the bathroom."

"And she can't hear me? With the music on, I'd understand, but now in the silence? No. Something's wrong."

"Is there a key to the room?"

"Yes. Silly me." She reached above the door. She retrieved a key from the narrow one-inch ledge, slotted it into the lock, twisted the doorknob, and pressed the door open. "Mom, time to rise and—" She lurched forward. "Mom? Are you okay? Mom! Emma, come quick!"

I rushed down the hall and into the room.

Addison was standing beside the ornate four-poster bed. "Mom, wake up. C'mon. Get up." She touched her mother's cheek and glimpsed over her shoulder at me. "She's cold." She recoiled. "Icy cold. I don't think she's breathing." Her voice quavered. "Help me. Please."

I hurried to the bed and gaped at Gianna. The white duvet lay neatly beneath her chin. Her skin was pasty. Her eyes were closed. Her hair was fanned out. There was no rise and fall to her chest. I pressed two fingers against her exposed neck but couldn't feel a pulse. My insides knotted. My palms grew sweaty. *Not again. Not. Again.*

After a long moment, I whispered, "She's dead."

"No!" Addison coughed out a sob and whirled away, one hand pressed to her mouth, the other arm clutching her torso.

"Has she been ill?" I asked. "Has she been under a doctor's care?"

"What? No. I don't think so."

"I'd better call nine-one-one. They'll have to rule out foul play."

"Foul play? C'mon, Emma, do you think my mother was murdered? How? With what? I don't see a weapon. She hasn't been shot or anything." She thrust a hand toward the way we'd entered. "The door was locked and the window's closed. Mother always bolts it before going to bed."

"How many people know where the key is?"

"I don't know. Plenty. None of us dared invade Mother's privacy when she wanted it. She often got headaches and needed to be left alone. But sometimes she asked to be waited on, so each of us knew . . ." Fresh tears fell. "Oh, Emma." A wail keened out of her.

I fished my cell phone from my purse and dialed. As I waited for the dispatcher to answer, I examined Gianna again and noticed she hadn't removed her lipstick before getting into bed. It was smeared.

"Does your father stay in this room?" I asked.

"Of course. They're married."

I scanned the bedroom, which was fit for royalty. In addition to the gigantic bed, there was a bureau, an armoire, and a secretary desk with a matching chair. The floor was hardwood. An expensive area rug with a floral pattern added a burst of color. Each bedstand held a stack of books in a variety of genres. Satin drapes graced the windows.

The dispatcher answered.

"Hello." I gave my name and added that we'd found Gianna McKay dead in her bed.

"She was alive when I got home last night," Addison said. "She spoke to me."

While answering the dispatcher's questions about address and location inside the house, I bent closer to Gianna and inhaled. I detected the aroma of lavender and a fresh sweet scent I couldn't pinpoint. On the brocade chaise lounge lay one of the herbal-infused pillows we'd distributed yesterday as party favors. Gianna had asked for a white one.

I regarded her hair again. Sometimes before I fell asleep I would sweep my hair up above my head so it wouldn't touch my face, but Gianna's hair appeared positioned, as one might see in a hair commercial.

The dispatcher asked me to wait for the police to arrive.

"Yes, ma'am, we will. I'm with Mrs. McKay's daughter." I pocketed my phone. "Addison, you didn't see your mother when you got home?"

"I didn't go in the room, if that's what you mean."

"Are you sure it was she who spoke to you?"

"I know my mother's voice," she retorted sharply, and instantly apologized.

"What time was it?"

"A little after five."

"When I reached out to her earlier, I thought she might have been crying."

"She sounded stuffy," Addison said, "but I didn't hear her weeping. She gets colds and infections often, so I didn't think anything of it. I'm like my father. Rarely sick."

"Your father is in San Francisco for meetings?"

"Yes. With a company willing to pay him to design a new golf course, like they need one more in the City. I should call him."

"Yes, you should."

Addison kept her distance but studied her mother's face again. "Do you think she . . ." She swallowed hard. "Do you think she locked the door and took a drug that made this happen?"

"Does she have sleeping pills?"

"No. She is . . . *was* . . . a health nut. Sure, she loved to eat rich food, but she didn't put anything artificial into her body."

Then why had Addison asked about drugs? I said, "May I look around?"

"Go ahead." She sank onto the chair beside the desk. Her shoulders heaved as she dialed her phone.

I pulled a tissue from a container beyond the stack of books on the bedstand, wrapped it around my fingers to prevent leaving fingerprints, and opened the stand's sole drawer. It was empty, except for a gilt-edged Bible and a pair of eyeglasses. I went into the bathroom and viewed the countertop, which held a mirrored tray filled with pretty perfume atomizers. In a two-bottle caddy to the left of the sink stood a container of white musk liquid hand soap and another of white musk lotion. There were no visible pill vials.

The only items in the medicine cabinet were vitamins. I searched the drawers and under the sink and found a bottle of fiber pills and another of probiotic ones and some eye contact solution. There were additional lotions and hair sprays, as well, but I didn't find even one container of Tylenol or Advil.

I returned to the bedroom.

"Daddy's driving home now. He's stunned." Addison began to tremble. "I . . . I can't believe it."

I waited with her for the police to arrive. It didn't take long.

Chapter 5

A siren blared. Brakes screeched. Doors slammed. I peered out the primary bedroom's window. One police vehicle had arrived. I recognized both people who disembarked and dashed to the front door to let them in.

Detective Dylan Summers, a handsome man in a silver fox kind of way, gawked at me. "You."

"Yes, sir." I'd met Summers a few months earlier when a friend of mine was murdered.

Officer Teresa Rodriguez, an attractive female officer not much older than me, joined him while pulling on latex gloves. As always, her flawless caramel-colored skin looked healthy and makeup-free. She wore her glossy black hair tied at the nape of her neck. Her uniform was freshly pressed.

"I'm here because I came to retrieve a check for my services," I said to justify my presence. "This way." I retreated into the home and down the hall to Gianna's room while explaining how she—Mrs. McKay—hadn't responded to her daughter's calls through the locked door. "We used a key." I indicated the ledge above the door. "It was up there. Mrs. McKay was dead when we found her. I felt for a pulse. There was none."

I entered the room before Summers and Rodriguez. He cut past me and pressed his fingers against Gianna's neck as I had. He refocused on me while typing a note on his cell phone. In the past he'd written his thoughts in a notebook with a pen—old-school. Apparently, he'd joined the twenty-first century.

"Sir"—I motioned to Addison—"this is the deceased's daughter, Addison Lacey." She hadn't budged. She was seated by the desk, dabbing her face with the wad of tissues she'd clumped into her right fist. "Addison, this is Detective Summers and Officer Rodriguez."

Man, I sounded cool, calm, and collected. I was anything but. Energy was surging through me. If Gianna had killed herself, I couldn't figure out how. Would we find an empty bottle of pills wedged between the mattresses? Or tucked beneath her delicates in the bureau? Or hidden in a pocket of a piece of clothing? What if someone did kill her? Though the room had been locked, according to Addison, plenty of people knew where the key was, so entering through the bedroom door was the most likely scenario. I doubted the police needed to hunt for hidden passageways. I imagined O'Malley and the housekeeper knew about the key. Did Peyton, Idha, or Frederick? Did Addison's soon-to-be ex-husband Wyatt know? He must have come to the McKays' home a time or two. He'd been super angry at Gianna on Monday night after he'd interrupted the dinner party. He'd accused her of driving a wedge between Addison and him.

"The doorknob, Detective Summers." I mimed a twisting motion with my hand. "Can you tell if fingerprints were erased from it?"

"My prints are on it now," Addison murmured.

"Yes, but if your mother's prints aren't on the door, then it means someone else wiped them off the knob."

Summers gave Rodriguez the directive to inspect the doorknob.

Then he smoothed the front of his shirt. He never wore a uniform. His outfit often consisted of a white button-down shirt and chinos. Simple. Approachable. "I'd like you to walk me through your accounts. Emma, you first."

I was shocked he'd used my first name, even though a few months ago my grandmother had insisted he treat me normally and not formally. Was he content to abide by her wishes going forward?

Another siren whooped. Doors slammed. In seconds two EMTs appeared in the hall beyond the opened door. "May we come in, sir?" the taller of the two asked.

Summers shook his head. "Not necessary, men. Resuscitative measures are not needed. I texted the coroner already. He'll be on his way. Please remain outside until we release the body."

They retreated, and my gaze landed on Rodriguez. She'd moved away from the door and was taking photographs of the surroundings. Was this truly a murder investigation? She snapped an image of the desk, the chaise longue, the armoire, and finally Addison, who sat hunched and miserable and unaware of the officer's attention.

Summers donned latex gloves while he listened to my account: arriving, calling down the hall, pounding on the door, locating the key.

"Ms. Lacey didn't hesitate?" he asked. "She knew exactly where the key was?"

"Yes."

"You entered."

"After Addison. She reached her mother first. Felt her cheek. The coldness frightened her. I checked for a pulse, as I told you. There was none. Gianna . . . Mrs. McKay looked almost peaceful. Her arms were as you see them, under the covers. No sign of a struggle." I hesitated, but in an effort to be transparent, I quickly added, "I searched for sleeping pills in the side table drawer and the bathroom cabinets but found none."

He groaned.

"I wrapped a tissue around my fingers. You won't find my fingerprints on anything." I spread my arms, palms up. "FYI, Mrs. McKay was a health nut. There isn't even a bottle of aspirin in the bathroom."

"Emma." Addison's voice was tiny and weak. "I see a check on the desk for you."

Summers joined her, inspected the check, and brought it to me. "This validates your side of the story."

I glowered at him. "I am not a suspect. Besides, it doesn't look like there has been foul play here," I stated, even though I'd suggested the idea to Addison earlier.

"I disagree." He resumed his inspection of Gianna and delicately pried her eyes open. "Bloodshot, as I expected. She was smothered."

Addison gasped. "What? Someone did kill her? When? While I was upstairs in my room?" She covered her mouth with her hand and turned ashen, as if she was going to puke.

Quickly, I explained that Addison was living with her parents temporarily until her divorce was final. "What did the killer use, Detective?" I recalled the scent of lavender lingering on Gianna and glanced to my right. "Could it have been a pillow, like the one on the chaise longue? Each of the women attending the happily divorced party received them."

"The what?"

"The happily divorced party," Addison murmured through split fingers. "My friends and I are going to Aroma Wellness for treatments and teas and . . ." She sobbed. "If only Daddy had been here."

"Where is he?" Summers asked.

"Coming home from San Francisco," Addison replied.

"Sir, do you detect the scent of lavender?" I asked to refocus the detective on the crime scene. "The pillow is herbal-infused." I wished I could pinpoint the other aroma I'd picked up. It was sweet and fresh—not perfume or cologne—but now, with all the people in the room, I couldn't identify it. "The pillows given to the party attendees all smell the same."

Summers bent and inhaled the air near Gianna's face. He summoned Rodriguez to bring him the pillow. She did, and he inspected it top and bottom, front and back. "This was not used as a murder weapon."

"How can you be sure?" I asked.

"There's no lipstick smear on it."

I returned my attention to Gianna and again wondered why she was wearing lipstick if she'd planned on going to sleep. A notion struck me. I tried to push it aside, but I couldn't. What if she'd donned makeup because she was meeting up with someone—perhaps a lover—while her husband was away? Did whoever it was break her heart, ergo, the reason for her tears when I'd phoned? Was that why she'd wanted to be left alone when her daughter came home?

"The killer could have removed the stain using dish soap and a toothbrush," I suggested. At the spa, we had to contend with all sorts of cleaning issues concerning massage table covers, sheets, and towels. Facial peels and body oils were difficult to wash out. I recalled seeing hand soap and lotion in the primary bathroom. "Does the pillow also smell sweet, like white musk?"

"I don't know," he said and held it out to me.

I sniffed lavender again but no remnants of soap or cleaning solutions.

Rodriguez rounded the bed and inspected the undisturbed king-size pillow on O'Malley's side of the mattress. "No smear on this one," she stated.

"Sir, another question." I raised a finger. "Wouldn't there have been a struggle if she'd been smothered? Gianna looks peaceful."

Summers instructed Rodriguez to take more pictures of the victim and asked us to keep our distance as he pulled down the duvet.

Gianna was dressed in a cotton nightgown and lying as I'd surmised, perfectly still, her arms at her sides. There were no ropes or straps restricting her.

I jutted out an arm toward the bed. "Her hands are at rest. Her fists aren't clenched. And her fingernails are perfect. Not one is broken. Plus, there aren't any scratches or marks on her arms." When the detective didn't dispute me, I continued. "Is it possible someone drugged her so she would be compliant, making it easier to smother her?"

"Don't theorize," he snapped.

"I'm not theorizing. I'm thinking out loud."

He grumbled under his breath, but I heard a word that sounded like *Lissa* and was pretty sure he was cursing my grandmother.

Rodriguez, who had witnessed Nana and me going toe-to-toe with the detective on previous occasions, kept quiet. She was a smart, stalwart officer who was in it to win it.

"The coroner will have to determine if drugs were employed," Summers stated. "They'll draw blood and do a urine test. Until then—"

"Do you see a needle mark?" I asked. "The killer might have injected her with a sedative."

"Emma, please." He sounded exasperated.

"What else might the killer have used to prevent her from breathing if not a pillow?" I asked.

"A hand. A cloth. An object the killer took with them." He picked up the white herbal-infused pillow and eyeballed Addison. "Do you have one of these?"

"Yes. It's . . . it's in my room." She rose shakily to her feet. "Like Emma told you, I'm staying here until the divorce is final next week."

"Get the pillow."

She bolted out. I heard her feet pounding the stairs. A minute later, she entered with a pink pillow and handed it to him. "No lipstick."

He smelled the pillow. "I can't detect cleaning solution, Officer, although I do pick up a hint of lavender." He shook it in Rodriguez's direction.

She concurred.

I regarded Gianna again. Why was her hair so perfect yet her lipstick smeared? Had the killer run out of time, or had he—

I paused. I supposed the murderer could have been a she.

Had he or she liked the idea of Gianna looking perfect but messy? Was this a preplanned murder or spur-of-the-moment?

"Ms. Lacey." Summers turned his attention to Addison.

"Yes, sir." Like frailty personified, she was standing knees locked, toes directed inward, shoulders trembling.

I wished I could comfort her but didn't want to incur Summers's wrath.

"I'd like to hear your version of last night and this morning." He motioned for her to speak.

"I got home right after Emma phoned me."

"She contacted you? Why?" He leveled me with a glare.

"I touched base with Gianna about the payment," I said. "She sounded like she'd been crying. I was concerned and informed Addison."

"Go on." He gestured for Addison to resume.

"When I got home, I knocked on the door." She could barely find the strength to speak. "Mother yelled that she wasn't feeling well and didn't want to be disturbed. She also let me know Daddy was staying overnight in San Francisco for a business meeting. I told her I knew about Daddy and added I'd have dinner in my room. She asked me not to play loud music, saying it would hurt my eardrums. I laughed. She knew me well enough to know I wouldn't listen to her. I grabbed a beer and a piece of cold pizza from the refrigerator."

"Didn't you say your mother only ate healthy things?" I interjected.

"She did. Not me. I'm a pizza junkie. I went upstairs, switched on Spotify, put on my headphones, and for hours listened to Taylor Swift sing her heart out while I worked on my card collection. I quit at two a.m."

"Your card collection?" Summers repeated.

"I design cards and sell them on Etsy."

"She's excellent," I said.

"You didn't hear anything more from your mother?" Summers inquired.

"No."

"Did you say good night to her?"

"No," Addison replied. "I mean yes, when I told her I was going upstairs to eat."

Summers mulled over her response. "Did you hear anything this morning?"

"No, sir."

"Did you have reason to kill your mother?"

"What? No!" She shot a pitiful, pleading glance at me. "No. Never. I loved her."

I reflected on the way Gianna had treated Addison at the dinner the other night. How she'd demeaned her daughter in front of all those people. Addison had stood up for herself. Had she harbored enough ill will toward her mother to kill her?

A line Riley uttered facetiously cycled in my mind. *Mothers. Can't live with them. Can't kill them.*

"I can think of a lot of people who did have a reason," Addison hurried to add. "Mother could be snooty and overbearing to nearly everyone. My ex, Wyatt, hated her."

"Your soon-to-be ex," Rodriguez murmured.

"Yes. Soon-to-be. He despised her. He blamed her for our breakup."

"Addison." I cleared my throat. "Did Wyatt ever visit this house when you were married?"

"Sure, a bunch of times."

"Did he know your mother suffered from headaches and locked herself in her bedroom on occasion?"

"Mm-hmm."

"Is it possible he knew about the key above the door?"

"Sure, probably." Addison screwed up her mouth. "Though I can't remember him ever going down this hallway. The guest bath is on the other side of the living room."

"That doesn't mean he didn't," I offered.

If Summers's stare was a laser, it would have cut me in half.

"Wyatt has ASPD," Addison stated, without preamble.

"Antisocial personality disorder," I clarified.

"I know what ASPD is." Summers's tone could've cut ice.

If I felt I could get away with being sassy, I would quip, "Don't shoot the messenger." But I couldn't. Not around him.

"I've always worried due to his disease and all the outbursts that he might—" Addison started to cough erratically. When the fit subsided, she went on. "I've always worried that he might kill someone someday."

"Do you need some water?" I asked.

She bobbed her head. "Yes. Please."

Presuming using a glass from Gianna's primary bathroom would be a no-no, I rushed to the kitchen to fetch one. Summers didn't stop me. There were no dishes in the sink. No dishes drying. I opened the cupboard for a fresh glass and glimpsed a matching pair of crystal tumblers. One had a remnant of lipstick on the rim. Odd, I thought, for someone as fussy as Gianna. I bypassed it and took a plain highball glass, filled it with water, and hurried to the bedroom.

As I handed it to Addison, I said, "I noticed a strange thing in the kitchen."

She sipped the water. "What?"

"A crystal tumbler had a lipstick mark on it."

"Mother never would have put it away in such a fashion," she exclaimed. "She always washed things to within an inch of their lives. She was very tidy and specific about those particular glasses. Daddy gave them to her on their fifteenth anniversary. I remember his words that night. 'As crystal is fragile and easily broken, so this gift reminds us to nurture our relationship and treat it with care.'" Tears glossed her eyes. "He could be so romantic."

I recalled Idha breaking a goblet the other night at dinner and winced. Had the incident, as I'd posited to my aunt, been an omen of things to come? "Does your mother have a housekeeper, Addison?"

"Yes, but she would have been fired for doing something so sloppy. Maybe the caterers who served us dinner Monday did it."

An idea formed. I addressed Detective Summers. "Is it possible the killer gave Gianna a drink with some kind of sedative and washed the glass quickly to remove evidence, doing a slipshod job?"

He didn't respond.

I continued. "If so, she might have known and trusted whoever killed her."

Summers zeroed in on Addison. "Someone like her daughter."

Chapter 6

Addison squealed. "No! I didn't do it!"

I asked Summers if she needed an attorney.

"I have a divorce attorney," Addison blurted out.

"A criminal attorney," I clarified.

Summers nodded. "It would be wise. She doesn't deny she was here. She had motive and opportunity."

"I didn't have a reason to kill my mother!" Addison screeched. When she settled down enough to say she would search for legal representation after her father arrived, Summers ordered me to leave.

Concerned about Addison but uneasy about the way the detective was glowering at me, I agreed to go. I fetched my rain slicker and, on my way out of the house, passed a bald man wearing a jacket with a badge affirming he was the coroner. Though I was curious to find out what the time of death was and whether a sedative had been used, I reminded myself it wasn't my business. Even though Addison and I had found her mother and I was helping Addison host her party, the victim wasn't my relative. On the other hand, I'd attended the fractious dinner Monday night and felt invested in learning the truth. Not to mention, Addison had seemed so fragile and near her breaking point when I left. Plus after all the soon-to-be-divorced party planning and additional spa treatments I'd provided or would provide, I considered her to be a friend.

If she didn't kill Gianna, who did?

A short while later, when I entered the spa, I found Meryl doing her best to calm her mother, but she couldn't seem to quiet her. Mah was mumbling and wringing her hands. Meryl was patting her back.

All my senses went on hyperalert. "What's wrong?"

"Plumbing." Mah jutted a hand toward the hallway.

"Plumbing?" I echoed.

"We have a plumbing problem," Meryl explained. "We sprang a leak under the facial room sink. The floor is flooded."

Mah said, "I contacted a plumber. He can't come now."

I made a snap decision. Now was not the time to tell them about Gianna's murder. "When can they make it?"

"They're super busy, so I . . ." Meryl released her mother and plucked the sleeves of her boho blouse. "I watched a YouTube video and did a patch job. It's holding, but we need a professional. I put towels everywhere."

Mah sighed deeply. "I canceled all facials for today."

I was the sole facialist. "Okay. Good." As upset as I was about the murder, I might not bring my best game to the treatment.

Mah exchanged a look with her daughter. "Is Emma mad at me?"

"Of course not!" I squawked. "Don't worry. Accidents happen."

"No." Meryl spread her arms. "My mother needs to know if you are upset because she continues to have trouble with the phones. She can wisecrack with the best of them, but putting someone on hold is throwing her for a loop. She accidentally cut off three clients."

"You'll get the hang of it," I said.

Mah made a dismissive sound.

"You will." I fanned the air breezily, though her inability to grasp such a simple task was making me question whether I needed to move her to another position and hire a new receptionist.

"Mah, I've got an idea." Meryl held up a finger. "You could put a phone bit in your act for next week's gig. You know, like Lily Tomlin used to do." Mimicking the famous comedian, she attempted an Ernestine the telephone operator impression. "Hello?" She snorted twice. "Yes, how may I help you? Hold please. Hello?" She stabbed another imaginary line and returned to using her own voice. "After your opening, you'll realize you have five callers on the line, and you can't remember who's who."

Mah scoffed. "I won't steal another comedian's signature sketch."

"It's not stealing. You're not going to do the nasal voice or use her words. Or, I know, how about a few one-liners?" She held up both hands. "Hello, what do you get when you cross a telephone with an iron?" She waited a beat. "A smooth operator."

Her mother groaned. "Go away. It is not a good joke."

"Emma laughed."

I did. I was in dire need of giggles.

"Tell Emma about Dante." Mah fluttered her fingers in my direction.

Meryl's buoyant mood went south, and her face pinched with pain. Her son, teenage Dante, was a handful.

"What's going on?" I asked.

"He hates me," she muttered. "My ex is doing the same old, same old. Demeaning me to Dante. I want a relationship with my son, but I don't know how to go about it. His father is devious and can't be trusted, and my shrink says he's gaslighting me, telling me I'm nuts to even consider he's pitting our son against me."

"Psychiatrist," her mother corrected.

"Shrink," Meryl reiterated. "She's trying to shrink my problems."

"He-e-ey," Mah said, dragging the word out in the same way Meryl would when preparing to tell an anecdote. "A guy asks his friend, 'Have you heard the joke about gaslighting?' 'No,' says his friend. 'Sure you have,' replies the guy. 'You're crazy.'"

Meryl moaned. “Not funny.”

I bit back a smile. They were always trying to one-up each other. “Dante will come around,” I assured Meryl. “Lots of kids rebel when they reach their late teens. He’ll return to you eventually. Promise. Now get to work.”

“Hold on.” Meryl raised a palm. “Did you get the check from Gianna?”

My insides snarled. *No time like the present.* Quickly, I brought them up to speed about the murder. The locked room. Finding Addison’s mother. Smelling lavender and another scent. The police’s arrival.

“Yikes!” Meryl clasped her mother’s hand. “Why didn’t you start with that, Emma?”

“The plumbing fiasco sounded pretty dire.”

“Right, of course it is. But you are the one who found her?” Meryl whistled. “Emma, it’s such bad karma. Totally cray-cray. What does this mean for the spa?”

“It doesn’t affect us at all.”

“It could. Addison and her friends are having all their treatments here. Gianna was supposed to pay for them. Somehow—I don’t know how—this will reflect badly on Aroma Wellness, like it did when your friend Willow was killed.”

Was she right? Worry swirled through me. Did I need to be proactive and stay on top of the police investigation to tamp down any rumors? A couple of months ago, when Willow was murdered, tongues had wagged and my business had faltered until I’d proved I hadn’t had a hand in her untimely death.

“Hello.” The door opened and a man strutted in. Not just any man. My father, Everett Brennan, in his late forties and ruggedly handsome. Silver strands streaked the sides of his wavy dark hair. His bushy eyebrows waggled as he crossed to me, sheer delight in his eyes. “How are you, baby doll?”

“I could’ve sworn you were in Timbuktu, Dad. You sent me a postcard featuring the Great Mosque of Djenne.”

“I was. I’m all done there. Now I have a few meetings with the foundation in Silicon Valley, but I thought I'd stop in and say hi to you before I head there. C'mere." He spread his arms.

I hustled to him, and he embraced me in a firm hug. His breath was warm on my neck. The aroma of Pierre Cardin—a blend of lavender, orange, basil, and bergamot—filled my senses. It had always been his cologne of choice. In my childhood fantasies, I'd hoped to find a guy who wore the same. I didn't have a Daddy complex. I simply liked and trusted him, and it was a known fact that scents often triggered cherished memories and affected our attraction to others.

He held me at arm's length. "What's troubling you?"

I couldn't start with the murder. "We have a plumbing problem."

"On it. Fetch me a tool kit."

He studied the layout of the spa as I guided him down the hall. "The place looks great. Exactly like the photos you sent me. Is Sierra working out okay?"

"She's brilliant."

"And how's Lissa?"

He and my grandmother got along well. She didn't hold a grudge against him for leaving my mother and me. She understood how devoted he was to his causes and knew how terrific he was about communicating with me.

"Thriving. She avidly runs the library and book clubs."

"At her age?"

"Don't let her hear you say that. She is forever young."

He chuckled.

"She volunteers in the library garden, too. She hates weeds."

"Don't we all? Useless growth." He didn't ask about my mother, and I didn't offer.

I retrieved the tool kit from a cupboard in the hall, and we entered the facial room. "Yikes. Mah and Meryl weren't kidding. We've reached out to a plumber, but they're booked."

"Fret not. I've got this." Dad grinned. "Trivia for one hundred, Alex."

Fond recollections of sitting by my father's side watching *Jeop-*

ardy! when Alex Trebek was the host whooshed through me. Dad always uttered the right answers. "What's the category?" I asked.

"Water." He lowered himself to the floor and scooched face up under the sink.

"How does it look?" I asked. "Meryl said she patched it."

"It's not holding. We'll need some sealant."

I rummaged through the tool kit, found a tube, and handed it to him. "What's the clue?"

"This portal contains more than four hundred million water quality records from more than two million locations, sourced from more than sixteen hundred water quality data providers, including every state, territory, and more than one hundred Tribal Nations." He hummed the *Jeopardy!* tune while applying the sealant. "Ding, ding, ding. Time's up."

I spanked the counter. "The Water Quality Portal."

"Phrase it as a question."

"What is the Water Quality Portal?"

"Good girl. You've been boning up."

"Purely on bodies of water. I knew you wouldn't be able to resist that line of questioning. Either that or you would focus on capitals of the world."

Dad poked his head out and squinted up at me. "Are you dating anyone? Have you heard from—"

"No. Let's not talk about him." My last boyfriend, a talented man who could play anything on the piano but wasn't a musician by trade, was currently saving rainforests. I'd confirmed it recently via Facebook. He'd posted loads of pictures. When we broke up, it was semiamicable. Semi because we'd argued. Loudly. I'd wanted to open the spa. He'd needed to explore the world. To be honest, I wasn't sure I ever wanted to date again. I certainly didn't think about marriage or raising a family. I was young. I had plenty of years to navigate those tricky waters.

Dad ducked under the sink. "Does he write you postcards like I do?"

"No, he's not good at communicating. When we bid each other goodbye, we both meant goodbye." At least I had, although I dreamed of him and his chiseled physique and the intimate way he would pull me in close and kiss me on the forehead. *Shh, shh, shh, Emma,* I cautioned, and mentally pushed romantic memories from my mind. "I'm content to occupy my time with business and friends."

"Sure you are."

I sobered. "Hey, Dad, something horrible happened today."

He inched out from beneath the sink.

I told him about finding Gianna McKay.

"Sweetheart, why didn't you say so in the first place?" He scrambled to his feet and embraced me again. "Two murders inside a few months?" He caressed my hair. "You must be devastated."

"I feel as if I'm a magnet for bad luck."

"Or you're Jessica Fletcher and experiencing the Cabot Cove effect."

Said effect was a humorous way to describe a fictional phenomenon, stemming from the TV show *Murder, She Wrote*, where the small town that the protagonist lived in experienced a bizarrely high number of murders.

I swatted him. "Now is not the time to be glib."

"Perhaps not, but you're smiling, and to think clearly, you have to find your sense of humor." He hugged me one more time. "I happen to know Gianna McKay's husband, O'Malley. I consulted him on a water issue in South America, where he was designing a golf course. How's he doing?"

"Shell-shocked, I imagine."

"I presume Dylan Summers is on the case." Carmel Police had a number of officers, but Summers was a senior detective.

"He is, but . . ." My voice trailed off.

"But what?"

"Dad, this could affect my business." I told him about Meryl's concern.

He scrubbed his chin. "Nah, Dylan will shield you."

"Why will he need to shield you?" a woman asked while knocking on the door to the spa room.

I knew the voice. My stomach plummeted. I turned. "Kate!" My mother preferred everyone to call her by her given name. I could get away with saying *Mother* on occasion, but never Mom. "Um, hi!"

She caught sight of my father and aimed the tip of her umbrella at him. "You! What are you doing here?" I sure hoped the umbrella tip wasn't poisonous. Dressed in a black suit, a white silk blouse, heels, and a huge black tote, she looked ready for battle.

"Hi, Kate." Dad's voice was as smooth as honey. "Emma and I are catching up, and I'm helping repair the plumbing."

"What are you doing here?" she repeated. "In America, I mean."

"I'm heading to Silicon Valley later today and thought I'd swing by Carmel first. Nicest place on earth." He beamed, albeit cheekily.

Kate regarded him skeptically. "You're telling me you drove the two-hour trek from San Francisco International Airport just to see Emma?"

"Hour and a half. Traffic was good. Plus, she's the love of my life."

Kate growled. Man, he could irk her. After all, it was his choice to end the marriage. She'd dated a few men since he left, but most of the relationships had fizzled quickly. Being a well-educated English professor, she had attracted somewhat stuffy intellectuals. My father was a smart man, but he was not an academic by any stretch of the imagination. He liked the outdoors. He relished adventure. Golfing was the extent of Kate's exposure to the sun, and even then, she was covered head to toe in clothing and her face, neck, and hands were always lathered in sunblock.

"I was hoping to take you to lunch, Emma." My mother cocked a hip. "I want to talk about my latest course, featuring the works of Charlotte Brontë."

My father yawned deliberately. I *thwacked* his arm.

Snickering, he nudged me. "Go. I'll finish up here and drive north, but I'll return Sunday. No one at the company works on Sundays. Firm policy. Sunday is your day off, isn't it?"

"Yep."

"Why don't you and I take a hike?"

"I'd like that, Dad. I'll make a picnic."

He arched a skeptical eyebrow. "How are your cooking skills?"

"Better than they used to be. Sierra is coaching me."

As I ushered my mother out of the room, my father yelled, "Don't forget to tell your mother about your morning."

Kate cut me a hard look. "What happened?"

I offered a recap.

"Heavens. You found the body? No wonder you and your father were discussing Dylan Summers and his need to shield you." She huffed. "You have too much drama in your life, Emma. Why, this could affect your business. I told you when you dreamed up this idea that it was an iffy prospect, and—"

"Don't say it. This business is my soul. My center. It brings people joy. I am not giving up. I'll protect its reputation until my dying day." The poor choice of words rattled me, but I managed to keep a steady pace.

My mother sniffed derisively. "Isn't Addison Lacey the one who's having a happily divorced event at your spa?"

"Exactly."

"I wish I'd had a happily divorced party."

"Kate!"

She pulled a face. "From what I heard, her mother Gianna wasn't well liked. I never followed her modeling career, and I didn't do any business with her—she wasn't my Realtor—but rumors about her temper were rife. Even so, I doubt she deserved to be murdered."

"Does anyone?"

"Yes, bad people." She cut me a hard look. "Whatever you do, stay out of it. Your father is right. Dylan Summers is entirely capable of solving this crime all on his lonesome."

When I first met Detective Summers, I learned my grandmother knew him well. He was a regular at the library. Shortly thereafter, I realized my mother knew him, too. They both played golf and had met on occasion at one of the many public courses they toured. Carmel had over twenty-four public courses, including the renowned and expensive Pebble Beach Golf Links.

"Yes, I know he's competent." I didn't remind her I'd helped him figure out who'd killed my friend Willow. Why poke the bear?

When she reached the reception area, Kate glanced over her shoulder. "I don't want you spending time with your father."

"Mother, let it go."

"He's not a good influence on you."

"I beg to differ. I get my courageous spirit from the Brennan side of the family."

"I'll have you know the Reades are adventuresome."

The Reade surname, with its many variants, like Reid, Reed, and Read, was one of the most common surnames in Ireland, although Reade with an *e* was English and typically meant someone who was red-haired. Oddly enough, none of the Reades I knew had red hair. I think my great-great-grandfather might have.

"Your great-grandmother was an outdoor enthusiast," Kate stated. "And a premiere touring cyclist."

"Genetically, she was from the Murphy clan, and from what I can tell, the Reades are eggheads. Including Nana Lissa."

"Using one's brain is much more important than using one's brawn."

"Unless one needs brawn," I quipped. Thus the reason I'd been taking karate and tai chi classes. "I want to hone both aspects of my personality."

"'Vanity working on a weak head produces every sort of mischief,'" she intoned. "So wrote Jane Austen in *Emma*."

"Are we going to have a battle to see who can summon up the better quote?" I sassed. My mother loved to spar with me by referencing lines from famous books. Austen was her favorite author and the source of my name and why Kate had been motivated to give me so much of the Austen-themed décor in my apartment.

"Emma!" Mah whistled as I passed by the check-in desk. "Addison Lacey called. She asked if you'd return her call."

My mother waved a hand, encouraging me to take care of business. "We'll get lunch another time." On her way out, she peered one more time down the hall, clearly unhappy by my father's appearance.

I reached out to Addison. She bypassed formalities and informed me her father had arrived and didn't know any attorneys and neither did her divorce attorney, but she needed one desperately, seeing as Detective Summers was grilling her as if she was a person of interest. Could I recommend one? She knew I'd been in a fix during the summer. Without hanging up, I texted her the attorney's contact information.

"Emma," she sobbed, "I still can't believe it. Who would've done this to my mother?"

I recalled Kate's comment moments ago. Gianna McKay hadn't been well liked, which meant there could be multiple suspects. Who would be on the police detective's radar besides Addison? Gianna's brother? Her sister-in-law? Wyatt Lacey? Had any former business associates held a grudge?

Chapter 7

By the time I was closing up for the night, though my shoulders were aching and my brain was exhausted, I was looking forward to tending my garden and drinking in the night air while sipping a glass of wine. Hopefully, I'd catch a sighting of Dewberry again. It would lift my spirits. I was setting the alarm when my grandmother called me. I answered after one ring.

"I heard you had an eventful day." Her voice was warm and reassuring, but her concern filtered through. "Why didn't you contact me?"

"I've been super busy."

"You found the body?"

"Who told you?"

"Dylan. I ran into him at Percolate." Percolate was a charming café within walking distance, south of Ocean Avenue. Nothing in Carmel was very far, honestly. People hoofed it everywhere. "He was loading up on caffeine and said he was none too pleased you were at the scene."

"I'll bet."

"However, he assured me you made some good observations. He didn't mention what they were. He can be close-lipped."

"What an understatement." I waited for her to chide me further for not reaching out, but she didn't.

"I'm calling because a friend's winery is having a soiree at their tasting room tonight. How about you, Sierra, and I attend, and you can catch me up? Sierra already said yes."

"You are sly, Nana. You want to see how I'm doing."

She snickered. "Indeed. Sierra also mentioned a certain someone came to town, and your mother was close to exploding."

Hoo-boy. How many others had put two and two together after seeing Kate storm off and my father leaving later on?

"He's got meetings with his foundation in Silicon Valley," I told her.

"He's in for a split second and, like a tumbleweed, gone with the wind?"

"No," I replied, though she'd captured a fairly apt description of my father. "He's coming back Sunday and we're going hiking."

"Good. I know how much you miss him. I'll pick you up at seven." Nana Lissa ended the call.

I crossed the courtyard to check in on Yoly. "Good day?" I asked from the doorway.

"The best. About to close up."

"Don't forget to arm the alarm."

She tapped her temple. "It's emblazoned in my brain, but I can't tell you how weird it is that it's silent. I mean, when I'm leaving, I double-check the light on the panel to see if it's on. Otherwise, how would I know if it triggered?"

"The security company would call," I assured her. "G'night. Be safe."

When I arrived home, I immediately hung up my rain slicker. So much for there being rain in today's forecast. Of course, Vivi was eager to start playing. I picked her up, kissed her nose, set her on the floor, and switched on the automatic laser toy sitting on the kitchen desk. Vivi darted after the red lights the toy emitted around the room.

"Have fun," I cooed.

Knowing I was going out for a glass of wine, I decided to be smart and have a giant glass of sparkling water to hydrate. Sierra would be so proud of me. I carried the glass to the living room window and peered into the backyard. "Garden, you will have to wait."

I searched for Dewberry but didn't see her. Maybe she'd been assigned tasks by Merryweather Rose of Song, a mature guardian fairy who primarily hung out at the library. I'd met her for the first time a week after I'd seen Dewberry. According to my grandmother, Merryweather, the eldest of the fairies in the human world, could be rather bossy.

"Dewberry," I whispered, hoping she'd hear me and whiz into view, but she didn't materialize.

"Emma!" a woman yelled and knocked on my front door. "Emma!"

I hurried to it and peeked through the peephole. Ursula Josipovic, my upstairs neighbor, was standing there, twirling a curl of her hair with a finger.

I opened the door. "Is everything okay?" She rarely visited unless she needed a kitchen item. We were friendly and she came to the spa for a variety of services, but she could be very private.

"I'm fine." *Exotic* and *glamorous* were the words that had come to me when I'd first met her. She had dark, expressive eyes and a full mouth an actress would covet. Long brown tresses spilled from beneath the pumpkin orange scarf she'd tied around her head. "Do you like my new gown?" She had a lingering Eastern European accent, as if she'd worked hard to Americanize it.

"I like it very much."

"I bought yesterday." She pulled the seams of her colorful, floor-length, tent-style dress to show how expansive it was. The heavenly scent of patchouli wafted with the move. She favored the perfume, especially because it was an aroma that could enhance the mind and boost one's libido. "You have reminded me to be kind to myself, and I needed a present."

"Come in." I beckoned her. After she stepped inside, I closed the door and led her to the kitchen. I set my sparkling water on the counter. "Why did you need a present?"

"My fortune-telling business is languishing. I have posted the ads we discussed, but I do not entice all the new clients I need."

Now might not be the best time to spend money on a dress, I reflected, but kept my opinion to myself. "Care for a drink? Water? Wine?"

"Nothing, thank you." She picked up the cat and nuzzled her. "Hello, sweet Vivi." She'd had a cat of her own but gave it to her sister because she was traveling too often. Many of her clients lived in other states and paid beaucoup bucks for her to read for them in person. Perhaps that aspect of her work was suffering. She had been around town a lot more lately than in the past. "I wanted to inform you I have plans."

"What kind of plans?"

She set Vivi on the floor, and the cat resumed darting after the red lights swirling around the room. "You will see, but I think you will be pleased with me."

If she wasn't going to tell me about learning to read crystals from my aunt, I wouldn't press. "I'm delighted to see you smiling about whatever it is."

"Telling fortunes is not always pleasant. Sometimes I see very scary things. In my new venture . . ." She studied my face and her mouth turned down. *"Egek."*

"*Egek* what?" *Egek* in Hungarian translated to *heavens*. That couldn't be good.

"I did not look you in the eye before, being so focused on my own path. Emma, you must beware."

"Of what?"

"Danger looms. A man . . ." She paused. "No, a woman." She

wagged her head. "No, a man. I don't know which for sure." Thunder rumbled outside. Ursula shuddered. "Someone wishes to do you harm. Be alert." She embraced me briefly and left.

Shaken, I followed her, locked the bolts, and slogged into the kitchen. Gloom consumed me. I slumped into a chair. Someone wished to do me harm? Who? Would a shattered glass ceiling be involved?

A memory of one of my major relationship flops ran roughshod in my brain. In my freshman year of high school, I fell for a skinny boy named Liam. Besides being a track star, he was a science geek. He lived for biology. He wanted to become a surgeon. At the beginning of our relationship he was kind, but after a few weeks, I started to sense the real measure of him. He often got testy and had a penchant for dissecting things. First it was bugs, then frogs. When I realized he'd advanced to examining animals outside of class, I reported him to the principal. Liam found out and threatened me with a shard of glass. A week later his parents committed him to Atascadero State Hospital, a psychiatric hospital constructed within a secure perimeter. To this day, I could feel the tip of the glass against my throat. He was another of the reasons I'd pursued meditation and why I was motivated to champion the health of others.

I glanced at a quotation, one of many hanging on my kitchen walls: *Once you replace negative thoughts with positive ones, you'll start having positive results. ~ Willie Nelson*

My grandmother was the person who had encouraged me to post sayings, reminding me that the adages needn't come from worldly pundits. Singers, actors, artists, and other creatives often came up with heartfelt sayings because they, like me, were always on the alert for inspiration.

I whispered, "Yes, Emma, be positive. Be calm."

But it was difficult, because recently I'd started having nightmares about Liam. He'd attended Carmel High School. He knew where my grandmother lived. Was he the one Ursula saw in my future? Had he escaped from the asylum? What if the doctors had pronounced him healthy enough to return to society?

* * *

Euphoria Winery's tasting room was located south of Ocean Avenue on Dolores Street. It was of modest size and buzzing with good vibes when Nana, Sierra, and I strolled in. The décor was golden yellow with splashes of burgundy. The blond wood, tall tables with stools, and light-colored counters created a warm atmosphere.

A staff member in a stylish witch's costume—a black dress with red-and-white-striped stockings—offered to take our raincoats. All three of us had brought them. "This way." She motioned to a table reserved for us.

"This place is so fun," Sierra exclaimed. "And the decorations are adorbs."

The table was adorned with tiny pumpkins and miniature haystacks tied with raffia.

"Well, I clash with everything." Nana Lissa grimaced. She'd dressed in an ocean-blue sweater over cigarette pants.

"You do not," I assured her. "Especially given all the costumes the customers and staff are wearing. I wish we'd known to dress for the occasion."

"Uh-uh, not me." Sierra waggled her head. "I never don costumes."

"What are you talking about?" I plucked a green grape off its stem and twirled it at her. "You acted in plays in high school."

"I don't wear costumes outside the theater," she revised. "I prefer to be authentic."

"Wearing a costume is fun," I said. "It can reveal your creative side."

"Outside the kitchen, I don't have a creative bone in my body."

A server in black slacks, white shirt, and burgundy apron emblazoned with the winery's name approached. Kitten whiskers adorned her cheeks, and she'd applied a black heart shape to the tip of her nose. "Hi, ladies. The boss told me you were coming in." She was soft-spoken. I strained to hear her. She set a platter filled with fresh fruit and a selection of cheeses, each marked with a wooden sticker denoting the flavor, on the table. She also laid down a menu with explanations of the cheeses' origins and cocktail napkins.

"Love the tail," I quipped.

"Thanks." The fluffy appendage, which she'd pinned to the backside of her pants, flipped right and left with each movement. "The boss said to tell you she won't appear for a while. Hope you'll stay long enough to see her. I heard she's dressed as the Bride of Frankenstein. In the meantime, how about a flight of white wine selections?"

"Sounds delicious," I said.

Nana Lissa hummed her approval.

The server left, and the three of us tasted the cheeses. The truffle cheese was divine.

"How do you know the owner?" I asked Nana Lissa.

"She was one of the first members of the library's book club. She always adored reading nonfiction about wines and food, and she finally took the plunge and invested in this winery."

"Oh, man." Sierra smacked her lips. "This cheddar is incredible." She referred to a descriptive menu beside the platter. "Hook's Fifteen-year Cheddar. It has tang as well as sweetness."

After the server returned with three wooden planks set with four small tumblers, each filled with two ounces of white wine, Nana Lissa tapped the table. "Let's talk turkey. Emma, tell us everything. You went to the McKays' to collect a check. Addison knocked on her mother's door. When Gianna didn't respond, you let yourselves in and found her dead."

I had to admit I was tired of relaying what I'd seen—Gianna smothered, her hair fanned out, her lipstick smeared—but I decided revisiting the scene with my loved ones might help me remember a detail I'd overlooked, so I launched into my account.

"Poor Addison." Sierra sighed. "You don't think she did it, do you?"

"No."

"Except she was at the house when it happened. How could she not have heard?"

"The primary bedroom is on the first floor. She was upstairs, and she was playing loud music and wearing headphones."

"What is it with young people and eardrum-splitting music?" Nana Lissa tsked.

"There was deafening music on when I arrived this morning," I went on. "I was surprised the neighbors weren't complaining."

"Aha. So, she doesn't always wear headphones," Sierra concluded. "Could she have lied about that?"

"I don't think so. Loud music in the day is one thing. Booming music at night would have drawn attention and possibly a warning about disturbing the peace." I recounted how I'd seen the pair of crystal tumblers in the kitchen cabinet, one with remnants of lipstick, and I explained my reasoning about the killer possibly dosing Gianna with a drug to sedate her. "I wonder if the coroner has determined it to be true."

Sierra paired a wedge of Brie with a slice of apple, bit into it, and crooned, *"Ooh,* I'm in love!"

"Why do you think Gianna was sedated?" Nana asked.

"How else would she have lain peacefully while being smothered? Any of us would have fought the killer."

"Wouldn't the body have spasmed, even if sedated?" Sierra asked.

"Not if a paralytic was used," I said, sounding knowledgeable, though I was only parroting a theory I'd read in a mystery. "There weren't any scratches or bruises on Gianna's face or body I could see."

"Poor dear," Nana Lissa murmured.

Dear wasn't how I would've described Gianna, but *poor* . . . definitely.

We grew silent and glanced around the space. A few customers were dressed in costumes, among them a wench, a princess, Barbie, and Darth Vader.

Sierra pointed out the man who was wearing a cowboy getup. "Do you think he's the real thing?"

"Not with such pasty skin," I joked, and instantly cringed, recalling how Gianna's skin had been ashen and flaccid. Appetite squelched,

I set my glass of sauvignon blanc aside. "Nana, Kate told me Gianna wasn't well-liked. Have you heard the same?"

"When she was a model, people adored her. Sure, she could be a prima donna, but she was so beautiful, others catered to her whims. When selling real estate, she had a reputation for muscling other Realtors out of a sale or maligning their reputations, but I never dealt with her. I don't know firsthand and shouldn't spread rumors."

"Were she and Peyton good partners?" I hadn't included Gianna's friend on my list of suspects. Should I?

"From all I heard, yes. Gianna was the bait. Peyton was the closer. She was extremely devoted to Gianna." Nana Lissa downed a piece of Edam. "A yearslong friendship is golden."

"Why did Gianna quit the real estate business?" Sierra sipped her wine.

"She'd had enough," Nana stated. As a librarian, she'd amassed a lot of knowledge about everyone. Readers liked to confide in her. "What I heard was, she received a tidy inheritance."

I briefed them on the trust Gianna had set up for Addison.

"With her wealth," our grandmother continued, "she chose to live a life of leisure. It didn't hurt that O'Malley was drawing a very good income."

Sierra propped her hands on the table and lowered her voice. "Gianna's sister-in-law was livid with her the other night. Remember how she smashed a glass because she was so upset?"

"Not on purpose," I said, wondering why I was defending Idha. I supposed I admired her for standing up to Gianna. "She was championing her husband and her niece."

"Emma"—Nana focused her gaze on me—"if you want my two cents, I think Dylan will be open to more of your thoughts if you have any to share."

"I don't."

"But you may. This is the kind of mental processing you do with ease. You listen to people and weigh their responses. You determine their needs."

"Hey, Nana, what about me?" Sierra tapped the table. "I could solve a crime. I'm a chef, and chefs pay attention to detail. A sprinkle of this, a tablespoon of that."

Nana Lissa patted Sierra's hand. "Of course, dear girl, but you're not really a people person. To solve a crime, an investigator must have the ability to be attentive to a person's tone and demeanor."

"Bah!"

"Emma focuses on a person's health. It's an entirely different skill set."

"Did your fairy tell you that?" Sierra pretended to frown, as if Nana had hurt her feelings, but the scowl quickly turned into a grin.

"Do not mock me, young lady."

"Is she here?" Sierra asked.

"As a matter of fact, yes."

Merryweather Rose of Song, was, indeed, attending our soiree. Her iridescent, gossamer hair glimmered in the light. Her loose-fitting crimson dress went nicely with the winery's décor. Her polka-dotted wings were fanciful. I crooked a finger at her in greeting, and she stuck her tongue out at me. I squinted to chide her. Her laughter tinkled like wind chimes.

"Does she go everywhere with you, Nana?" Sierra's skepticism was palpable.

"Not just me. She is a guardian fairy who oversees all the people who visit the library," Nana Lissa replied. "She is not a one-human fairy."

"Get out of here. There's such a thing as a one-human fairy? What total silliness." Sierra smoothed the sleeves of her silver sweater. "Enough talk about imaginary things, and let's not discuss the murder any longer, either. It's giving me the creeps. Why don't we toss around ideas for growing the business? I think we should obtain a beer and wine license and stay open at nights and possibly on Sundays."

"No!" I protested. "We're stretched thin as it is."

"You're right." Sierra sighed. "And if I had to give up my Sunday cycling group, I'd be distraught."

"About the group"—I wiggled my nose—"I don't think you should stay in it."

"Why not?"

"Wyatt Lacey might be a murderer."

"Do you really think so?" She leaned in. Apparently, the distress she'd experienced a second ago while talking about murder had vanished.

"Someone with antisocial personality disorder can be impulsive and lack remorse," I said. "He might have a need for control. If Wyatt truly believed Gianna was the reason Addison was divorcing him, he might have lashed out."

"Even so, I'm going to continue cycling." Sierra lifted her chin. "Others in the group have said if I stick with it, I could be good enough to compete."

Nana Lissa and I exchanged a worried glance.

Chapter 8

In the middle of the night, I awoke with a start because I'd been battling snakes that were slithering from Ursula's tresses and lashing at me with their tongues. Was she right? Was someone going to hurt me? Was Liam at large? Unable to quiet my mind, I opened my iPhone and searched for him. As far as I could tell, he had no internet history. No social media profile. Unless he'd changed his name, I had to assume he was still housed in the asylum. He was not out and about. But to be certain, I called the state hospital where he supposedly resided.

A docile-sounding woman answered. When I asked if Liam was still a patient, she hesitated. She said she couldn't wake a patient. I assured her I didn't want to speak to him, adding that I really needed to know his whereabouts because he had threatened me in the past, and someone believed I was in danger now. She asked me to hold. A minute later she came back on the line and said he was still there, sleeping soundly, and there were no plans for his release.

Breathing easier, I thanked her and ended the call.

The morning arrived with clouds and the forecasted-for-yesterday rain, which instantly put a damper on my good mood. Don't get me wrong. I appreciated rain. It helped gardens grow and washed away dust that had settled on the streets and buildings, but I didn't like taking a morning walk on the beach in a drizzle or a downpour. Certainly not on a workday. My hair would look like a rat's nest afterward. So I skipped the walk, added gel to my locks, knotted them at the nape of my neck, and threw on leggings, flats, and a long-sleeved, no-iron, sage-green blouse.

I poured the coffee I'd brewed in my Keurig into a travel mug and said, "Let's get a move on, Vivi." I was taking her to work today. "I have clients to attend to." She was bent over her food bowl, eating the last few bites of her breakfast. Rotating her head slowly, she gazed up at me with those gorgeous eyes opened wide and meowed.

"Chop-chop. Eat up."

She mewed again, meaning she didn't want to be rushed.

"Don't you want to come with me?" I didn't take her to work often, but when I did, she usually enjoyed hanging out in the office.

She twitched her tail, rejecting the offer.

"Fine. You stay home." I spoke cat sign language as well as the next cat owner. "I'll put your red-light toy on a timer." It would provide a couple of kitty workouts during the day.

A short while later, I arrived at the Courtyard of Peace. Everything appeared to be in order. The rain had stopped. Either Sierra or one of the staff had already wiped down the wrought-iron chairs and tables. I waved to Yoly, who was unlocking the gift shop. She didn't respond. She was dashing into the shop to turn off the alarm system. I laughed. How many times had I told her she could walk? The system wouldn't trigger for at least sixty seconds. *One, one thousand. Two, one thousand . . .*

I approached the café. People with unopened umbrellas murmured among themselves while standing in line ready to be welcomed inside. A few were studying the chalkboard menu marked *Thursday Specials* that had been placed in the window. A pumpkin delight smoothie topped the list again. I texted Sierra to make me one of those when she got the chance—she didn't try to dissuade me this time—and continued on to the spa.

"Morning, Mah," I said as I entered and crossed to the reception desk. She was fluttering a feather duster over the furniture. I shrugged out of my rain slicker and hung it on a hat tree behind the desk. "What do you think? Will it rain on and off all day?"

"Yes. One hundred percent chance."

I glanced up and spotted a plaque on the wall behind the desk different from the one that typically hung there. It read: *Do not overrate what you have received, nor envy others. He who envies others does not achieve peace of mind. ~ Buddha*

"Where did the plaque about conscious breathing go?" I asked.

"I put it in the office where this one was hanging. I thought moving them around would help inspire your clients. Each week, they will read a new quotation."

"Brilliant."

She beamed.

"You look nice." I indicated her hair. "The combs are very attractive."

She fingered them. "Meryl thinks they make me look too girlie. When I was young, I was very poor. . . ." She signaled me to wait for a punch line. "After years of struggle, I am no longer young."

I giggled. "Good one."

"You have a mindful meditation today."

"With Addison. Yes, I know." I'd seen the appointment entered in the calendar before leaving last night. It was exactly what she needed.

"She called a bit ago and asked if she could include her friend Riley and her aunt. I told her yes. It is all right, is it not?"

"Of course."

"Someday perhaps you will do a meditation for me and Meryl. It might help her deal with Dante."

"What a great idea. Let's schedule it. Um, any messages?" I noticed the answering machine was blinking.

"*Ack*, Emma, yes, there are many. The machine tells me there are five, but I cannot figure out how to access them." She screwed up her face.

"Breathe," I insisted, though I was once again wondering what to do about her. It wasn't hard to operate the contraption. Push a button, listen, write down the message, press an arrow, and go on to the next. I'd have Meryl teach her one more time.

"Good day to you!" Meryl emerged from the hall, filing her nails with an emery board. She was wearing what I presumed was another of her flea market bargains—a flower child–style lace vest with tassels over a white T-shirt and jeans. "The plumber has come and gone. He inspected your father's work and declared it particularly good."

I would have expected nothing less. What my father did in remote areas of the world required him being capable with his hands.

"Why didn't your father stay?" Meryl asked. "He was here such a short time. Less than a day."

"He's coming Sunday," I said, but I wasn't completely sure he would. Who knew what might cause a hiccup in his plans? "We'll go on a hike and picnic."

"Nice."

"Daughter," Mah cut in, using a regal tone, "Emma says she will give us a mindful meditation soon. We need to pick a date."

"It'll be free," I offered, in answer to Meryl's questioning look. "My treat."

"Yeet! You're on."

Before I could mention the messages issue, Addison pushed through the spa door. Riley trailed her. Both women were in jeans and sweaters. Their umbrellas were dry.

"My aunt is almost here." Addison waggled her phone. "She texted she's running late."

For someone who had lost her mother yesterday, Addison seemed a tad too chipper. The notion she'd killed Gianna skittered through my mind, but I pushed it aside.

No, Emma. Don't go there.

"I'm so glad you were with Addison yesterday," Riley said, reaching for both of my hands. She gave a firm squeeze and released me. "She really appreciated your support. She's heartbroken."

"Darn it, Riley, I told you . . . I told you not to . . ." Addison burst into tears. So much for being cheery and in control.

Riley threw an arm around her friend. "I'm sorry, honey. I didn't mean to upset you."

Addison peered at me. "I can't seem to stop crying. I'm like an automatic faucet with no Off button." She fished in her tote for a tissue and blotted her face. "Are my eyes red?" She turned to Riley.

"They're fine."

"They were so red earlier."

"The cold compresses I gave you did their magic."

"I was wondering, Emma"—Addison squished the tissue into a fist—"could we have tea on the patio after the meditation session?"

"Of course."

"Will you join us?"

"If it's not raining." We hadn't fitted the tables with umbrellas. Perhaps we should. "I don't have a facial treatment scheduled until eleven."

"Perfect." Addison clasped Riley's hand. "What do you want us to do now?"

"Sit down," I said. "Drink a glass of cucumber water. We'll start when your aunt arrives."

Addison's cell phone jangled. "Sorry." She frowned. "I thought I'd put it on mute. It's my father. Is it okay to answer?"

I nodded.

She pressed the screen. "Hi, Daddy. *Hmm?* No, I'll be okay. Yes, I'll eat. Promise. Riley will make sure I do. She's like an obnoxious mother hen."

Riley pulled a face.

"Yes, ring me after your business dinner." Addison ended the call and pocketed the phone.

At the same time the door swung open and Idha Gibson stepped inside looking as elegant as ever, her long black hair pulled sleekly off her face, her shoulders square, her high-end black outfit stunning.

"My darling girl." Idha swooped Addison into a hug. "I'm so sorry for your loss. Your uncle Frederick is beside himself with grief. Your mother was always his rock. His anchor. How are you doing?"

"Daddy says one foot in front of the other." Addison's voice cracked. She cleared her throat, as if to rid it of lingering emotions, and broke free of her aunt. "Work?" She indicated the briefcase hanging on Idha's right shoulder. In her left arm, she was toting a stack of books.

"Yes. I was at the library poring over a client's manuscript. I needed a few references to fact-check it."

"You're not carrying an umbrella," Addison said, stating the obvious.

"It's not going to rain."

Mah muttered, "One hundred percent chance."

"While I was there," Idha said, "that nice Detective Summers spoke with me."

Addison wrinkled her nose. "He's not nice. He's . . ." She eyeballed me, as if begging for another word.

"Firm," I inserted. "Firm, smart, and dedicated."

"And handsome," Riley cooed.

Addison *thwacked* her friend's arm. "Cut it out. He's old."

"Excuse me." Idha glowered at her niece. "He and I are the same age."

Addison's cheeks tinged pink. "I didn't mean to imply—"

"It's okay. I'm feeling pretty old lately." Idha offered a reassuring smile.

"Why was he at the library?" Addison asked.

"He was checking out a book."

This early in the morning? I reflected. Not a chance. I would bet he'd been approaching Idha's house, eager to question her about her relationship with Gianna. However, when he saw her leave and guessed where she was headed, he opted to approach her at the library to make his interrogation less off-putting.

"What did you two discuss?" Addison pressed.

"He wanted to know where your uncle was Tuesday night when your mother . . ." She shook her head solemnly.

"Why would he ask you about Uncle Frederick? Why not ask Uncle Frederick himself?" Addison's voice sounded strained. "And how could he possibly think Uncle Frederick killed Mother? He wouldn't hurt a fly."

Or a mosquito, I reflected, recalling O'Malley's quip about having a secret weapon to combat them. Why wouldn't Frederick get the details from O'Malley? Did his pride forbid him?

Idha shrugged one shoulder. "I believe the detective is ruling out suspects one by one."

"What is Uncle Frederick's alibi?"

"He and his astronomy buffs were holding their weekly Zoom session. Knowing they would chat for hours, I went to see a movie I knew he wouldn't enjoy."

Interesting how she was offering an alibi for herself while providing one for her husband.

"What a relief." Addison sighed. "I'm glad people know where he was and can vouch for him."

"Ladies"—I clapped softly, eager to turn off my suspicious and overly active mind—"why don't we start the mindful meditation?" Detective Summers was on the case. I didn't need to be.

Idha trailed me. "Emma, Addison claimed her mother was smothered, possibly with a pillow, and told me you believed Gianna might have been drugged. Detective Summers wouldn't reveal anything to me, not even the time of death."

"Between five and nine," Addison said. "I overheard him discussing it with the coroner. But of course it wasn't around five because Mother spoke to me through the closed door when I got home—"

I turned and held a finger to my lips. *"Shh*. Everyone, quiet your minds. No more talk about the murder. The goal of this meditation is to awaken the inner workings of our mental, emotional, and physical spirit. Regular worldly thoughts"—and thinking about murder, I reasoned—"shouldn't interfere."

"Yes, of course," Addison whispered, and mimed sealing her lips.

The meditation room was my favorite space in the spa. Six recliner chairs sat in a cluster at the far end. In the center lay a large square of rubber flooring. The room featured soft green walls. Glass shelving held a variety of crystal singing bowls. A few were no more than three inches across. The larger ones were a good twenty inches in diameter. Bronze singing bowls, which were known to spread healing, made beautiful sounds, but they didn't appeal to me. An array of geodes adorned the room to add to the positive energy vibe.

After dimming the lights, I invited everyone to settle onto the mat and sit in a half lotus or *Ardha Padmasana* pose. "Bend your left knee and place your left foot under your right knee," I instructed. "Then bend your right knee and place your right foot under your left knee." This pose enhanced flexibility in the hips, ankles, and knees and was one of the best asana a person could do when working toward the full lotus—both feet propped on top of one's thighs. "Now place your hands on your knees, palms upward, and close your eyes."

They followed each instruction.

In a gentle, steady tone, I invited them to fill their lungs with fresh air and exhale, adding that meditation could help unleash the natural curiosity of one's mind.

"This has been a traumatic time for all of you. You are sapped of energy and possibly at a loss as to how to feel. Should you cry? Should you get angry? Let these thoughts fade away for the moment and focus on your heart and soul. Let's restore the inner peace by concentrating on your strengths and talents. Pay attention to the love you have for the others in this room. The love you have for your family."

As the words spilled out of me, I couldn't help but picture Gianna lying on the bed looking so peaceful. I also couldn't help wondering whether her daughter might better process the situation if Gianna had taken her own life instead of being the victim of murder. Addison was undoubtedly curious about who had killed her mother and why. Was she suspecting those closest to her, even her aunt?

Emma, stop. Now is not the time to think about the crime.

"Breathe," I intoned, and then invited them to join me in repeating a series of meaningful chants. "I let go. I am letting go. I am letting everything go."

They repeated each phrase.

After asking them to inhale deeply and exhale again, I provided the next chain of words. "I am present in this moment. I am aware of my breathing. I feel the breath in my chest."

I followed with another. "I feel my shoulders releasing. Relaxing. The tension is melting away."

We continued in this fashion for twenty minutes.

Nearing the end, I guided them through one final inhalation and exhalation. "Repeat after me. I am at peace."

Their voices were soft as they echoed the words.

I rose and toggled the dimmer switch to bring the lights up slowly. "You may open your eyes."

They did and smiled at one another.

Without rising from the mat, Addison grabbed the hands of the other two. Her skin was rosy and her eyes clear. "I love you both so much. Thank you for doing this with me. I feel . . . hopeful."

Hopeful for answers, I imagined.

They rose to their feet, and Addison led the way out of the room.

Two tables were available on the patio, and the rain Mah was certain would return hadn't begun yet. Addison chose the table closest to the fountain, saying she loved the sound of the water. I offered to fetch treats from the café.

Sierra met me at the counter. "We're slammed. Sorry I didn't deliver this earlier." She handed me the pumpkin delight smoothie I'd asked for. "What do you need?"

"Tea and treats for four."

"How are you holding up?" she asked as she prepared a tray.

I told her about leading the mindful meditation. "I'm always calm after doing one."

"And Addison?" Hands busy, she motioned with her chin toward the patio.

Addison, Riley, and Idha were checking their cell phones.

"Fragile." I sipped my smoothie, taking a moment to appreciate the heavenly spices and smooth texture. "This is delicious."

"Glad you like it."

Sierra arranged whole wheat scones on a plate. "These are blueberry-lemon scones and they aren't beautiful."

They definitely weren't.

"But they are delicious. I make them with Greek yogurt." She was adding a few of the items she'd provided at the previous tea and stopped abruptly, her gaze fixated on something outside. "Hey, what's he doing here?"

I turned and caught sight of Wyatt Lacey marching across the patio. In his black-and-yellow cycling gear, he resembled a giant wasp—a very angry giant wasp. A bicycle tire was slung over one shoulder.

"No, no, no. Bring this tray out for me, would you?" I dashed through the door.

"Addison!" Wyatt bellowed.

Addison stiffened in her chair. "What are you doing here?"

I was out of breath when I arrived at the table. "Hello, Wyatt," I said to distract him.

He wheeled around and acknowledged me before returning his attention to Addison. "I'm sorry to hear about your mother's death."

An automaton would've sounded more sincere.

"How did you find me?" Addison demanded. "Are you following me?"

"No. I . . ." He splayed his hands. The bike tire shimmied to his elbow. He returned it with a yank to his shoulder. "I was out riding earlier and was passing by when you and Riley were climbing the stairs. I figured you had a treatment, so I waited an hour and returned."

"I don't want to talk to you, Wyatt."

"I heard your mother was murdered. Is it true?"

Riley said, "Yes."

Startled by her interruption, Wyatt directed his next question to her. "How?"

"She was smothered," Riley replied.

"Leave, Wyatt," Addison ordered.

A woman at a nearby table gripped her friend's arm and pointed past me.

I spun around and caught sight of Detective Summers and Officer Rodriguez striding across the patio. They must have seen Wyatt bolt up the stairs to the courtyard and decided to pursue him. Good. Haul him away. Keep him a safe distance from Addison.

Summers drew to a halt near the table. "Ms. Lacey, I'm placing you under arrest for the murder of your mother."

"What?" I squawked.

"I didn't do it," Addison cried.

"How did you know she was here?" I asked, and peered hard at Wyatt. Had he informed the police of her whereabouts or had Idha? She'd run into Summers at the library. I cut a look in her direction.

Idha shook her head. "I didn't tell him."

"Me either." Wyatt held up both hands.

"We triangulated her phone," Rodriguez offered.

Summers shot her a stern glance before readdressing Addison. "Please stand."

Addison obeyed. "Sir, I have no motive." Her voice skated upward. "None. I loved my mother."

"You hated her," Wyatt rasped.

"Not true." She scowled at her soon-to-be-ex-husband. "I didn't. I loved her."

"That's not what you said to me."

So much for Wyatt keeping their conversations private. What a jerk.

"He's lying, Detective." Addison spanked her hands together. "He's a born liar."

"Quiet, all of you." Summers mimed a *T* for time-out. "Ms. Lacey, we discovered your mother was going to cut off access to your trust fund."

"What?" She exchanged a look with Riley and refocused on the detective. "Why would she?"

"Don't you mean *how could she*?" Riley asked, and reached for her friend's hand.

"Officer"—Summers motioned to Rodriguez—"please explain."

Rodriguez tugged the hem of her uniform jacket and cleared her throat. "If the trust is a revocable living trust, which it is, a trustee can change the beneficiary at any time via an amendment. The beneficiary does not need to be notified of the change."

Had she memorized the definition at Summers's insistence?

"But there is a co-trustee," Riley argued. "Wouldn't he have to agree?"

"I presume he would," Summers said. "Ms. Lacey, I won't cuff you if you'll come peacefully."

"I didn't do it. I really didn't. I'm telling the truth." Tears leaked from Addison's eyes.

"How did you find out about the trust?" I asked the detective.

"Peyton Pelagatti informed us."

"Uh, sir, she informed you," Rodriguez corrected. "Not me."

"Yes, me, because I am lead on the case," Summers revised. "She said Gianna McKay told her on Monday that Addison was irresponsible and not worthy of the trust."

So much for Peyton being like an aunt to Addison. Had she offered up this information out of the goodness of her heart, or as a ploy to steer suspicion away from herself? She and Gianna had worked together until Gianna ended the partnership. Had her business suffered because of Gianna's exit? Did she hold a grudge?

"Mother never said anything of the kind to me," Addison argued. "Peyton's lying. Yes, my mother and I had differences of opinion, but she knew I was responsible. I have a thriving business."

"Ms. Pelagatti says your business is floundering."

Addison chewed her lip. "It's not earning enough to allow me to live on my own without some help, but it's not floundering. It will see a profit inside a year. And I'm diligent. I work every day for at least eight hours. I reach out to clients. I manage my social media. My father . . ." Addison held up her cell phone. "I need to call him. He'll know if what you're saying is true."

"You may call him from the precinct."

"Detective," I interrupted, "grant her the phone call now." I motioned to the customers on the patio. Many were staring intently. Some were taking photographs. I'd bet a few were recording videos. "Goodwill goes a long way."

Summers caught my drift. A police department could always use positive PR. Relenting, he gestured for her to call her father.

Addison reached O'Malley. "Hi, Daddy, it's me. I'm sorry to bother you, but the police are going to arrest me." She explained why.

"Put him on Speaker," Summers demanded.

She complied.

"Mr. McKay, Detective Summers here. I'm listening to your answers."

"Hi. Yes. Fine. Addison, sweetheart, I don't know anything about the trust other than your mother inherited the funds from her father." O'Malley sounded anxious. "She never told me what she intended to do with it."

"Was she truly disappointed with me? Was she vindictive?" Addison mewled.

"She never wanted you to marry Wyatt," her father stated. "I think after your divorce was final she might have come around, of course, but just last week—"

"Are you saying she was punishing me for a bad decision?"

Wyatt cut in. "I was the best thing that ever happened to you!"

"He's there?" O'Malley shouted. "What're you doing there, Wyatt? Detective Summers, I'm warning you, he's not to be trusted."

"Why, you . . ." Wyatt growled.

"Hush, Mr. Lacey," Summers ordered, and moved closer to Addison's phone. "Mr. McKay, I'm taking your daughter to the precinct. When we spoke yesterday, I suggested you would do well to find her a good attorney. It is still the case. Good day, sir." He commanded Addison end the call and hand over her cell phone.

She bid a tearful goodbye to her father, but before she ceded her mobile, she yelled, "Hold on, sir! Wyatt, did you know what my mother was going to do with the trust? Did you kill her before she could, so I would still inherit everything and be able to bail you out of your failing business?"

"My business is fine," he snapped. "Six stores, all in the black."

"Ha!" She arched an eyebrow. "In what fantasy world are you living? Lest you forget, my divorce attorney and I reviewed your books. Talk about floundering."

"I did not kill your mother," he rasped. "Besides, if you go through with the divorce, I won't benefit from any windfall you might receive. And I have an alibi for last night."

"Between the hours of six and nine?" Summers asked.

Apparently, the coroner had narrowed the window.

"I was watching business news." Wyatt lifted his chin defiantly. "The Dow was down six hundred points. The Nasdaq lost three percent. Two auto manufacturers released new electric SUVs with broader appeal."

"Watching the news isn't an alibi." Addison aimed a finger at him. "You could've read all of it on your app."

"I did not kill your mother!" he shouted.

"Neither did I."

Chapter 9

With the onset of the afternoon rain, a gloom fell over my staff. When one or more of them were not providing massages and other treatments, their muted chatter centered around Addison's arrest. I didn't think she was guilty and voiced my opinion, but many employees questioned whether I was biased.

At the end of day, while neatening my office, it dawned on me that if Addison remained in jail, I might need to cancel all the appointments for her friends and family, as well as the happily divorced cocktail party. Fortunately, I had Gianna's deposit to cover any losses. I caught a glimpse of the corkboard mounted on the wall next to the window. It held pastel-colored, three-by-five cards, each outlining tasks I needed to do for the spa, café, or gift shop. On the blue were water-related items, like checking all plumbing and fixtures and reordering oils and massage creams. After the fiasco in the facial room, plumbing inspections would be a weekly chore. On the pink, I'd written gift shop objectives. We needed to do inventory and reorders at least once a week, and we ought to prettify the displays by rotating items to new locations. On the pale green cards I'd spelled out the café matters I thought were important. I sent twice weekly texts to Sierra asking for her input. Doing our own health and cleanliness inspections ahead of any governmental assessments, she replied, were top of the list.

Staring at the cards, I felt inspired to write down the myriad questions racing through my mind about Gianna's murder. When Willow died, I'd found it helpful to clear the board of my to-do lists and fill out cards for each individual I considered a person of interest. However, since none of my queries at the moment could be attributed to suspects—I didn't have a clue who might have killed Gianna—I chose white cards.

I sat at the desk and used a special pen gifted to me from a guru.

 # 1: Would the trust fund motive be enough for Summers to hold Addison without a murder weapon?
 # 2: What physical evidence did the police have?
 # 3: Had the coroner discovered any knockout drugs in Gianna's system?
 # 4: Had Summers found any prescription bottles in Addison's room or elsewhere on the premises?
 # 5: Had Gianna consumed alcohol?
 # 6: Had the forensics specialists determined whether there were other fingerprints on the doorknob leading into Gianna's room?

Above the existing cards, I affixed the new cards to the corkboard in a single row. Organization mattered when corralling one's thoughts, my mother had drummed into me. How else could a student write a proper thesis? I took a step backward and hoped the visual images would trigger my subconscious deducting skills. No such luck.

Before heading home, I decided to swing by the gift shop and pick up a small token for Addison to show my support. I planned to visit her at the jail tomorrow during my lunch hour. The Carmel-by-the-Sea City Detention Center primarily held individuals who were pending transfer to other facilities. I hoped she would be released on bail before that happened.

"Hello?" I called as I slipped into the shop.

Yoly was dusting the glass shelving. She swung around, her expression grim. "I heard about your friend. I'm so sorry." She swiped a fingertip along the shelving, double-checking her efforts.

"Thank you." Although Addison wasn't an official friend, I was starting to believe she might become one. I liked her spunk. I cared about her future.

"The news spread like wildfire after the police showed up."

"I figured it would."

"It didn't hurt business," Yoly went on. "At least half of the customers this afternoon stopped in to get the scoop."

Swell. Aroma Wellness, the go-to place to infuse peace and harmony into a customer's life, was now the rumor mill for a murder investigation. Was my mother right? Would the business suffer? Should I give up trying to make a go of it and find another career?

No. No way. A steely resolve gripped me. I would not quit, if only to prove Kate wrong.

Yoly pushed her long braid over her shoulder and scrutinized me. "You look tired."

"I am, but I'll muscle through. I'd like to pick a supportive stone for Addison. One to protect her and bolster her hope."

"I doubt Detective Summers will allow you to give it to her," Yoly said, "but as your aunt Sophie would tell you, having it as one's own, if solely in the knowledge of owning it, can stimulate positivity. You could put it in a nice dish. One of her friends could place it in her bedroom until her return."

"Do we have hematite or black tourmaline?"

"We have the latter. Good choice." She rounded the glass case holding all the gemstones and crystals. She retrieved a smooth black stone from a grouping and also produced a card explaining the stone's powers. She put a small ceramic jewelry dish into a gift box and added the stone and card. "Black tourmaline is powerful and excellent for promoting emotional stability."

I added, "It can also make the aura and space around a person's living area affirming." My aunt had made sure I understood the properties of all stones, even if I never learned the skill of reading crystals. "If placed on or near the front doorstep, it should provide all sorts of protection, which might be necessary in the event Wyatt Lacey should dare to approach her again."

Yoly scrunched up her nose. "I don't like him. He looks menacing."

"*Unstable* is a better word."

"One of the customers confided he's got ASPD."

I wondered if the diagnosis was influencing Detective Summers's view of him.

"How can he run a successful business with that kind of psychological baggage?" Yoly asked. "I mean, aren't antisocial people lying, dishonest, and cruel? Don't they thrive on making others hurt?"

"Not all. Some can be charming and industrious. Consider Tony Soprano, Hannibal Lecter, or Sherlock Holmes."

"Holmes was antisocial?"

"He wasn't diagnosed, but he was definitely outside the norm when it came to interacting with others, and he was brilliant."

Bringing up Holmes distracted us, and we went off on a tangent, idly chatting about the first stories we'd ever read with him as the protagonist—both of us enjoyed reading mysteries. Unlike me, Yoly also devoured romances.

When the conversation hit a lull, I bid her good night, and she reminded me we'd sold out of nearly every essential oil bottle I'd crafted and I needed to make more.

"On it."

Ten minutes later I pushed inside the front door of my unit, and Vivi bounded to me. I switched off the alarm, shrugged out of my wet slicker, and bent to nuzzle her. "Your best friend Sierra is coming over."

She'd texted she was stopping by with much-needed wine and snacks.

"Knock, knock," Sierra called from the foyer and tramped into the kitchen. She plopped her large carryall on the floor and shook herself like a wet dog. Water flew off her russet-colored boho blouse. She fluffed her sleeves. "Ahem, you're supposed to lock up when you enter."

"I got home one second before you. Did you twist the bolt after you arrived?" I hated that we had to secure our doors, but Carmel wasn't as gentle as it used to be. Crime was on the upswing in all communities across the globe.

"Of course I did. I am much more conscientious than you are."

"Ha! *Not.*" I pulled a face. "Why are you wet? Why didn't you carry an umbrella or throw on a jacket?"

"To come downstairs? What a bother. A little water never hurt anyone."

"Except the Wicked Witch of the West."

She cackled, which pleased me. I loved when I could get a chuckle out of her.

"I brought your favorite Scheid wine." She pulled a bottle from the carryall. "Chardonnay from Isabelle's Vineyard. I also have quiche and crispy salmon appetizers warm from the oven. I made them before leaving the café."

"You're a godsend."

"And the pièce de résistance, a lemon ginger turmeric tart." She placed it on the counter.

"Yum to all. I love turmeric." Like a lot of colorful plant-based foods, turmeric was rich in phytonutrients and had anti-inflammatory and antioxidant properties. *Trivia for three hundred, Alex,* I mused and thought of my father. How was he doing with the foundation? Would he keep our hiking date or leave on another mission before then?

While I removed two blue-rimmed Wedgwood china plates and a serving platter from a cupboard, Sierra unscrewed the metal cap on the wine bottle. She fetched two of my new Irish crystal goblets—I'd gifted them to myself a month ago because I'd neglected to give myself a present for my birthday in April, having been overly preoccupied with opening the spa—and she poured each of us a glass.

"Here." She handed me my drink and began plating our meals. "Tell me all."

I took a sip of wine and savored the intricate fruit flavors. "All of what?" I arched an eyebrow.

"The fracas on the patio today. Customers gossiped about it the entire afternoon."

"Follow me." In our text exchange, I'd explained I needed to make additional essential oils tonight.

I put a can of tuna into a bowl for Vivi and carried it and the wineglasses through the living room to the rear door. Sierra and Vivi followed. The cat lifted her nose in the air, inhaling the delectable aromas. I set the exit alarm, and we crossed to the rear door of my studio.

Unlock—turn off the beeping system—enter—lock. The routine was dull and exasperating, but I knew if I didn't do it, Sierra would chastise me. How I wished my place hadn't been broken into during the summer. Things might've been different. I recalled the intrusion and shivered. Until the security company installed a system, I'd felt so vulnerable. Now, heeding Ursula's warning that someone might wish me harm, arming the system was the only answer.

My studio had the same floor plan as my main unit, but I'd set it up differently. The kitchen featured sea-green accents and served as the laboratory. I'd added a freestanding basin, metal tables, and storage racks. The living room was the staging ground where I kept amber-colored glass bottles, containers for creams, and a copper essential oils still.

"I forgot there's nowhere to eat." Sierra placed the food on the counter.

I set down the wineglasses. "There are stools." I'd relocated the bistro dining table to the bedroom, which I'd converted into a storage area complete with freestanding shelves holding vials of essential oils, as well as a refrigerator to keep items cool.

"Here, beautiful." I beckoned Vivi and placed her bowl on the kitchen floor.

She didn't hesitate. She dove in. Between mouthfuls, she offered a trill of thanks.

I settled onto a stool and dished up a slice of quiche. I took a bite and beamed. "Delish! Kale?"

"Kale, leeks, and shitake mushrooms."

"Love the Gruyère cheese." I shook my fork at her. "There's a spice I'm not recognizing."

"Good taste buds. It's white pepper. Brilliant, right? You can't see it, but it's heavenly." Her cell phone rang. She removed it from her pocket, scanned the screen, grumbled, and put the phone face down on the counter. "Is Addison devastated?"

"She's in shock, I'm sure." I filled her in about the trust fund.

"So that's what everyone was talking about. I kept hearing people say, *Money, money, money. Always follow the money.* Do you think it's true? When she learned her mother was going to cut her off, did she blow a gasket and smother her?"

Briefly, in the afternoon, I'd considered the possibility, but whoever had killed Gianna hadn't gone berserk. The method of death was orderly, lacking emotion. Addison was a planner. She cut and recut pieces for her cards. She liked the cards to be creative but exact, meaning she would probably be a methodical murderer. Idha fact-checked her clients' work, a tedious discipline. O'Malley designed golf courses. I doubted he winged it or strayed from doing precisely as he outlined for his clients. Frederick was a scientist, signifying he was meticulous by nature, but he had an alibi. Peyton was a Realtor. She had to dot her *i*'s and cross her *t*'s when writing up a contract.

Did anyone else in Gianna's sphere fit the profile?

"How much is the trust fund?" Sierra asked.

"I don't know. Riley said a tidy sum." I took another bite of the quiche and swallowed. "During a facial a few weeks ago, Addison told me the monthly amounts she receives helped her leave her husband and maintain her lifestyle while she builds her business. I hate to admit it, but if she learned her mother was planning to cut her off, it would be a darned good motive to want her dead. However, before the police escorted her away, Addison turned that theory on its head. She speculated it could also be Wyatt's motive, because if he was able to persuade her not to divorce him, he would have access to the funds."

"She's not going to change her mind about the divorce, is she?" Sierra sipped her wine.

"You heard Wyatt at dinner Monday night. He vowed to kill himself if she didn't come home."

"Yeah, and she threw ice water on the idea." Sierra popped a salmon appetizer wrapped in a strip of bacon into her mouth and chewed.

"Yes, she did. But will she remain resolute?"

The notion of Addison being guilty plagued me, and my appetite waned. I wiped my hands, took one more sip of wine, and rose to my feet. "You keep eating. I'm going to the living room to start up the still."

Aunt Sophie had imparted how helpful oils were. Some fought harmful bacteria. Others rejuvenated the skin. Certain oils, like lavender and peppermint, could add a dash of spice to a food dish. Sierra used many in her healthy treats.

I decided to put together camellia oil, rich with properties that would enhance the skin's natural ability to safeguard itself from irritants while reducing reddening and more. It was also a good choice for people with inflammatory acne. A number of our clients asked for help for their teenagers who were battling skin issues. It just so happened, in addition to some lovely azalea bushes, the fourplex's backyard boasted a thriving camellia bush. I'd gathered seeds from it last week—the best time to harvest them was in autumn—and I'd refrigerated them so they wouldn't rot.

I pulverized the seeds into a powder, placed enough of it into the copper still to fill it halfway, and covered the powder with water. Next, I adjusted the setting and brought the water to its highest heat before switching it to low. The potion would brew, doing its magic for three hours and then, like Vivi's laser toy, automatically switch off. Bright and early tomorrow morning, I would remove the essential oil floating on the top of the cooled liquid, pour it into vials, and refrigerate it.

Loudly, Sierra screamed, "No!"

Heart pounding, I raced to her. "What's wrong?"

She was punching her mobile. Literally punching it. If she got upset while cooking, she was mindful not to throw whatever she was holding across the room. Spoons, knives, pots, and pans could hurt one of her employees. A cell phone was a different matter. She'd hurled hers months ago and it had shattered and cost her a pretty penny to replace. Holding it while punching it was a much wiser solution. But why was she doing so?

"I repeat, what's wrong?"

"Connor," she snapped.

"Connor?"

"My ex-boyfriend chef, Connor Coke."

"I know what his last name is, you goon." I'd always thought his surname was funny, seeing as the Coke name in Old English meant *cook*.

Sierra had met him at the culinary institute and they'd planned to build a life together until, suddenly, Connor decided to move to New York alone to make his fortune. He never even asked Sierra if she wanted to go with him. He'd hoped to become a Michelin-worthy superstar. So far, no luck.

"He's reaching out." She waggled her cell phone.

"And . . ."

"No. Absolutely not! I can't."

"Can't what?"

She spanked the counter. Vivi darted to the living room, no doubt to hide in her cat bed in the nook of the end table.

"Cool it. You're frightening the cat," I chided.

"Well, Connor is scaring me."

"Calm down and tell me what you can't do." I used quotation marks around the word *can't*.

"I can't call him. I won't. If I hear his voice . . ." She paused. "The last time we spoke . . ." She couldn't catch her breath. "The last time . . ." She tried again but faltered.

I put an arm around her shoulders. "Breathe."

"I can't. I really can't. I'm—" She clutched her chest. "I'm having . . . I'm having . . ."

Ursula's words rushed through my mind: *Someone wishes to do you harm*. Had she been mistaken about someone hurting *me*? Maybe she'd seen someone in my cousin's future. Though we looked nothing alike, Sierra and I were as close as sisters. An oracle might confuse the two of us in a visualization.

"You are not having a heart attack," I assured Sierra. "Or a panic attack. You're upset, but you're fine." She was petite and might fool others into thinking she was frail, but she was strong. A fighter. She could manage a kitchen staff like a general. I turned her away from me and began massaging her shoulders. I really worked my thumbs into the muscles to release the tension. "Go on. The last time you spoke, what did he say?"

"The same thing Wyatt said. If I didn't come to New York to be with him, he'd kill himself."

"What?" I squawked. I spun her around. "Why is this the first I'm hearing of it?"

"He didn't do it. Obviously. But what if he threatens to do it again? Given all the sad things happening this week, I might believe him and cave."

"You won't give in. I won't let you. I'll remind you about the way he abandoned you. The way you felt betrayed after he left. The way his leaving undermined your entire self-worth. You are better off without him."

A few phrases I'd posted at Aroma Wellness came to me. I recited one. '*The woman who does not require validation from anyone is the most feared individual on the planet*—Mohadesa Najumi." Najumi was a British financial technology reporter working for *HuffPost*. "And don't forget this gem: *Sometimes good things fall apart so better things can fall together.* Thus said the witty and wise Marilyn Monroe."

"Witty and wise." She snuffled out a laugh.

I released her shoulders and spun her around. "You and I are now a team because he didn't realize your value. Lucky me."

Sierra gripped my hands. "Thank you for being my support system. By the way, you should share those quotes with Addison."

"Good idea."

Chapter 10

I didn't sleep fitfully—no nightmares, no images of personal attacks or murder—but I woke up Friday with a stiff neck and puffy eyes. Rain was still falling and dampened my mood. Rather than go for a walk, I took a long, hot shower. The water released the tension but didn't remove the puffiness. I dabbed a drop of lavender oil beneath each eye—it was excellent for reducing swelling—and massaged it into my skin. Tonight while I prepped for bed, I'd apply a dash of rosemary oil, great for promoting calm and relaxation.

"Vivi, my love," I cooed to my sweet cat. She was lounging on the comforter licking one paw. "I'm going to finish the essential oil prep and then I'm going to throw together a quickie breakfast and head out because I have a full day. Want to join me?"

"*Mawr*," she purred and gawked at me like I was nuts. She loved the sound of rain and intended to loll around all day.

"If it's dry later, we'll go out to the garden and look for your fairy friend."

She twitched her tail as if saying, *No big deal*, leaving me to wonder whether her seeming disinterest was because Dewberry was sneaking into the unit and they were playing daily. Merryweather Rose of Song could materialize easily, regardless of doors and windows. Could Dewberry do the same?

When I arrived at the spa, Meryl was answering phones. Like me, she had dressed in leggings, but the comparison ended there. Her blousy top was a riot of color and swirls, while mine was black and emblazoned with the words, *Read, Eat, Sleep, Meditate, Repeat.*

"Where's your mother?" I asked, hanging my damp rain slicker on a peg behind the reception desk.

"In the treatment room crying."

"What happened?"

"She messed up a couple of appointments. Dottie Summers thought she'd booked a facial at eleven o'clock, but it turns out Mah penned it in at ten." Dottie, a neighborhood watch advocate who lived near me, was Detective Summers's mother. "Luckily, I fixed it. I contacted the eleven o'clock customer to see if she could switch to an hour earlier and she could, so you'll give back-to-back facials today."

"About your mother—"

"Don't fire her, Emma." Meryl pressed her palms together. "She's really trying. But she's never held a job like this. To keep afloat and support her comedy career, she worked as a waitress and a bartender. She can juggle plates and liquor bottles with aplomb, but phones and schedules do not compute in her wacky brain." She twirled a finger beside her temple.

"I heard you." Mah emerged from the hallway, her face splotchy, her lips twisted into a scowl. "My brain is not wacky."

"Why didn't the brain take a bath?" Meryl jested. "It didn't want to be brainwashed."

Mah made a dismissive sound. "You and your infantile jokes. Grow up."

"I would," Meryl replied, "but I'm as tall as I'm going to get."

I snickered.

"I'm sorry, Emma." Mah hung her head. "I made more mistakes." She began scratching her forearm.

Upon closer inspection, I realized she had a brand-new tattoo featuring prayer hands laced with a ribbon. On the ribbon was scrawled Dante's name. What a supportive thing to do for her daughter. When I got the chance, I would swing by the gift shop and see if we had any white lace agate I could give each of them. Thanks to its gentle energy, the stone offered comfort to those who were grieving. If we didn't have any, I could substitute amethyst.

"Don't worry. It takes time to get the hang of things," I assured her, though I was very concerned. We couldn't afford to have clients upset due to scheduling. If a treatment went wrong—occasionally a reaction to oils, lotions, and facial scrubs occurred—we'd apologize and offer a freebie, but we couldn't provide gratis therapy for messed-up appointments.

Meryl tapped the computer screen. "We have five sign-ups for Tuesday's mask-making class."

"Great to hear."

"And the waivers are in the top drawer."

Prior to holding any classes where I taught students how to make facial masks, I'd needed to structure our liability insurance to protect the business from potential lawsuits related to product safety or claims. I'd also conducted stability and safety testing with friends and family to ensure the products we would make were safe. Even though the FDA didn't regulate cosmetics and require approval of them before they went to market, I'd wanted to make sure anything I sold at the spa had general approval first. Also, our attorney had suggested creating waivers and requiring class attendees to sign them, although she reminded us waivers would not relieve us of gross negligence or fraud.

"When should we schedule the next class?" Meryl asked.

"A month from now."

Once we opened, I'd planned on providing classes weekly to

teach customers how to make what I concocted in my studio, but that had been a pipe dream and costly. Sometimes only one customer signed up for the class. When I announced the class would occur less frequently, we received a lot more interest. The law of supply and demand worked in a small business like ours. In the upcoming class, in keeping with the Halloween season, I would show the students how to make a pumpkin facial scrub.

"Boss"—Meryl tattooed the counter with her fingertips—"I came up with an idea about another way to bring in income."

"Daughter." Mah clicked her tongue. "Do not call Emma *boss*. It is disparaging."

"No, it's not. It's endearing. Très chic."

"Chic." Her mother inhaled sharply.

"Ooh, Mah," Meryl said playfully, and aimed a finger at her mother's face. "You sniffed. Are you reading my mind?"

"I am not. I would never invade."

"No, I was kidding. The idea I want to mention is"—she inhaled as her mother had—"Smell-O-Vision. Have you heard of it, Emma?"

"No."

"During the nineteen fifties and sixties, motion picture companies tried a number of gimmicks to lure in viewers. Mike Todd Jr. Have you ever heard of him?"

I wagged my head.

"He was Elizabeth Taylor's stepson from one of her many marriages. Mike Todd Sr. was the producer of *Around the World in 80 Days*."

Trivia for one thousand, Alex, I mused.

"Anyway, Junior was innovative, and he coined the phrase *Smell-O-Vision* because he used familiar scents to enhance the audience's experience. For example, you see someone eating vanilla ice cream and then you smell vanilla. Or you watch a couple walking through a field of flowers, and voilà, you pick up the aroma of daisies or roses. Alas, it didn't catch on. In fact, it flopped. But I was thinking it might work for us." She painted the picture with her hands. "If we could advertise the scents you offer at the spa by doing demonstrations around town, like maybe from a pop-up cart, it could drum up business."

"Sounds expensive," Mah complained.

"How much could a pushcart and a vendor cost?" Meryl asked. "The staff could take turns hawking our wares when we have slots on our schedule."

I said, "I'll put it on the list."

Sometimes Meryl's suggestions were doable, like videotaping a tour of the spa or partnering with another business for a promotional campaign, but finding enough hours in the day to implement all of them had been a challenge. Even still, I liked the way her mind worked. Creative people were inherently imaginative and always thinking outside the box.

Meryl lit the sage candle by the computer and waved the scent in my direction. "Yoo-hoo, Emma. Are you feeling clearer mentally? Less anxious? Is this aroma uplifting your mood?"

I inhaled and exhaled.

"Yes," she coaxed. "Make your nose work overtime."

I drew in another breath and closed my eyes as a memory came to me.

"What are you thinking about?" Meryl asked. "Your eyelids are fluttering."

I opened my eyes. "The crime scene."

"What about it?"

"I smelled lavender near Gianna's face."

She tilted her head. "Sage made you think of lavender?"

"No, inhaling did. And I recall detecting another scent."

"Sage?"

"Sage did not spark the memory, Daughter," Mah said.

Meryl stuck out her tongue.

"I can't place it," I said. "It was fresh. Gianna had white musk hand soap and lotion in her bathroom, but I don't think that's what it was."

"Addison was there." Meryl cocked her head. "Did she get a whiff?"

"I'm not sure, but I'm going to ask her right now." I slipped on my rain slicker, drew the hood over my hair, and hustled toward the exit.

"Remember, you have a ten o'clock facial," Mah yelled.

The Carmel-by-the-Sea police precinct was located on Junipero, north of Ocean Avenue. The building was in need of repair, but so far the Town Council hadn't been able to drum up the funding. I stepped into the foyer and eyed the photographs on the walls. There were no Halloween decorations of any kind. *Bah humbug.*

After explaining the reason for my visit to a clerk, a middle-aged officer relieved me of the gift I'd brought, as well as my purse and my slicker and secured them in a locker. Then she escorted me down a plain hall and told me to wait outside a door. She knocked, opened the door, stepped inside, and reappeared a few seconds later.

Riley exited directly behind her. "Hi, Emma." Her skin was sallow, her curly hair uncombed, and her dress hung on her thin frame. Had she lost weight fretting about her friend? "When Addison heard you were here, she told me to go." Tears flooded her eyes. "I love her so much. I will do anything it takes to get her out of here. Even lie."

"Don't even think about—"

Before I could utter the word *lying*, she nudged the officer to lead her out of the building.

"Riley, wait. I brought this for Addison, but they won't let me give it to her." I pulled the gift box from my purse. "Could you take it to her house and place it in her bedroom?"

"Sure," she said flatly.

I entered the small private room, which was fitted with a table and four chairs. There were no two-way mirrors. No security cameras. While walking along the hall, the officer had informed me that the room was primarily for attorney-client visits and insured privacy.

Addison was seated at the table, her hands resting on top, clinging to a tissue. The prison-supplied blue shirt and pants did nothing for her complexion. Her right eye was twitching.

"Hi," she murmured. "I'm so glad you came."

"How are you holding up?"

"I'm fine," she said, and rubbed her eye in an attempt to calm the twitch. "Daddy finally got hold of the attorney you recommended. She couldn't make it in time last night to get me released, but she's heading to court today to enter a plea of not guilty. Daddy will go with her, but he's on his way here first." She ran her fingers through her hair. "Do you think she'll be able to get me out on bail?"

"I don't know." I didn't have a clue what other evidence or proof of motive the police might have on Addison. "May I ask you a question?"

"Sure."

"It's about the moment you realized your mother was . . ." I paused.

"Dead. Don't be scared to say the word. I say it a lot. Dead, dead, dead."

I reached for her hands.

She pulled them off the table and tucked them into her lap. "What do you want to know?"

"When you approached the bedside, did you detect the scent of anything?"

She shook her head. "I didn't think she smelled dead, if that's what you mean. She didn't even look it. I thought she was asleep."

"Do you remember when I asked Detective Summers if he picked up a whiff of lavender?"

"Uh-huh."

"You didn't comment. Did you smell it?"

"No." She pursed her lips, considering the question. "But I didn't lean in very close."

"You touched her."

She shivered. "She was so cold."

"You didn't pick up lavender or any other scent? Something fresher, like white musk?"

"I don't know what that smells like." She rested her hands on the table and began shredding the tissue. "Why does it matter?"

"What cologne does Wyatt wear?"

"He doesn't. He says men's perfumes are a waste of money since he showers and changes clothes after every ride. Him and his cycling," she snarled.

"It's his career. His business."

"Yes. I suppose." She discarded the ruined tissue on the table and folded her hands. They wiggled restlessly.

"Do you know what kind of soap he uses?"

"Dove for Men."

I knew the scent. It had hints of eucalyptus and cedar. A guy I'd dated for a nanosecond had used the same soap.

The door behind me opened. The same officer appeared. "Your father is here," she said.

O'Malley pushed past the officer. A man heading for the gallows couldn't have looked worse for wear. His hair was mussed, his eyes bloodshot, and his skin slack.

"Sir, one visitor at a time."

"I'm not a visitor. I'm her father." He eyed me suspiciously. "Emma, what are you doing here?"

"She's being supportive, Daddy," Addison said.

He was wearing a Patagonia rain jacket. The collar of the yellow golf shirt beneath was smudged with dirt, as if he'd tried to clean off a stain but failed. He caught me staring and touched the blot with a fingertip. "Forgive my appearance. I was finalizing funeral arrangements at the cemetery and talking to the landscaper about what plants he would install by the headstone. I didn't have time to change, and I didn't want to . . ." His face pinched with pain. "I didn't want to go home."

My heart ached for him and Addison. They would have to cope

with uncomfortable grief for a long time. I doubted they would ever be able to escape the memory of how Gianna died.

"I'm staying, Officer," O'Malley said. "Emma stays, too. Please leave." He was the type of man who wouldn't accept another outcome.

The officer wasn't packing a gun. She wasn't big enough to muscle him out. So she left, but I wondered if she would seek out a superior who could manage O'Malley's gruffness.

"Hi, sweetheart." He rounded the table, kissed Addison's cheek, and returned to the chair beside me. He sat down, pulled a cloth handkerchief from the rear pocket of his chinos, and dabbed his eyes. "Your mother will be put to rest in a few days, once the coroner's office finalizes its examination." He choked out a sob and pressed a fist to his lips. When he recovered, he dropped his hand. "Nothing will take place, no funeral, no memorial, until you are cleared of this crime."

The door behind us opened again. Detective Summers strode in. Same outfit as usual. Same stern demeanor. I'd seen the man smile in the presence of my grandmother. I knew he could do so. His mouth wasn't broken. "What are you doing here, Emma?"

"Visiting."

"You and Ms. Lacey are friends?"

"We are."

Addison seemed pleased with my response. "Detective, my attorney is going to court to plead not guilty."

"I heard."

"Dylan," O'Malley said. "I'm sorry to hear about you and your fiancée." I wondered why Addison's father knew the detective on a first-name basis and was familiar with the man's personal life. Maybe they played golf together.

"Thank you," Summers said.

"I'm sure you'll patch things up. You're a good match."

Summers eyed me. "One of the two of you needs to leave."

"Sir," I said, eager to steer the conversation back to the case. "Before I go, could you tell me if you found the murder weapon?"

"Not yet."

If a killer disposed of a weapon in the ocean, or buried it, or tossed it down a well, the police might never recover it, meaning it wasn't required to prove guilt beyond a reasonable doubt.

"We have confirmed that all the female guests who are invited to the"—he cleared his throat—"happily divorced party are in possession of their pillows."

"I gave him the list of names," Addison said.

"My team has viewed each one. None have lipstick stains."

Interesting how Riley hadn't mentioned he'd questioned her when we bumped into each other.

"Lipstick stains?" O'Malley arched an eyebrow.

"There should have been a tinge of it on the murder weapon." Summers addressed Addison. "Is it possible you forgot a name?"

"No, sir."

"Detective," I said, "as I mentioned at the crime scene, the killer might have been able to clean the stain with soap and a toothbrush. Did you or a colleague smell each of the pillows?"

Summers screwed up his mouth.

"Would knowing how to erase a stain require expertise?" O'Malley cut in.

I said, "Not really. There are YouTube videos showing the steps to take."

Summers regarded him. "Why do you ask, Mr. McKay?"

"Peyton Pelagatti happens to be OCD," O'Malley replied. "Obsessive compulsives can be germaphobes. Gianna told me Peyton would wipe down her kitchen counters ten to fifteen times a day if she didn't think they were clean enough."

A college friend of mine was the same. Her hands were always a dry, cracking mess because she used harsh products frequently.

"Are you suggesting she killed your wife?" Summers asked.

"She's a bitter, jealous woman who has always coveted Gianna's way of life."

"Did she also desire you?" Summers asked.

"No, no." He laughed in a self-deprecating way. "But the rest of it. The trappings. The prestige."

Summers pulled his cell phone from his pocket and typed a few words into Notes.

"Daddy, you're wrong. Aunt Peyton was Mother's lifelong friend." Addison spread her arms wide. "She didn't kill her."

"She is not your aunt!" he snapped.

"You're right," Addison said meekly. "I know. Slip of the tongue. I'm sorry."

"And lest you forget," O'Malley continued, "Peyton was the one who informed the police about the trust fund issue. She is the reason you are in jail."

Excellent point.

"I mention it, Detective"—O'Malley focused on Summers—"because Peyton and Gianna fought Monday night. They often argued about Peyton's son. Peyton believed Reginald would've been a better husband for Addison. She held a grudge about Addison rejecting him. She blamed Gianna, as if she should have borne the responsibility for Reginald and Addison not hooking up. In truth, Reginald didn't rise to his fullest potential and would've been a lousy match."

Chapter 11

Detective Summers stopped O'Malley from theorizing any further and demanded we both leave. O'Malley didn't resist. Neither did I. In the foyer of the precinct, I asked Summers if I could chat with him privately. He frowned, clearly not open to the idea.

O'Malley paused before exiting and glanced over his shoulder. "Emma, bless you for being there for my daughter."

I nodded. "I'm sorry for your loss."

He mumbled, "Thank you," and continued on his way.

"Sir," I said to Summers, "at least tell me if the coroner determined Gianna was drugged."

His gaze grew steely. "Emma, how many times do I have to tell you that you are not involved in this investigation? You have no right to ask."

"I'm simply wondering what was used, if anything."

He brandished a hand. "No, Emma. It's a flat no. Because of

your grandmother, I have bent over backward being civil to you, but I'm advising you—you and her—to stay out of this."

"But—"

"I don't care if you and Addison Lacey are now bosom buddies because you're throwing her a happily divorced party. I don't give a hoot if you are the most compassionate person in the world and have a deep-seated need to right wrongs. I've got this. Do you hear me?"

I felt the urge to salute but refrained. A sassy response was not warranted.

"For your edification, it sometimes takes thirty days to get a toxicology report," he added before retreating into the bowels of the department.

Disheartened, I hoofed it to Aroma Wellness. The drizzling rain did nothing to boost my mood. Instead, I held a discussion with myself aloud because sometimes it was the best way for me to reason things out. "Why, Emma, why do you press? Why do you need answers?" I knew why. The detective had pegged me correctly. I wanted to right the wrongs of the world. "Acknowledge who you are," I muttered. "Own it. Don't beat yourself up for being a caring soul. It's what makes you *you*, and if he doesn't like it, he can—" I bit off the remainder, refusing to utter anything negative. Summers was a good detective. He didn't deserve my wrath.

I turned north on Dolores Street and began talking myself through a mindful meditation. "Shift your attention to what you can control. Repeat after me, *I am capable. I am alert. I can see the big picture.*"

By the time I was climbing the stairs to the Courtyard of Peace, I was calm and focused. An hour later, while I was cashing out the first facial client, Mah swept through the front door. She was sipping a smoothie she'd obtained at the café. I comped each of the staff one tasty treat a week, as well as one treatment a month.

"Dottie is here." Mah gestured toward the patio. "She's out there by the fountain."

"In the rain?" I'd been so focused on my meditation, I'd missed seeing her.

"She's keeping dry."

I peered out the plate-glass window. Dottie Summers, a dainty octogenarian who looked nothing like her detective son, was perched on a chair and holding a polka-dotted umbrella overhead. She was so frail, I feared the light breeze might blow her over, but I'd learned over the past few months that she was as tough as nails with a dynamic voice to match. I opened the front door and stepped out, protected by the overhang. "Dottie!" I hailed her.

She rose and wended through the tables to the entrance.

"Aren't you cold?" I took her umbrella from her, shook off the moisture, and stowed it in the rack by the door.

"Not a whit. I dress accordingly, and I treasure the pitter-patter of rain. It soothes me. Now, let's get to it." She stamped her feet and let the rain fall from her jacket and trousers onto the mat Mah must have laid out. "I'm here to have my first brightening facial ever. Everyone promises it will be restful."

"It will, but I must admit I'm surprised you booked the appointment."

"Why? I've been telling everyone about the last time I was here." Her exuberance was infectious. "I'll be doing a sound bath again real soon." She hummed as if she was a singing bowl being awakened by a crystal rod. "Not a bad imitation, right? The sound is lodged right here in my brain." She tapped her temple.

"Not bad at all, but Dottie, what I meant was, you haven't had a treatment other than the sound bath. You know, like a massage or a pedicure. So why a facial?" I guided her to the lockers, where she stowed her jacket—she opted to keep her purse with her—and then on to the therapy room.

She beamed. "I know at my age I shouldn't be vain, but my skin looks a bit weary."

"I think you're beautiful." I wasn't lying. She glowed with good energy. "I'll leave the room and you remove your top. Then lie on the bed and drape the sheet over yourself."

She giggled nervously, as many first-time clients did.

I waited a minute, knocked on the door, and heard her say, "Come in."

While I swept her hair off her face and wrapped it with a terry-cloth turban, I explained the treatment. "We'll concentrate on a deep cleansing, which will remove impurities and dead skin cells."

"Pfft. Never say dead to a woman in her eighties."

"Tired," I revised. "Afterward, I'll apply the latest skin peel. It's very gentle. It won't make your face too red, and you will be able to enjoy a walk in the sun immediately, as long as you wear sunblock."

"If we ever see the sun again."

"The forecast is for sunny skies by end of day."

"One can hope."

I switched on the steam machine and peered at her through a magnifying lamp. "You've done a nice job taking care of your skin."

"Not bad for an old broad," she joked. "I've used sunblock since it came on the market."

"Good for you. Now, you might be wondering how peels work. Let me explain. The peel I'll apply will dissolve the bonds between the skin cells. Usually, a peel includes ingredients like alpha hydroxy acids or fruit acids like apples or pumpkins."

"I love apples. My favorites are Envy. Nice and crisp. Pumpkins? Meh. There are way too many pumpkins around at this time of year."

"Not a Halloween fan?"

"I like the candy. I hate the gruesome masks." She shuddered. "Why does everyone find them so fun to wear? I've never understood it."

I grinned and continued. "This peel also contains vitamin C as well as green tea, which adds protective antioxidants to your skin."

"Go for it." She folded her arms mummy-style across her chest.

I turned off the steam machine and opted not to do extractions. She didn't need them. Not to mention, paper-thin skin like hers could bruise easily.

"Emma," she murmured as I dried the beads of steam off her

face. "I'm pretty sure Dylan wouldn't want me telling you this, but I must."

"Dottie, if it involves his investigation into the murder of Gianna McKay, you shouldn't."

"Why not? He's not the boss of me. He used to say those words to me when he was a boy. *You are not the boss of me, Mom!* Well, I say what's good for the goose is good for the gander," she said playfully. "And after all, you were the one who found Gianna McKay's body. You have a right to know."

Even though her son would disagree, I didn't hush her, too eager to get the scoop.

"Last night, I went to the precinct because I was meeting Dylan for dinner. He was outside, talking with Teresa Rodriguez. Not loudly—it was definitely a private conversation—but I have the ears of an elephant." Dottie cackled. "Anyway, he didn't see me approaching, so I stood still and heard him say, *The coroner determined what drug was used.*"

"Really?" I couldn't tamp down my surprise. "He told me it could take thirty days to get a tox report."

She opened her eyes. "I imagine someone high up pressed for answers. Dylan is friendly with the mayor, and the mayor was Gianna's boyfriend years ago."

"Really?"

"Years ago," Dottie clarified. "Way before she married O'Malley."

"Oh." What else could I say?

"I knew you were wondering whether a drug was used," she went on, "because your grandmother mentioned it to me at the midday book club at the library. I don't go to the night ones. I get too tired to concentrate." Dottie was an avid reader. She preferred historical fiction. Often when we bumped into each other in the neighborhood, she would pop off the titles of the latest books she'd devoured. She was a big fan of our local historical romance author.

I didn't say a word, worried I might disturb her train of thought.

"Then he said, *Flunitrazepam.*"

"I'm sorry, what?"

"Flunitrazepam. I researched it. It's generic Rohypnol, the date rape drug."

Oh my golly.

"I didn't hear anything further," Dottie added, "because Teresa spotted me and ended their conversation."

Wow. Double wow.

I applied the peel, making sure not to dab any too close to her eyes. "I wonder where the killer might have obtained such a drug. They wouldn't have needed a whole bottle, of course. One pill would've done the trick."

"I thought the same thing," Dottie murmured. "Sadly, these kinds of drugs are easy to acquire illegally. Why, Hattie Hopewell was telling me the other day how her nephew . . . or was it her grandson . . . no, I think it was her nephew . . . or a friend of her nephew . . . it doesn't matter." She tittered.

Hattie was the head of the Happy Diggers Garden Club and active in the neighborhood watch program for the area where Dottie and I lived.

"Hattie told me the person in question was walking down the street in Monterey when someone offered him one of those kinds of drugs. Can you imagine? What's next? A vending machine?"

The notion turned my stomach. How were people supposed to feel safe if drugs were readily available, no questions asked? And how could the person buying the illegal drug trust that the pill or pills weren't laced with fentanyl?

"I hope this helps you in your quest, Emma."

"My quest?"

"Yes, dear. After solving Willow's death, you have a reputation. I presume, because you were the one to find Gianna McKay's body, you will turn over every stone until you unravel this crime."

"I didn't find her. Her daughter did."

"But you were there, and I hear you are friends with the daughter. If so"—she opened her eyes and stared up at me—"be bold."

"But your son—"

"Will appreciate the help."

Yeah, not.

After Dottie's facial, I went to the café to pick up some lunch and was surprised to see my grandmother sitting with Sierra at a bistro table. Though the rain had abated, Nana Lissa was wearing rain boots as well as a yellow slicker over her clothes. An umbrella with a hook handle hung on the frame of her chair. The two were whispering, their heads close together.

I tiptoed up. "Care to share the secret?" I asked conspiratorially.

Sierra started and bumped the table, which caused the teacup in front of her to rattle. She steadied it. "Oh, hi! It's not . . . we weren't . . . Nana told me Addison has been released."

"On bail?" I asked.

"No, completely released. Exonerated."

What? Why hadn't Addison texted me? Perhaps she had too much on her mind, or she might have gone to help her father with funeral details. "Do you know what evidence cleared her?"

"Nana thinks someone must have been able to verify she was where she said she was at the time of the murder," Sierra replied.

For the entire time between six and nine? Interesting. It couldn't have been her father. He was in San Francisco.

"That doesn't explain why you were whispering." I wagged a finger between the two of them. "Spill." I borrowed an unused chair from another table and sat.

"We were discussing the trust fund issue," Nana Lissa said. "It seems curious that Peyton knew of it, because neither she nor Gianna raised the issue at Monday's dinner."

"I'm not following," I said.

"Gianna certainly wasn't refraining from lambasting her daughter, if you recall." Sierra tapped the table. "She verbally drubbed Addison. The way she body-shamed her was over-the-top cruel.

"Peyton had her claws out, too," our grandmother added.

"*Mm-hmm.*" Sierra bobbed her head.

"With such intimate knowledge of the issue, why didn't she use it as a weapon and put Gianna on the spot? For that matter, being the controlling person Gianna was—"

"And volatile," Sierra chimed.

"And volatile, yes," Nana Lissa said. "Why wouldn't she have brought up the issue in front of the entire family, if for no other reason than to further humiliate her daughter?"

"Exactly," Sierra said. "Doesn't withholding the trust seem like an issue Gianna would have hurled as a warning?"

I agreed.

Nana Lissa sipped her tea and set down the cup. "You know, there were a couple of Gianna's prior business acquaintances at the library this morning, and they were implying whenever Gianna had an opinion, she shared it. And I mean, whenever." She attempted a dismissive head-slide movement.

Sierra hooted. "Nana, you are one smart cookie, but you cannot pull off that kind of attitude."

Our grandmother threw her the stink eye.

"Go on." Sierra flicked a finger.

"These business acquaintances—one was a Realtor, the other a lender—asserted Gianna behaved the way she did because she was an only child, meaning spoiled. She acted as though the world owed her."

Tongues sure are wagging around town, I reflected.

"I almost forgot!" The words popped out of Nana. "A woman who Gianna played canasta with was also there. Not a friend, merely another player. She claimed Gianna would go berserk if her partner didn't play well."

It never failed to stun me what a close-knit community Carmel-by-the-Sea was, not to mention how many people gossiped.

I said, "I'm sure the police are asking Peyton when and where Gianna fed her this information. It had to have been Gianna who did so. I doubt the co-trustee would have divulged such sensitive material to anyone who wasn't a family member."

"I should hope not." Nana clucked her tongue. "For all we know,

Peyton is simply throwing Addison to the wolves to take suspicion off herself."

"You could be right," I said.

"But why?" Sierra lifted her teacup, ready to take another sip. "Why would she have killed Gianna? Isn't that always the issue? What was her motive?"

I recalled the contentious spat on the patio I'd broken up Monday between the women I'd dubbed *frenemies*. Were Peyton and Gianna like them? Over the years, they'd probably had plenty of ups and downs. What if Gianna asked Peyton to come to the house Tuesday to console her over some broken heart issue—I wasn't sure I was right about the setup, but she had been crying when I'd called—and Peyton saw an opportunity. She knew O'Malley was out of town. Most likely she knew Addison's noisy work habits would distract her. She might even have spied Addison in the window. She slipped into the house and, knowing where Gianna kept a spare key, entered Gianna's room. She comforted her, gave her a drink dosed with Rohypnol . . . and waited. When Gianna was asleep, she placed the small pillow she'd brought along and smothered her. Were the police revisiting the idea that Peyton, being OCD, might have cleaned her pillow like a professional?

I leaned back in my chair. "Where would she have gotten the drug?"

Sierra's eyes widened. "Say what?"

I pitched forward and filled them in on the bombshell information Dottie had revealed during her facial.

"Bless Dottie's soul," Nana Lissa whispered. "Dylan won't be pleased if he learns she revealed sensitive information."

"I bet Dottie can handle his moods," I said. "She's got spunk."

"Emma, I've been thinking"—Sierra set down her cup—"if you really believe a happily divorced gift pillow was used to smother Gianna, you should reach out to the Etsy designer who made them and see if she sold another to a customer in Carmel."

"Why me?"

"You've done business with her, goofball. She knows you." Sierra grinned. "Plus, you're Carmel's best amateur sleuth."

"Get out of here!"

Sierra snickered.

Nana Lissa nodded. "What a great idea."

I glanced between them as I considered another scenario. What if the designer had sold a second one to Peyton?

The door to the café opened.

"Emma!" Ursula flounced inside, the skirt of her floor-length caftan wafting like a sail. She'd fastened her hair in a bear clip. Long, wavy tendrils graced her cheeks. She made a beeline for our table. Heads turned, as they often did for her. "Emma," she repeated breathlessly. "Meryl told me you were here. We need to speak."

"Nothing has harmed me," I assured her. Liam was still locked up. I was not in danger.

Nana Lissa and Sierra exchanged a concerned look.

"Ursula envisioned something," I explained. "But I think she was mistaking Sierra for me. I think she visualized the issue with Sierra's ex."

"What issue?" our grandmother asked.

"He texted and says he wants to meet with her. Tell them about it," I prompted.

"It's not . . ." Sierra shrugged. "It's nothing."

Ursula studied Sierra's face for a brief time and closed her eyes tightly. She lifted her chin as if meditating. A few seconds later, she opened her eyes. "Your boyfriend will not cause you harm. He won't even cause you heartache. There is love in your near future, but not with him."

Sierra's face lit up. "Really?" She clasped her chest and offered a ridiculously sappy expression. "With *moi*?"

I squelched down a laugh.

"Rest assured you can meet up with your ex," Ursula said. "You will have the confidence to tell him to bug off. As for you, Emma . . ." She clicked her tongue.

My stomach did a flip-flop. *Don't tell me bad news. Please. I don't want to hear it.*

"Fine," Ursula said. "No predictions."

Whoa! Had she read my mind?

"We will focus on me instead," she went on. "I am suffering. I am feeling dejected. I have come for a meditation. Do you have time?"

My pulse settled down. "For you, always." I rose from the table. "Let's go to the spa. We'll do a sound bath." It would be a meditative experience, but an entirely different one from the mindful meditation she had participated in on a previous occasion.

"Bless you."

Nana Lissa called after me, "Don't forget our special book club!"

"How could I?" I tapped my temple. "Steel trap." I'd been looking forward to this book club, which would take place at Open Your Imagination, the fairy garden shop on the other side of Ocean Avenue. I never passed up a book club featuring a mystery. Due to the prevailing Halloween furor, my grandmother had picked an appropriate title, *The Ghost and Mrs. Mewer,* a clever cozy mystery set in a pet-friendly town.

The sun was peeking through the few remaining clouds on the way to the spa, helping to dispel the vibes Ursula was putting out. I let Mah know my destination and guided Ursula to a treatment room. She sighed when she entered.

"I must confess . . ." She hesitated, worrying her lower lip between her teeth.

"Confess what?"

"I want to become a crystal reader. I am learning how to do so."

"Good for you. Who's your teacher?"

"Your aunt."

"Oh? Do tell." I spread my arms, inviting a response.

She shook a finger. "Do not act surprised, Emma. I know she informed you."

I held up both palms. "Guilty as charged."

"She says it will take time to learn. A very long time." Ursula heaved another sigh. “I do not have patience. It is not my forte, as you say.”

“Let’s work on it today. Sit in one of the recliners or lie down on the mat. You can even curl into a ball. It’s up to you. Right now, I want you to immerse yourself in the experience as the sound encourages your body to relax. Drink in positivity. Unlike what I do in a mindful meditation, I won’t speak a lot. This is a time for your mind to guide your soul.”

“All right.” She chose a chair and smoothed the lap of her caftan. “Ready.”

“Let your feelings come and go.” I dimmed the lights, fetched a rod to stir the crystal singing bowls, and slowly circled the room. One by one, I activated the sounds. Each bowl emitted a unique tone and energy. “Notice any sensations in your body as the sound vibrates through the air and into your being.”

As I gently rubbed the rod around the rim of the bowl, it created a continuous resonating sound, a tone so harmonic, it felt like layers of different pitches were blending together.

“Focus on the sensations you’re experiencing. Do not let your mind wander. Stay present.”

Forty-five minutes later, when the session ended, Ursula stood up looking refreshed and calm. “Thank you. I can do this, Emma.” She pressed her hands together. “I will continue to serve my regular clients and travel as necessary until I have accomplished my new goal.” She clasped my shoulders and blew me a kiss. “You are magical.”

“Hardly.”

Without warning, she released me and recoiled, as if I was made of hot coals. “Emma, no. It *is* you I see.” Her teeth made a sizzling sound. “*You.* Not Sierra. And it is not good for you. Be wary. Be very wary.”

Chapter 12

I didn't have time to mull over Ursula's second warning because Addison and her pals Riley, Cara, and Tatiana streamed into the spa. Each was wearing a colorful shirt-style dress. Addison's was adorned with music-loving tots, Riley's with mermaids riding sidesaddle on seahorses, Tatiana's with toddlers playing soccer, and Cara's with myriad images of children reading Dr. Seuss books.

"Emma!" Addison raced to me and hugged me briefly. "I've been released."

"No charges!" Riley squealed.

Cara cried, "Completely exonerated!"

Tatiana hushed them. "Girlfriends, keep it down. People are relaxing here."

Addison giggled. "Right. Sorry, Emma."

"I heard the news," I said. "I'm so happy for you." I eyed their clothing. "Cute outfits. No Halloween theme today?"

Each of the women raised their wrists to show off matching silver charm bracelets adorned with pumpkins.

"Cara bought them to celebrate," Addison said. "And she had a local designer make these dresses."

"How thoughtful."

The women were bubbling over with joy.

"Speaking of thoughtful," Addison went on, "I found the stone and dish you asked Riley to put in my room. Thank you."

"You're welcome. Who cleared you?" I asked.

"According to my criminal attorney—she's wonderful, by the way—a neighbor glimpsed me in my room on a couple of occasions. Apparently, she walks her dog a ton. Whoever she was alleged each time she caught sight of me I was wearing headphones and swaying to music. She also said I looked intent on the project I was working on."

Riley patted her friend's shoulder. "Addison chair dances while she works."

"Apparently," Addison went on, "an alarm went off across the street around eight, but I never heard it. I didn't even look up. Can you believe it? The neighbors were robbed."

"Murder is worse," Riley responded.

"Of course. Much worse. I . . ." Addison swallowed hard. "Because two incidents occurred on the same night, I asked the police if the robbery was connected to my mother's murder, but the detective didn't think so."

What an interesting theory. Would the murderer have offed Gianna and fled to the house across the street to trigger the alarm to create a distraction?

"Addison, how much do you know about your trust fund?" I asked. "How is it doled out? What are the limitations?"

"Sheesh, talk about nosy," Riley said, giving me the evil eye.

"Riley, simmer down," Addison said. "Emma's tuned in to investigations. I'd expect her to ask. She cares. To answer your question, Emma, I know I can't access the whole thing until I'm forty.

Mother—" Her voice caught. "Mother set it up with guardrails. She wanted me to have a clear head when I finally got hold of the money, claiming I'd know better how to spend and save, suggesting, of course, at my current age I'm not respon—" She clapped a hand over her mouth and quickly lowered it. "She never called me irresponsible. Never!" She looked between her friends, who cooed their support. "Mother said she herself was a spendthrift at my age. That's the point I was making."

"Did you ever have conversations with the other trustee about the disbursement plan?" I asked.

"No. He sends me a modest monthly check. I won't need it as soon as my business takes off. I've been working social media like crazy, connecting with influencers and everything."

"She's super dedicated," Riley chimed.

"Dedication doesn't always pay off," Tatiana said, an intense sadness in her voice.

"Yeah." Addison offered her friend a supportive smile. "Tat regrets giving up her soccer career, but what else could she do? She couldn't work herself to the bone, right?"

Riley murmured, "I wish we all had trust funds."

"Okay, everyone, put a lid on it. Enough maudlin babbling," Addison said. "Emma, we were hoping to get treatments on the books for tomorrow morning."

"You already have them," I reminded her. I hadn't erased any off the calendar . . . except Gianna's facial. "Your aunt has a massage planned, too. I'm not sure about Peyton. She hasn't responded to my messages."

"Peyton," Addison grumbled. "Why did she throw me under the bus?"

"I think she murdered your mother," Riley opined.

"Cut it out." Addison swatted her. "No, she didn't. Don't say such a thing."

"Then who did?" Cara asked.

"Wyatt!" Addison blurted out. "He hated her."

Riley shook her head. "I don't think he would've had the guts to slip into the house with you there."

The others agreed.

"Sure he would," Addison countered. "He of all people knows how concentrated I can be on my work, and how I always listen to music full blast. It's one of his bugaboos about me."

Tatiana crooned, "But he loves everything else."

"To distraction," Riley added.

Was the attorney certain a female neighbor had exonerated Addison? What if Wyatt was the person who'd claimed to have seen her multiple times in the window, but the police were keeping that information to themselves?

The door to the spa flew open and Peyton stormed in. "How dare you, Addison!" She halted beside the beverage cart, dry umbrella in hand. Though she was wearing an expensive cashmere overcoat, it couldn't cloak the wretchedness of her hunched form. "How dare you tell the police I killed your mother!" Peyton's puffy face was flushed.

Addison flinched. "I didn't."

I took in the peeling skin on Peyton's hands, a clear sign of using too many cleaning products.

"Cool your jets, Peyton." Tatiana stepped in front of Addison, ready to take one for the team.

Cara and Riley flanked her.

"H-how did you know I'd be here?" Addison stammered from behind her offensive line.

"I reached out to your father when I heard you were released from jail," Peyton stated.

Addison grumbled. "I knew I shouldn't have given Daddy my itinerary."

Riley grunted in support.

"If you didn't sic the police on me, why did they come to my house?" Peyton persisted. "When they wanted to see the party favor pillow you gave me, I didn't understand why, but I didn't protest. I was more than compliant. So why did they come a second time and ask to see it again? Why demand to view my cleaning supplies?"

Dawning gleamed in Addison's eyes. "Emma speculated the killer might have cleaned the pillow, and Daddy said you're OCD, so—"

"Ladies, *shh!*" Meryl rushed into the reception area. "You are way too loud," she said under her breath as she gestured frantically toward the rear of the spa. "I could hear you in the nail room. Please lower your voices."

I waved for her to return to her customer, wondering where Mah was but not wanting to interrupt this heated exchange.

"Why would the police care if I cleaned the pillow or not?" Peyton asked.

"Because . . ." Addison deferred to me.

"Because," I used my inside voice, "it's possible the killer smothered Gianna with one of the pillows, and—"

"She was smothered?" Peyton gasped. "I didn't know she . . . oh . . ." She pressed her thin lips together.

"And the pillow might have had a telltale smudge of lipstick on it," I added.

"It wasn't me," Peyton said. "I didn't do it. I didn't leave my house Tuesday night. I was home alone, knitting and listening to a podcast."

Why did her response sound prepared? "Can you prove it?" I asked gently.

"No, I cannot." She leveled me with a bitter look. "No one lives with me. No one was visiting. I was by myself. What did you not understand about the word *alone*?" She returned her focus to Addison. "Darling, I loved your mother with all my heart."

Addison narrowed her eyes. "Not true. The two of you fought like cats and dogs."

"Like siblings. Both of us were single children. Both craved a best friend. We were BFFs. You and Riley know what I mean."

"All I can say"—Addison broke through the fearsome threesome, shoulders squared—"is I don't yell at Riley. Ever. I don't treat her like my lackey, either, the way my mother treated you. I don't diss her behind her back. And I would never lie like you did to the police and say my mother was going to dissolve the trust fund. So Aunt . . ." She stopped herself. "Peyton, leave. You are no longer welcome in my life."

"Why, you spoiled brat." Peyton grabbed the pitcher of flavored ice water to her right as if ready to hurl it.

I bounded toward her and wrenched it from her grasp. "No, ma'am. Time to go."

Peyton started to shake. She clenched one hand with the other. "I'm sorry. I don't know what came over me. I'm sorry. So very sorry."

"Leave," Addison repeated.

Peyton did, and as she shuffled toward the steps, I wondered again whether she'd killed Gianna. Had she finally had enough of the woman? Had she held a pillow to the woman's face and snuffed the life out of her?

Out of nowhere, Addison threw herself into my arms and bawled. "Please, Emma," she said between jagged sobs. "Please find out who killed my mother."

The rest of the afternoon flew by. At six I hustled home and changed into an outfit appropriate for the book club. We wouldn't be making fairy gardens at Open Your Imagination. We wouldn't be getting our hands dirty. We were strictly partying. The shop typically hosted their own book club events on Saturday afternoons and served tea, but Nana Lissa had finagled a special evening for our group, complete with wine. Similar to soirees we would throw at Aroma Wellness, no liquor license was required as long as the party hostess brought the refreshments and the shop didn't charge a fee.

Vivi meowed to be fed. I complied and poured her a glass of water. She lapped greedily. Heaven forbid she drink from a bowl. Then I lifted her and tapped her nose. "You are coming with me."

When Sierra, Vivi, and I arrived at the fairy garden shop, I caught a glimpse of Detective Summers entering the Hideaway Café across the street alone. Would a revival of his failing relationship make him less cranky? Okay, he wasn't necessarily cranky. He was abrupt and authoritative, and he had every right to be the latter, but I did not appreciate when he was terse. He must have felt me staring because he turned and gave me a curious look. No, it was more than curious. It was dark and foreboding. Definitely a warning to stay in my lane.

I swallowed hard, wondering whether he had learned Dottie told me about the drug found in Gianna's system. If so, would I face dire consequences tomorrow?

"Go." I prodded Sierra. "Inside."

I'd visited Open Your Imagination a couple of times, once when I'd browsed for curios and on another occasion when I'd made a fairy garden for my grandmother. I'd found the most adorable book-reading fairies and bookshelves. She had loved the surprise.

The owner of the shop, Courtney Kelly, pert and bright in black capris and a long-sleeved silver sweater adorned with a sequined orange pumpkin, greeted us as we entered. It was obvious by the wares in the shop how much she loved all things fairy. There were whimsical wind chimes, fairy-themed books, jewelry, planters, and more. And yes, there were decorations acknowledging the season: miniature skeletons, coffins, and ghosts. A Happy Haunting garden in a wide-mouthed pot featured fairy lights, black cats, a ghoulish house, and a gigantic spider.

"Hello, Vivi," Courtney cooed to the cat. "I've heard so much about you. Pixie and Fiona will be pleased to meet you." Pixie was her Ragdoll cat. Fiona was a righteous fairy. Even though I could now see Dewberry, I hadn't set eyes on Fiona yet. For the longest time, I'd questioned whether she was real. "Place the cat on the floor, Emma." Courtney motioned. "Let her explore."

I did, and Vivi, as if guided by GPS, romped through the showroom to the patio.

"Follow me." Courtney, who wore her hair in a short feathery style, tucked a loose strand behind her ears. "We closed at six. The shop is yours to enjoy privately."

The patio, rich with magical ambience, was covered with a pyramid-shaped glass roof. Fairy lights twinkled in all the ficus trees. A fountain burbled to the left. Bakers racks held a wealth of figurines and environmental items for miniature gardens. The verdigris wrought-iron tables were set with candles. At the far end of the patio, Courtney had arranged a table with food and wine. Our grandmother stood beside it.

"Girls, you look lovely," she said when we joined her. "Did you dress together?"

Both Sierra and I had donned skinny jeans, boots, and amber sweaters. When she walked through my door, we laughed and decided we didn't have time to change. Tonight, we'd be *twins*.

"Here." Nana Lissa handed us each a glass of white wine. "Before the book club gets started—"

"Emma!" my mother called while walking down the ramp to the patio.

"Darn," Nana whispered. "I wanted to pick your brain before the others arrived. I can't stop thinking about Gianna's murder."

Kate pecked me on the cheek and smiled at Sierra. "What did I interrupt? You three look like the proverbial cats who swallowed the canaries."

Who in the heck uses the word proverbial *nowadays?* I mused but bit my tongue.

"C'mon, what were you discussing?" she pressed.

"Nothing," I replied.

Kate twirled a finger in my face. "You were discussing your father, weren't you?"

"No." I felt my cheeks warm.

She frowned. "Why did he slink back into town? What does he want?"

"He's not here. He's in Silicon Valley, taking care of business."

"But he's returning Sunday. He's—"

"Mother!" I held up my hand to stop her. "Give it a rest. You don't like him. I do. I will spend time with him, and he'll be on his way."

Her huff spoke volumes.

Sierra was doing everything not to cackle. Even my grandmother appeared ready to burst out laughing.

"Wine, dear?" Nana Lissa offered a glass to Kate.

She took it. "What in the world is this book we're discussing tonight?"

"Didn't you read it?" Nana Lissa asked.

"Yes, but why did you assign it? I mean, it's called a cozy mystery. What in heavens does that mean? Murder isn't cozy."

"I enjoyed it a lot," I said. "What's not to like about Apparition Apprehenders coming to Wagtail during Halloween to investigate supernatural local legends? Ghost hunters are a hoot."

"Don't tell me you believe in ghosts, too?" my mother scoffed.

"Too?"

"You say you believe in fairies."

"I do."

Sierra blew a raspberry. "Between you and me, Aunt Kate, I think she's full of baloney."

Kate beamed, happy with her niece's support. "You haven't seen one, either?"

"Not a flit or a flutter."

As if on cue, a fairy appeared.

"Do you see *her*, Sierra?" I asked.

"See who?" My cousin scanned the area. At least her recent dismissal of the supernatural didn't mean she wasn't eager to believe.

Could it be Fiona? I wondered. She wore a sparkly silver dress and had gossamer wings and bluish-silver hair. She was about the same size as Dewberry. Giggling, she whizzed above the two cats doing loop-the-loops. Each animal pawed at her. In an instant, she retreated into the ficus trees.

Sierra scoffed. "Don't tease me, Emma. Let's revisit what Nana wanted to talk about. The mur—" She stopped abruptly.

"Were you going to say *the murder*?" Kate asked.

Nana clicked her tongue. Sierra blanched.

"Tell me what you were discussing," Kate prompted.

Courtney joined us and nabbed a glass of wine. "Actually, I was hoping we might be able to chat about Gianna McKay's murder, too, before the book club begins. What do you know so far?"

"Yes, what?" my mother asked.

I rolled my eyes. Was everyone a true crime addict and curious for details?

"I was thinking"—Nana Lissa swirled the wine in her glass but didn't sip—"O'Malley could be the killer."

"Her father?" Kate scoffed. "I can't see it. I know him. He's a good man."

"He and Gianna sure went at it Monday night," Nana added. "You heard them, girls."

Sierra bobbed her head. "Remember what he said when Addison asked him why he and her mother stayed married?" She lowered her voice to imitate the man. '*Because your mother and I hate each other fifty percent of the time, and tolerate each other the other fifty. True love."* She snorted. "As if! It's sure not the kind of love I want."

Nana Lissa said, "On the other hand, not all couples who fight get divorced."

"Maybe you don't." Kate sneered. "But many do."

I shot her a look, begging her to be civil.

She threw up both hands. "We were oil and water, your father and I. You were our one saving grace."

My eyes went wide. Was she giving me a compliment? They were so few and far between. "Nana, Addison's father was in San Francisco at the time of Gianna's murder. I think we can rule him out."

"Right. I forgot."

"Emma, if only . . ." My mother sighed.

"If only what?" I asked, ready for the other shoe to drop.

"Nothing."

"If only I'd become a professor of literature like you? If only I didn't have my head in the clouds thinking I could run a wellness spa?"

The silver fairy I presumed was Fiona flitted from the ficus and landed on my mother's head. She did a jig, which made me laugh.

Kate did not find my mirth humorous in the least. "If you're going to taunt me, I'm leaving." She set her glass on the table. "For the record, I liked the Wagtail book and was prepared to talk about the possibility of ghosts. But now? Forget about it." She turned on her heel and stomped across the patio to make her escape.

Nana Lissa's mouth quirked up on the right. "Don't mind her. She's always had a temper."

I thought of Gianna again. And O'Malley. Both had fierce tempers. But then, so did Peyton Pelagatti and, come to think of it, Gianna's sister-in-law Idha.

Chapter 13

Bright and early Saturday morning, I dressed in leggings and a light jacket, loaded Vivi into her carry bag, and walked with her to the beach. I kicked off my sandals, slung the straps over one finger, and proceeded to the water so I could dig my toes into the sand. The lapping of the surf was soothing. Vivi purred gently against my chest. The sun was rising behind us and gracing us with autumnal warmth. Lots of people were already out—singles, couples, and groups—and dogs of all sizes were frolicking in the sea foam.

After a half hour of restorative deep breathing, I went home, showered, and downed a protein smoothie. Shortly afterward, I felt ready to face what was going to be a very busy day.

"Want to come to work with me?" I asked my sweet Birman.

She mewed, clearly content to laze about the unit.

"Fine. Be that way." I threw a catnip mouse across the floor. She raced for it, nailed it between her forepaws, and tumbled with it under the chair. "See you soon."

Mah was manning the desk when I entered the spa. *Frazzled* didn't exactly capture how she looked. Her eyebrows were pinched together in concentration, her tongue wedged between her teeth. I noticed all the phone lines were lit up and asked if she needed help. She assured me she didn't.

"All right, but I offered."

I slipped around the corner toward the office and paused to listen as Mah answered another call. Her tone was clipped. Exhausted. I made a mental note to chat with Meryl about the situation. We needed an unruffled receptionist who could represent the serenity Aroma Wellness offered. I didn't want to fire Mah, but I had to control the situation. Maybe she could help Yoly in the gift shop. Did I have enough income to afford another receptionist? I didn't care. I'd work my magic.

I went to the office and paid bills, then I decided to message the Etsy designer. I opened her Etsy shop, ChaCha's Chotchkes. I wasn't sure if ChaCha was her real name or a pseudonym.

Me: **ChaCha, everyone loves the pillows you made.**

I wasn't going to tell her someone was smothered with one. I didn't want her to think I was accusing her of anything.

Me: **Question for you. Recently did you sell anyone else, in or around Carmel, a lavender-infused pillow? Let me know when you can.**

I hoped she would respond quickly.

At half past nine I glimpsed the corkboard. Above it was a plaque reading: *You must do the things you think you cannot do. ~ Eleanor Roosevelt.* The quote had inspired me to imagine Aroma Wellness and to believe in my ability to achieve my dream. Now, it was prompting me to imagine the big picture where Addison was concerned. I cared for her and wanted to bring her peace.

Think, Emma. Who killed her mother and why? The why matters.

I moved to the corkboard and removed all the task cards but left the white cards with questions about the murder in place. I still needed them for reference. On fresh, pastel-colored three-by-five cards, I wrote three suspects names. Blue for Wyatt. Pink for Peyton. Green for O'Malley. Should I consider Idha or Frederick? Idha hadn't liked her sister-in-law. Had Frederick suffered under his older sister's tart tongue and smothered her to make her stop? Could he have faked his Zoom chat with fellow astronomy aficionados? What about Gianna's former business associates or clients, or someone from her past? Did any of them hate her enough to murder her?

Giving in, I created a yellow card for Frederick and a violet card for Idha, and marked a beige one with a big question mark to represent all the other people I didn't know in Gianna's sphere.

On the blue card I wrote: *Wyatt's alibi weak. At home watching financial news. Boring. Motive: blamed Gianna for ruining his marriage. Did he know about the trust fund?*

On the pink card I scribbled: *Peyton's alibi is also weak. Home alone knitting. Cannot prove. No witnesses. Motive: jealous of Gianna's success; angry about Gianna dismissing her son. She told police about the trust fund which threw suspicion on Addison. Truth or fabrication?*

On the green card I jotted: *O'Malley was in San Francisco at a meeting. Can someone corroborate his alibi?* I paused. Detective Summers must have questioned people to verify the man's whereabouts. I resumed writing. *Motive: They were no longer in love.* I hesitated again. Wouldn't a simple divorce solve the issue? On the other hand, if he was worried about how his wife was treating their daughter and if he knew about the trust fund issue and believed it could hamper Addison's future . . .

I added that tidbit.

To Frederick's and Idha's cards, I jotted down their alibis: *Frederick was home Zooming online with astronomy buffs. Idha, knowing he would chat for three hours, went to see a movie.* I added the motives I'd imagined and added: *Witnesses?*

I moved away to review my handiwork and felt drained. I knew nothing more than when I'd started. Writing everything down hadn't triggered any memories pointing to the killer, and my subconscious hadn't divined a darned thing from the white index card questions.

Frustrated, I dusted off my hands, refastened my hair in its clip, and went to reception.

At ten, I greeted Addison and her pals. After their sessions—I gave Riley a citrus facial, while Addison, Tatiana, and Cara opted for shiatsu massages—Addison announced they were going to have tea on the patio. Sierra had made them a special batch of healthy eclairs.

"They're sugar-free and low-fat," Addison assured them.

Her friends groaned.

"I ate one on a previous occasion and adored it," she went on. "Afterward, let's go to the gift shop. Daddy wants me to buy each of us bath salts or candles or anything else that might shore up our spirits."

For someone who'd broken down yesterday about the loss of her mother, she was managing quite well. The notion she might have killed Gianna yet again bloomed in my mind, but I whisked the idea aside. Addison was not a killer. She was merely enjoying the relief when someone who has browbeaten you your entire life stops doing so.

Death to bullies, I thought, and shuddered. It sounded like a chant one might have yelled during the Inquisition.

Later when I was crossing the patio to pick up lunch at the café, I spied Addison and her gal pals roaming inside the shop. Addison was admiring a large crystal formation. Cara was showing off a tiger's-eye necklace. Tatiana was raising and lowering a bonsai tree as if it was a barbell, causing Riley to laugh hysterically.

Good for you, I thought. *Let off steam.*

The café was humming when I entered. At the counter, Sierra was conversing with a ropy man in biking gear. His tawny hair was a mess. A smoothie and a helmet sat in front of him. My cousin saw me and waved. I held up three fingers—code for *Bring me whatever special sandwich you are offering*. I loved food. All kinds of flavors. And I had no allergies. I could enjoy taste testing her new creations worry-free. Sierra cried out my order to her sous-chef and redirected her attention to the customer. Was she flirting with him? Her eyes were twinkling.

I moved toward the end of the counter to wait for my order, putting me within earshot of my cousin.

"Go on." She rotated her hand. "Tell me more about Wyatt Lacey. He hated his mother-in-law for . . ."

I missed the rest of her sentence.

"Where'd you hear that?" Sierra glanced in my direction and winked.

"From a guy we bike with," the cyclist replied.

"*We*?"

"I'm in the Pedaling Pioneers cycling group."

"I'm a member, too," she said excitedly. "I haven't seen you."

"I can't commit to every week because I'm also in a running club."

"I run."

"Cool. Anyway, get this, my pal also claimed Wyatt loves his wife"—the cyclist made air quotes around the word *loves*—"even though she walked away from their vows."

"Sounds like this friend of yours has a pretty close relationship with him."

"He's known him for years. I think they went to grade school together." He sipped his smoothie. "Wyatt wants his wife to come home. Got it. He implied she should be grateful her mother is dead. Now she won't have all those hoops to jump through."

"Hoops?"

"According to my friend, Gianna McKay could be very"—he pursed his lips, as if debating which word to choose, and came up with—"*demanding*."

"Are you saying Wyatt killed his mother-in-law to win his wife's affections?" Sierra asked.

"It's sure a possibility. It's not what I'd do. Therapy is always the way to go. It helps. For couples and individuals."

"Do you go to marriage counseling?"

"Nah, I'm not a couple." He grinned. "But I am a therapist. You should hear the stories I could tell . . . but I won't."

Sierra smiled.

Yep. There was definitely chemistry between them.

The cyclist polished off his smoothie and left at the same time one of the staff brought me my to-go lunch.

Sierra whistled softly to grab my attention. When I drew near, she said, "Did you hear that customer's account?"

"I did, but Wyatt has an alibi." I spelled it out.

"Flimsy!" she trilled. "Police can shoot holes through it."

Exiting the café, I considered what the cyclist had alleged. Was Wyatt insane enough to believe killing Addison's mother would make her fonder of him?

As if I'd summoned Wyatt with my musings, I caught sight of him lingering outside the gift shop. Peering in one of the windows.

Uh-uh, not on my watch. I marched to him and barked, "What do you think you're doing?"

He wheeled around. "I . . . I just . . . I have to . . ." he sputtered. "I want to talk with Addison."

"No. Go. Leave these premises. This is my business. You're not wanted here."

The door to the shop flew open, and Addison stormed out. "Wyatt, are you stalking me?"

"No."

"How did you find me? Have you planted a tracker in my belongings?" She shook her crocheted purse.

"No."

"Addison," I cut in, "I heard a cyclist who belongs to the Pedaling Pioneers—I didn't get his name—say Wyatt told another member he hated your mother."

"I don't," he said. "I didn't. It's not true."

"Yes you did." Addison's voice skated upward. "On Monday night when you barged in on our dinner, you said she drove a wedge between us."

I'd forgotten about the exchange, more concerned with her parents' threat to obtain a restraining order.

Wyatt drew to his full height, jaw jutted forward, which made him look powerful and mighty angry. "I have an alibi, Addison. I already told you. I was watching the news."

Addison scoffed, "Did anyone see you? Is there a soul on this planet who can confirm you were home? How about the woman across the street from you who lurks in her window? Or your nosy neighbor who takes pictures of everyone's deliveries? Maybe one of them saw you."

He didn't answer.

"Like I suspected. Liar." Addison turned to Cara, Tatiana, and Riley, who were huddled in the door of the shop, staring down Wyatt.

Riley formed the letter *L* with her fingers. "Loser."

Addison turned back. "Bye-bye."

Wyatt's fists clenched. His face flushed red-hot. After a long ten seconds, he lowered his head like a chastised dog and fled down the stairs.

Addison eyed me. "Emma, I've been meaning to ask, where is tonight's tai chi class?"

I'd forgotten she'd wanted to participate. "Walking distance from here. Come to the spa at six, and we'll go together."

"Riley, do you want to join?" she asked her pal.

"No, thanks. Saturday is wine-and-dine night with my honey."

Addison pulled a face. "Cara, Tat?"

"Busy," each said.

"See you by my lonesome," Addison said to me, and herded her friends into the gift shop.

At the same time Sierra rushed from the café while wiping her hands on her apron. "What's going on? I saw Wyatt storm off."

I filled her in. "The biker guy you were talking to was cute, and he was into you."

"Not."

"Def." I aimed two fingers at my eyes and pointed them at her. "I'm not blind. I have twenty-twenty vision. Maybe you need to get your peepers checked. Hey, maybe he's the one Ursula envisions in your future. Did you get his number?"

"As a matter of fact, he left his business card under his drink."

"Woot!"

The modest-size tai chi studio, located in a building consisting of studios leased out to many other types of classes, was filled to the max. In addition to Addison and me, six women and four men of varying ages were in attendance. I recognized many of them, though none of us could claim we were regulars. I tried to show up every two weeks, but work and family obligations occasionally interfered. The twelve of us formed three rows. We'd all worn loose clothing and were barefoot. Addison and I took spots in the middle line.

"Welcome, everyone." Zane Ashford, our instructor, was handsome in a surfer kind of way. He had firm abs, if the snug-fitting sleeveless mesh shirt he had on was any indication. His sandy-colored hair looked like he'd brushed it with his fingertips. Gorgeous tattoos adorned both arms. I was pretty sure he had another job—not surfing—but I'd never had the opportunity to ask because, after class, students often swarmed him. "Before we begin, let's connect with our bodies."

Two women in the front row giggled. The taller one whispered to her friend, "I'd like to connect with his body."

Addison side-eyed me and made a gagging face. "Honestly?"

"Get used to it," I joked.

"Stand with your feet apart, knees slightly bent," Zane ordered as he did in every session. He inhaled and exhaled.

The nice thing about being the student instead of the group leader was that I was able to fully let go. I mirrored Zane and instantly experienced an inner sense of peace.

"Relax your shoulders and feel the weight of your body sinking into the ground. Imagine you are a tree. Your feet are the roots of the tree."

"I'm an oak," the taller woman in the front row inserted, "grounded firmly in the earth."

"I'm a willow," her companion said, "able to bend with the breeze."

Zane didn't comment. He didn't even crack a smile. He was used to this particular pair of women's interruptions.

Addison, in tree pose to my right, grumbled, "I wish they'd let him do the talking. They're getting on my nerves."

Breathe, I mouthed without uttering a sound.

Addison mock-glowered at me.

"Feel your head being gently drawn upward by a string," Zane said, his voice as smooth as silk. "And inhale deeply while letting go of any tension or distractions."

"Like Wyatt?" Addison whispered.

I threw her a look.

She held up a palm and bit back a smile. "I'll be serious. Promise."

"Tai chi is a practice of movement and stillness," Zane said. "Let your body be soft, not rigid. I like to think of our bodies as water flowing gently around obstacles, moving with ease."

For a full half hour, Zane directed us through the steps. We posed in the Horse stance, or Ba Bu, and then the Bow stance, or Gong Bu, a lunge-like stance used to develop balance and proper weight distribution. Occasionally, he approached a student to realign a position. Lightly. Never exerting pressure.

"Slowly move into the Golden Rooster pose. Remember to focus on your *dantian*."

Addison regarded me quizzically.

I pointed to a spot a couple of inches above my belly button—*dantian* was an energy center or sea of *qi* in Chinese medicine—and showed her the stance, right leg lifted, arms extended at my sides. I teetered.

"Balance is a key element in tai chi." Zane appeared at my side and steadied me by pressing his palm underneath my right elbow.

I detected a masculine aroma akin to Pierre Cardin cologne and nearly swooned. *Uh-oh. Nope. Not happening.* I refused to be attracted to my tai chi teacher. I needed a space where I could just let loose. "Thanks," I said without a hint of emotion.

"As you shift your weight from one leg to the other, notice how this helps you develop control over your center of gravity." Zane continued to circle the room. "It won't happen if you're tense. Relax. Focus on your breath and try to keep your mind clear."

He resumed his place at the front of the room and led us through a variation of the Yang-style form, a series of slow, flowing movements that helped promote focus, flexibility, and coordination.

By the time the class ended, I was dripping with perspiration.

Zane said, "Some of you have asked if I will teach combat tai chi. Probably not. To be fair, tai chi emphasizes deflecting and redirecting an attacker's force rather than confronting it with power. This is a valuable point to remember. Do you agree?"

"Yes, *Sifu*," the class said in unison, *Sifu* being the word for teacher.

"Excellent." Zane grinned. "Thank you all for coming. See you next time, and remember: Tai chi is a journey, not a race."

Addison stopped outside the studio and whistled. "Well, girlfriend, the class was enlightening to the max. Here's my takeaway. If I need to stave off Wyatt in the future, I will deflect and redirect rather than confront him with my super power."

"Good for you."

"I've got to say, none of my previous classes were as good as this one, and Zane, wow." She popped the fingers of both hands, miming an explosion. "He's special. The art on his arms looks Hawaiian, with all the volcanoes and smoke, but he sure doesn't look Hawaiian. And his gorgeous head of hair? Double wow."

I laughed.

"By the way, did you notice he didn't provide support for anyone other than you? Oh, sure, he touched their hands and repositioned them, but he did not prop them with his palm."

I had noticed but had pushed the thought from my mind.

"What does he do other than this? I mean, he's more than an instructor, isn't he? Teaching tai chi can't be his sole source of income."

Why was she asking so many questions? Was she interested in him? True, her divorce was nearly final and, like so many women coming out of a bad marriage, she was probably champing at the bit to return to the dating scene.

"He has another job," I said, "but I'm not sure what it is."

"Well, ask! He's interested in you, so return the favor. You got this." Playfully, she bumped me with her elbow.

Okay, I'd read her wrong. She wasn't interested in him for herself.

A half hour later, as I was inserting my key into the front door lock of my unit, Ursula's warning to beware haunted me. At the same time, Zane's words replayed in my mind: *Deflect. Redirect. Don't confront with power.* Could I do it if the situation warranted?

"Emma!" Ursula called from above.

I jolted. Heart pounding, I peered up at her.

She was leaning over the railing, the tails of her silver scarf dangling like spiderwebs. "Emma, you have been weighing on my mind. Therefore, I did a crystal reading for you."

"Can you do so without me picking the stones?"

"Yes. I am allowed to select the crystals intuitively based on questions I believe you want answered."

I grinned. "Which questions do you think I have?"

"Will your business survive? Will the killer be found? Will you be able to help Addison Lacey become the best version of herself?"

I gawked. Those were posers. "And?"

"Yes, yes, and yes, but not necessarily in that order." With her pronouncement, she retreated into her apartment, leaving me breathless.

Chapter 14

As much as I wanted to sleep in on Sunday morning, I couldn't. My father texted he was on his way from Silicon Valley and would pick me up in thirty minutes. I dressed, packed a picnic lunch for us, inserted it into a backpack with two water bottles, and fed Vivi. She was not happy to hear I was going out and not lounging with her for the day. I told her she was more than welcome to join us on our hike. The little snoot turned away from me, tail high in the air as if to say, *Walk? With you? On this perfectly gorgeous Sunday? Heaven forbid*.

I heard a *honk-honk* outside, blew my sweet cat a kiss, armed the security system, and hurried outside. I climbed into my father's rental Jeep and leaned across the console to peck him on the cheek. "Did you have a good meeting?"

"Meetings. Plural. They were eventful."

The day was going to be glorious. The weather, a temperate sixty-eight, was sublime. The changing colors of the foliage were vibrant. We decided to go to Point Lobos State Natural Reserve. The loop trail was the best hike in the area, hands down. World-class photographers scoured the reserve to capture the perfect picture. No dogs or bicycles were allowed. And best of all, no drones. How I hated those pesky devices. They destroyed any feeling of privacy.

We chose the North Shore Trail, which would take us along the rugged coastline to Sea Lion Point. On the hike, my father provided mini lectures on a variety of rare plant areas. I listened, but I was more interested in the view, the whoosh of the waves, and sightings of sea lions frolicking in the surf . . . all while wondering what my father had meant by *eventful*. I didn't press, hoping he'd expound further in time.

Plein-air artists had laid claim to lots of locations. One easel setup made me giggle. The artist was sitting on a stool attached to the easel itself. When she heard me laughing, she explained it was called a *donkey* easel. *Trivia for one hundred, Alex.*

"How is life, baby doll?" Dad asked.

"Other than—"

"Finding a body. Yes. I mean the rest of life. Are you interested in anyone?"

"No." Although I couldn't get Zane out of my mind no matter how hard I tried. "Have you read any good books lately?" I asked to change the subject.

"The complete works of Sherlock Holmes."

"I've wanted to catch up on all of them."

"Make the time. *The Adventure of Silver Blaze* is my favorite." He raised a finger. "'The curious incident of the dog in the night-time,'" he intoned. "Sherlock noticed what everyone else failed to perceive." He chuckled. "Do you?"

"Do I what?"

"Pay attention to the clues?"

"I'm pretty good at solving the mysteries I read before I reach the end."

He regarded me slyly and wagged a finger in front of my nose.

"You know that's not what I mean. You're been thinking about Gianna McKay's murder. Don't deny it. Use me as a sounding board. Right now. You've got a keen eye and a tender heart." He tapped his chest. "Those two attributes make a good detective."

"Don't tell Kate."

"Kate, schmate. She doesn't value your soul." He squinched up his face. "Don't get me wrong. I know she loves you, but she doesn't see you." He bracketed the word *see*. "So, what did you notice no one else did?" He tapped my temple. "Use your brilliant brain, which you got from me. Don't ever forget that."

We continued walking, and I told him all I remembered from the crime scene, the lack of medicines in Gianna's cabinets, the smudge on the crystal tumbler, the scent of lavender and the aroma of something else.

"You see?" He nudged my shoulder with his. "The nose knows. How many detectives other than drug-sniffing dogs could pick up scents like you do?"

Soon we found a picnic area. As I was laying out our lunch on a table, I noticed a family sitting at another table nearby. The toddler's costume made him look like the human epitome of a fire truck.

I said to the adults, "You've got to get your money's worth, right?"

"They would sleep in them if they could," the mother replied.

"Though the fire truck is a little unwieldly." The father chuckled.

"It's from the TV show *Firebuds*," the mother said.

"I've heard about it," I replied. "One of our customers brings her kids with her to sessions—she can't afford a treatment *and* a sitter—so she makes sure they remain quiet and enthralled with interactive presentations from the show."

"Are you a therapist?" she asked.

"Heavens no. I own Aroma Wellness, a spa in town. We offer massages, facials, mindful meditations, and more."

"I'll have to check it out."

I turned to Dad. He was studying his cell phone. His forehead was wrinkled. "Everything okay?" I asked.

"Yep." He turned the phone face down on the table. "What's to eat?"

"Pita sandwiches stuffed with olives, spinach, cucumbers, tomatoes, and feta, tossed with a garlicky vinaigrette."

"Gourmet." He grinned. "Anything for dessert?"

"I picked up a couple of cookies at Aroma Café before I left last night. Gluten-free double chocolate chip cookies."

"I love me some chocolate." He rubbed his hands together greedily.

We ate in silence and listened to the squawk of seagulls and peals of wonder from other hikers. One yelled, "Whale!"

"Not in October," I said. "My guess? It's a sea lion."

My father chuckled.

After dining, we took an amazingly long time to wend our way to the parking lot. I snapped pictures with my cell phone and, out of nowhere, I was plagued by images of the crime scene. Dad didn't notice. He had resumed browsing his messages. What was he hoping to receive?

Near the beginning of the trail, I eyed my father, who had slotted his phone into his pocket. "It's my turn to ask questions."

"Okay."

"What did you mean by the word *eventful* earlier?"

"The meetings were good."

"You're still employed by the foundation, aren't you?"

"Yes."

My father was a better conversationalist than this. Why was he being cagey?

"C'mon. What's up?" I asked. "Truth."

He faced me. "They want me to head it. The whole kit and caboodle."

"What?" My jaw fell open. "They want you to do the field work *and* be the CEO?"

"Nope. They want me to hang up my traveling shoes and run the thing, lock, stock, and barrel. Their offer is a big number."

"How do you feel about the idea?"

"I'm not sure. I'm mulling over my options." He clasped a hand on my arm. "I'd get to see more of you if I didn't gallivant everywhere."

I arched an eyebrow. "What else is helping you with your decision? Fess up."

His mouth quirked up on one side. "Aha! You are a natural detective."

I knuckled his arm.

"On my travels, I met a woman. She's an eco-scientist based in San Francisco. I'd like to see more of her. We're on the same wavelength. I'll tell you everything over dinner."

I cocked my head. "Everything?"

"As much as I can without blushing."

We returned to Carmel to change for dinner, I to my apartment, he to the Lamplighter, the quaint hotel where he was lodging. Then we met at Saison, a restaurant in a charming arcade on Ocean Avenue. The restaurant's décor was simple yet elegant, with deep blue walls, palms in giant blue pots, and cherrywood tables, sans tablecloths. However, to honor the season, there were strands of orange pumpkin lights swooping from the ceiling to the walls. The bar was bustling with activity. The sushi-style counter facing the open kitchen was filled with diners. The staff's congenial repartee ignited ripples of laughter.

A stunning Asian woman in a blue cheongsam dress—a traditional style for Chinese women—led us to our table and asked for our beverage order. Dad requested a bottle of prosecco and two glasses. She nodded and scuttled away.

"The concierge at the Lamplighter raves about the food here." My father perused the menu. "The mahi with grilled pineapple wedges is calling my name. You?"

"The seared scallops had me at yum." They would be served

with grilled artichoke hearts on top of smashed red potatoes. "So, tell me about this eco-scientist. What exactly does she do?"

"She oversees the collection and analysis of materials threatening the environment in California. Stanford grad. She looks a lot like the hostess who seated us, in fact."

"Wow. Go for the gold, Dad. Does she—"

"Hold on a sec." He rose to his feet. "O'Malley." He extended his hand to O'Malley McKay, who was passing by the table. "I'm sorry for your loss."

They shook, and O'Malley said, "Thank you, Everett." His skin was ghostly pale compared to the black polo shirt and trousers he was wearing. "Hello, Emma."

"I would've reached out," my father continued, "but I didn't have your number. I didn't think to ask my daughter."

"I appreciate the sentiment more than I can say."

"I heard you were in San Francisco at the time."

"Yes, sadly. I had meetings all day, and though I could've driven home, I was under the weather and had meetings scheduled for the day after, so I told the hotel staff not to disturb me and retired early. Of course, learning of Gianna's . . ." The word caught in his throat. "Of her death the next morning, I canceled all my meetings and drove straight home. Poor Addison is bereft. Emma, you have been a rock for her."

Hardly a rock. More like a camp counselor. But there were all sorts of ways to cope with loss. Burying one's sorrows in healthy treatments was a positive way to do so. It occurred to me to give Addison a box of daily inspirational cards. I had a set designed by Oprah Winfrey, and they'd helped me through some trying times. We sold similar ones in the gift shop.

"Are you alone, O'Malley?" Dad asked. "Care to join us?"

"I'm meeting an associate." He gestured to a sandy-haired man in a windbreaker and chinos sitting at the bar. "Had to wash my hands before dining. I've been looking at soil samples all afternoon."

"He's building another golf course in San Francisco, Dad."

"Don't they have enough already, man?" my father kidded.

"I won't say no to a project."

"Or a paycheck."

O'Malley attempted to chortle but failed. "Just think of my legacy if I could make a track that outshines Harding Park or San Francisco Golf Club. All drought-tolerant grasses, of course."

I studied his face wondering, as my grandmother had, whether he could have killed Gianna. Was it out of the realm of possibility for him to have driven down from San Francisco, murdered his wife, and returned? At what time had he told the staff not to disturb him? Had anyone seen him between the hours of six and nine Tuesday night?

"What are you thinking?" Dad asked me.

I blinked. "What? Oh, nothing."

O'Malley narrowed his gaze. "Yes, you are. You're wondering if I'm lying."

What had given me away? Had I been staring at him, or could he, like Ursula, read my mind? "No, sir, I wasn't."

"Addison raves about your ability to sort out the truth."

Honestly, my supposed reputation was getting out of hand. I'd helped solve one murder. One. Of a friend.

"To set your mind at ease, I'll prove my whereabouts." He held up his cell phone and dialed a number. He put the call on Speaker.

A female receptionist answered, "Hilltop Hotel. How may I direct your call?"

O'Malley identified himself and asked for the hotel manager. The receptionist put him on Hold. O'Malley waggled his mobile. "He's a friend. He'll set you straight."

A man with a silky voice came on the line. "O'Malley. I'm so sorry to hear about your wife."

"Robert, thanks." O'Malley bobbed his head.

"What a shock."

"Heartbreaking." He licked his lips. "Robert, I'd like you to confirm a fact about my stay Tuesday night."

"How are you feeling? It wasn't the flu, was it?"

"No. Probably something I ate. But to your point, I asked the staff not to disturb me, right?"

"You told me personally. What's the issue?"

"Is there any way to confirm I was at the hotel?" O'Malley asked.

"Well, I saw you when you came down for a glass of ginger ale. So did the bar staff. About eight thirty, I think." The hotel manager cleared his throat. "Why?"

"Some friends wanted to know. What time did I phone you from my room earlier?"

"Around four thirty. I'd just concluded a staff meeting."

"Thanks, Robert. See you soon." He ended the call.

It was impossible to drive from San Francisco to Carmel in less than two hours during rush hour, meaning he would have needed to kill Gianna by six thirty at the latest in order to return to the City in time to appear in the bar to request a ginger ale. However, if he'd asked not to be disturbed at four thirty, he couldn't have made it to Carmel until well past six. The date rape drug didn't work in a matter of minutes. He would have needed to hang out for a while before smothering Gianna. Perhaps she had been in a deep sleep when he'd arrived home and hadn't been drugged, except Dottie confirmed the drug had been found in Gianna's system.

O'Malley said, "I loved my wife, Everett. We were coming up on a big anniversary." His eyes misted over. "Our marriage was not entirely paradise, as your daughter witnessed at dinner on Monday night, but we were happy. I never would have killed her. To deny a daughter her mother? Unfathomable."

"Sir, who do you think did it?" I asked.

"I'd place bets on Peyton."

"She was Gianna's best friend," I said to my father, and summed up Peyton in a few words.

O'Malley's mouth quirked up on one side. "Best frenemy at times, too. They were always at odds."

"Why?" I asked.

"She was jealous of my wife's success and ease in society, as well as of our enduring marriage. Peyton's wedded bliss ended in divorce after three years. Plus, she has a temper."

What an understatement.

"If not her, then my soon-to-be ex-son-in-law Wyatt is my guess," he went on. "He hated Gianna for the way she pitted Addison against him."

The cyclist had stated the same at the café earlier.

"He is certifiably unstable," O'Malley added. "Why, a year ago he threatened to lock Addison in a room for the rest of her life if she didn't follow his rules."

"He did not!" my father exclaimed.

"Yep. Gianna and I managed to intervene and convince her it was time to divorce him."

My father exchanged a look with me.

"He sure seemed ready to lash out at my wife Monday night," O'Malley said. "Remember when he burst into the dining room, Emma?"

I'd had nightmares about it.

"He's a sick puppy." O'Malley frowned.

My father clapped him on the arm again. "Hang tough. I'm sure the police will sort this out."

O'Malley nodded somberly and proceeded on.

When he was out of earshot, Dad whispered, "Convinced?"

"Of . . ."

"He was right. You were wondering if he was the killer. I could see it in your eyes. But I think you can rule him out."

Chapter 15

My father refused to let me walk to my fourplex alone even though I assured him it was safe. We came across a couple of people strolling their dogs on 4th Avenue, but no one else.

"Told you!" I tapped my front door. "Safe."

"Better safe than sorry. Sleep tight, baby doll."

I entered my unit, disarmed the security system, and announced, "Vivi, I'm home!"

She rocketed to me and brushed her head against my ankle.

I swooped her into a hug, scanned my cell phone, and noticed I'd missed a message from my grandmother reminding me of our coffee appointment in the morning. I set Vivi on the floor, texted Nana Lissa I'd be there, and prepared for bed.

Though I agreed with my father that O'Malley McKay appeared to be innocent of murder, I dreamed about a helicopter transporting him and his Acura from San Francisco to Carmel in a matter of minutes. The deafening *whoosh-whoosh* of the propeller continued to echo in my head as I awoke to Vivi parading between me and the headboard.

"I tossed and turned, huh, kitty? Yes, I know it upset you. How about you accompany me to work today, and you can take care of me?"

She meowed her approval of the plan.

After throwing on yoga pants and a burnt-orange T-shirt emblazoned with pictures of vintage apothecary jars and herbs and the words *Know your roots*, I tucked the cat into her carryall, slipped on my favorite tourmaline-and-moonstone bracelet—both crystals were good for anxiety—and hustled to Percolate.

Nana Lissa was seated at a booth, chatting with Detective Summers, who was standing holding a to-go cup in hand.

"Morning, sunshine," my grandmother crooned. "Hello, Vivi."

The cat responded merrily.

I slid onto the banquette opposite my grandmother and set the carryall by my feet.

"You and I are drinking lattes." Nana pointed to the one she'd purchased for me, served in a wide cup. The floral pattern the barista had made with the foam was gorgeous, and I was jealous, wishing I had the knack.

"Did you see the pumpkins in the window, Nana?" The owner had sponsored a pumpkin carving contest for the staff last week, where one employee could win a paid weekend off. "My fave was the skeleton hugging the pumpkin."

"I liked that one, too," she said.

The winner was a ghoulish pumpkin, its eyes, nose, and mouth outlined in black, similar to something out of *The Nightmare Before Christmas*.

"I preferred the one with the haunted house image," Summers said.

Nana Lissa clicked her tongue in jest. "You would. It's intricate."

"What are you implying?"

"You are the epitome of thorough down to the last detail, Dylan."

"Yes, I am. Glad you noticed." He took a sip of his drink and peered at me over the rim. "Too bad your granddaughter doesn't hold the same opinion. In fact, I'm sensing she wants to tell me something." He leveled me with his gaze. "Spill."

"Me?"

"You, but you don't have to, because Addison Lacey already contacted me and told me what a cyclist in the Pedaling Pioneers revealed about her soon-to-be ex-husband. And yes, we are checking out Wyatt Lacey's alibi."

I said, "He claims he was home watching business news."

"Feeble," my grandmother muttered.

"I'll be the judge," Summers said.

Movement drew my gaze, and I gawped. "Detective, there he is." I pointed. "The cyclist with the tawny hair and the helmet tucked under one arm." The guy was moving forward in the line. "He's the one who told my cousin about Wyatt's motive."

"I hate coincidences," Summers groused.

"I didn't lure him here," I said with a bite.

"I know him," Nana Lissa cut in. "He's a regular at the library, as well as at Percolate. A charming young man. He's read everything about cycling. *The Secret Race. The Zen of Bicycling.* You name it, he wants to know about it. He believes cycling is good for the soul."

"He's a therapist," I stated.

"A very good one." She smiled. "We've had many profound conversations."

"Thank you, ladies. I'll go have a chat with him." Summers leveled me with a stern look. "In the meantime, Emma, keep the flow of information coming." He crossed the café to have a word with the cyclist.

My mouth fell open. Had he actually asked for my help? Or had his closing remark been a taunt, given that I hadn't filled him in the moment I learned Wyatt's alibi and motive?

Nana Lissa sipped her latte and leaned forward on her elbows. "Bring me up to speed. Let's start with the business."

"The spa is doing great." Our baseline required us to be booked ninety percent of the time. "We should consider hiring a few more masseuses, at least a couple who could step in should one of our regulars need time off."

She made a note on her cell phone. "Payroll?"

"We're faring well."

"Everyone's getting paid on time, even you?"

"Even me."

"Are there any orders we can't afford?"

"They're all in the budget. Breakage could be an issue, but so far, so good." I rapped on the table with my knuckles, and then filled her in on Meryl's Smell-O-Vision idea.

"I know where we can obtain a cart for free. One of the library patrons owns a pushcart business. The company supplies them for weddings and street fairs and such. She owes me a favor. I introduced her to her husband."

"Brilliant." I loved how Nana didn't consider herself a silent business partner. I appreciated her input.

"How are you doing?" She took another sip of her latte.

"Fine."

"Liar. You're worried about the business."

"No. Maybe. Sort of." I filled her in on my concern about the spa's proximity to another murder, and the fact that Addison was counting on me to solve the murder. "Why hasn't Detective Summers solved it yet?"

"Investigations take time." She cocked her head. "But you're concerned about something else."

How many mind readers am I going to encounter? I mused.

"Tell me how your day went with your father," she prompted.

"With Dad? Fine. We had a great hike."

"But . . ."

I told her he was considering moving to Silicon Valley full-time and taking the helm of the foundation.

Nana Lissa snickered. "That will make your mother supremely happy. *Not.*"

"Why? He wouldn't be living in Carmel proper. But between you and me, I think he'd hate not traveling like he does."

"I agree."

"However, he met someone, Nana." I described the eco-scientist in the manner he had.

"Good for him. He deserves happiness."

I sipped my drink. "I'm so grateful you don't hold him responsible for ruining his and Kate's marriage."

"They never should have wed in the first place. They were oil and water, and I told them so."

Like Gianna had told Addison.

"But I'm glad they did marry, because I have you." She reached for my hand and squeezed.

I slid my hand out of hers and drew my latte closer. "Let's talk business for a sec longer, Nana. I'm not sure Mah Kim is going to work out. She seems nervous all the time. She's bungling phone messages. I don't want to fire her, but—"

"Give it a week. See how it goes. You might be surprised. She might make the decision for you."

I arrived at the spa fifteen minutes before we would open and put Vivi in the office. She would enjoy exploring for a few minutes until she settled in the cat bed I'd placed behind the desk. The door had been closed overnight so the scent of vanilla—one of her favorites—was heady. "I'll return soon," I cooed, and strode to the reception area.

"You're looking spa-tacular, Emma," Meryl intoned.

"You are spa-arkling," Mah added with dramatic flair.

"If you need to relax, a spa pedicure will really nail it." Meryl smirked.

I frowned at them. "You're both being loony."

"Obvi." Meryl chuckled. "Forgive us. Neither of us has had a stand-up gig in the past few weeks. We're eager to find new material."

"I'd stick to your old routines. They're clever. Spa jokes?" I waggled a hand, palm down. "Meh."

The two of them giggled hysterically. I couldn't help but join in the laughter.

"Your friend Ursula called." Mah gestured to a note she'd written on a pad. "She'd like to invite you and some friends over tonight so she can practice a crystal reading. Does eight o'clock work?"

"Yes." I wondered why Ursula hadn't contacted me directly. She couldn't possibly be worried I'd turn her down. I texted her to say *yes* to the RSVP, and added I'd invite Yoly and Sierra.

"You have a full day ahead," Mah went on. "A facial at ten. Another at two. And Addison is coming in with her uncle in a few minutes."

"With her uncle?" I tilted my head.

"He's spa curious." Quickly, Meryl waved a hand. "Not a joke. He wants to learn more about why Addison's friends are enjoying coming here so much. Addison booked a massage for him and a mani-pedi for herself. They're at the café having tea right now." She motioned to the plate-glass window at the far end of reception with the view of the café, a novel design feature Sierra had suggested, saying it would invite customers to be intrigued by the other venue.

I caught sight of Addison sitting at a table with Frederick. The two appeared to be deep in conversation. He was hunched over, his elbows on the table, his hands folded. His skin was slack and pale and his jacket rumpled. Addison rested her hand atop his. Sierra spied me looking and waved. I responded in kind. Addison spotted me, as well, and held up a finger to convey she and her uncle would come to the spa in a minute.

I turned back to Meryl and Mah. "Other appointments?"

Meryl rattled off the list. Ten massages. Four mani-pedis. One mindful meditation. "And Yoly would like to meet with you if you have time."

"Absolutely. Tell her after eleven." I glanced at Mah, who appeared calmer today, perhaps because she wasn't answering phones at the moment.

Feeling unexpectedly antsy, I decided to cleanse the reception area with a smudging, an ancient ritual meant to assist healers in enhancing intuition and connecting with the spiritual realm. I lit a bundle of dried white sage and, with a bowl in hand to catch the ashes, walked the perimeter of the space. While doing so, I studied the area to ensure all the accoutrements were in place. The pitcher was filled with fresh cucumber water. The beverage cart held fixings for tea as well as coffee. Someone had fluffed the pillows on the chairs near the door. Satisfied with everything, I returned to the desk, put the remaining sage into the bowl, and placed it on the counter. The bundle would burn out eventually.

Next, I flipped over the *Open for Business* sign on the front door and drew back the door to allow Addison to enter with her beleaguered-looking uncle.

"Is it okay to come in a bit early?" Addison asked.

"You bet."

"Uncle Frederick, you remember Emma."

"Yes, of course. Your business model is lovely."

"Thank you."

He surveyed the space, his mood brightening a tad. "The idea of three locations in one—a shop, a café, and a spa—is very appealing. I particularly like the fountain on the patio."

Addison protectively clasped his elbow with her hand. "Doesn't it smell wonderful in here, Uncle Frederick?"

In addition to the burning sage, I picked up the faint odor of whiskey clinging to her uncle's clothing. Perhaps he'd spilled some on his jacket last night and, for whatever reason—distraction or grief—hadn't thought to don a fresh outfit today.

"Emma," Addison said, "my uncle was hoping to get a steam or a sauna, but I told him this isn't that kind of spa."

"No, sir. We're not like a gym or even a fancy resort hotel. We have a limited menu."

"So I signed my uncle up for a massage. Since Mother died, he's been . . ." Addison glanced at him, waiting for him to take the lead. When he didn't, she said, "Sad and weary."

"I'm tired today because I drank too much last night." He attempted a smile.

Was last night's binge a habit or a one-off? He'd imbibed a lot on the night of the dinner at the McKay's house, too.

"I fed him carbs at the café." Addison patted his arm. "You'll feel better after your treatment, Uncle Frederick."

"Have you ever had a massage?" I asked him.

"Once or twice when on vacation with my wife."

"They love to travel all over the world like your father, Emma," Addison added.

"My wife is very disappointed with me." Frederick sighed.

"C'mon, Uncle Frederick, don't be a sad sack. Aunt Idha adores you." She crossed her fingers. "They are perfect together, like two peas in a pod."

"She was disappointed with your mother, too," he murmured.

Addison released his arm. "Yes, we all know she could be critical of Mother and the way she held everyone to high standards. Peyton could be disparaging, too."

"She blames your mother for my regretful path in life."

"You love your work," Addison countered.

"Yes, but I don't have ambition. Initiative." He seemed locked on some perplexing train of thought. "Idha wants me to aspire to greatness, but my sister . . ." He sighed. "Quite often she made me feel less than. She was demanding."

And controlling and volatile, I reflected.

"Idha said her superiority was a façade," Frederick went on. "Gianna pretended to have confidence, though she lacked it. She was always haughty. She belittled everyone. She was the reason Idha—" He blinked, as though waking from a trance.

"Idha what?" I prompted.

"My wife says I'm not a good role model for our son."

"Not true." Addison addressed me. "Their son is a handful, but he's very sweet. He's an artist and can be erratic."

How old was the boy? Addison hadn't mentioned him before.

Tears spilled from Frederick's eyes. He mopped them with a soiled handkerchief he pulled from his jacket pocket.

"There, there." Addison consoled him like a mother might soothe a child.

Listening to the drama spilling out of this man and witnessing the way his niece was taking charge was, in a word, fascinating. Watching an episode of *Dr. Phil* couldn't have been more engrossing.

"I'm afraid she might have done something horrible," Frederick whispered.

Addison gasped. "Who, Mother?"

"Your aunt."

I shared a concerned look with Addison and asked, "What did she do, Frederick?"

"She went to a movie by herself the night Gianna was killed. She showed me the ticket stub, a six p.m. screening. I found that odd, as if she felt the need to prove where she was." He jammed his lips together and released them with a smack. "I don't believe her."

I recalled being suspicious of Idha after she'd freely offered an alibi for herself. "Do you know the name of the theater?" I pressed.

"The one in Monterey. The art house place. Cinema something. She watched *The World Dies Wanting*."

I wasn't familiar with the movie, though I'd been to the theater to see a retrospective of films from the sixties. *Bonnie and Clyde, Psycho,* and *The Graduate*.

"She went to dinner afterward."

"Did she say where?" I asked.

"Portofino. On the wharf."

"If she's telling the truth, there will be witnesses," I assured him.

Addison looked shaken by her uncle's despondency. "Emma, maybe you could find out for us."

"I—"

The front door opened. Other clients were entering.

Loath to have them view the maudlin scene playing out, I said, "I'll do what I can," and I beckoned them to follow me to their treatment rooms.

Chapter 16

After the ten o'clock facial, I went to my office, dabbed a drop of soothing lavender essential oil behind each ear, and picked up Vivi. She wriggled, eager to resume her nap on her pillow. I obliged and crossed to the corkboard. Staring at the three-by-five cards, I wondered if Idha's motive was strong enough. Had she been so angry at her sister-in-law's treatment of her husband that she'd smothered her to death?

Someone knocked on the door. Yoly poked her head in. "Got a sec?"

"For you, I have a whole hour."

She guffawed. "This won't take long."

"Sit." I motioned to the chair pushed up against the wall and took a seat behind the desk.

Yoly dragged the chair closer, perched on the edge of it, and rested her hands on her knees.

"Nice blouse," I chimed. Like me, she regularly donned leggings, but T-shirts weren't her thing. She liked to highlight her femininity with flouncy tops. Today's linen number was soft peach with floral embroidery, teensy covered buttons, and billowy sleeves. "Perfect with your skin tone."

"Thanks. Um, about my future . . ."

"Aha. You're here as employee to boss?"

"Yes." Her cheeks tinged nearly the same color as her top. "I've decided I'm not going to become a massage therapist after all. It's not for me."

"As good as your hands are?" I praised her readily whenever she gave me the occasional neck rub. "Don't tell me you're quitting the spa and going to work at the bakery with your sister?"

"No, no. I'm staying." She held up her hands, palms forward. "But I've become interested in candle making and thought I could run the gift shop while learning the trade and becoming an artisan. If you'd allow me, I could even sell them at the shop—on consignment, of course."

"Why candle making?"

"I've always been obsessed with them, and now I'm consumed with the process of mixing wax and choosing fragrances, and the pipe dream that I'd be creating beautiful items to help people relax. It'd be, I don't know, gratifying. Meditative. I love the image of people lighting a candle I've crafted and feeling more at ease. I've been experimenting with all sorts of waxes—soy, beeswax—and I'm playing around with different essential oils to create custom blends. Your oils, by the way. Each candle will have its own uniqueness. I'll make sure everything is eco-friendly and ethically sourced."

I beamed. Her enthusiasm was compelling. "Terrific business plan. Love it. And don't fret about not pursuing massage. It's not for everyone."

"Thank you for understanding." She stood up and caught sight of the corkboard with the note cards. "What's this? The same thing you did for Willow's murder?"

"Similar. I'm concerned for Addison and her family. I'd like to find closure for them. Detective Summers asked me to provide him with my theories."

"No way! Really?"

Granted, believing he gave me a no-holds-barred green light was probably a stretch.

She clapped her hands. "He sees your value. Finally." She inched closer to the board. "Five suspects. That's all you can come up with?"

"I didn't know Gianna well. There could be others, ergo, the big question mark on the beige card."

"Have you asked Addison for her input?"

"She thinks Wyatt or Peyton is the culprit."

Yoly tapped the violet card with Idha's information. "I've been to the theater. It's really nice. Intimate. I bet someone would remember if she was there."

"A visit is on my to-do list." I rose from the chair. "Also on my slate is learning how many things we're running low on in the gift shop. I'll need to submit orders." A number of the items we offered couldn't be shipped overnight.

"Follow me," she said, and led the way out of the spa and across the patio.

Courtney Kelly and Hattie Hopewell were waiting to enter the shop. I greeted them and took in Hattie's attire. Somewhere in her sixties, she often dressed like she was going to weed a garden. Today's T-shirt boasted the Garden Club logo. As she followed Yoly inside, I read the saying on the backside of the shirt: *Gardening is my therapy*.

Amen, I thought, wondering when I'd find the time to address the garden at the fourplex.

"What can we help you with, ladies?" Yoly headed for the sales counter.

The fairy I'd seen at Open Your Imagination swooped into the shop and hovered near Courtney's shoulder. It had to be Fiona. Did she go everywhere with Courtney?

"We've come to buy some crystals." Courtney brimmed with excitement.

"Dottie Summers swears by them," Hattie added. "As do many of our other friends."

"Which reminds me, Emma." Yoly snapped her fingers. "Dottie ordered an Aroma Wellness prosperity gift basket for her niece. She needs it Wednesday morning, first thing. It's the niece's fortieth birthday, and Dottie wants her to dream big."

Hattie and Courtney crooned, *"Aww."*

"We don't have all the items," Yoly went on.

I said, "Give me a list and I'll order them."

"Done." Yoly returned her attention to Hattie. "Miss Hopewell, I'm all ears."

"Call me Hattie, darling. I'm not very old." She chuckled and looked between Yoly and me. "Which should we buy?"

"Crystals are like galaxies." Yoly used her hands as she described them. "Each contains a unique system of energy, creating vibrations that coincide with the place where they were created. Sometimes they even call to you."

Courtney studied the items in the case. "The crescent moon shape is lovely."

"Good choice."

"What's that one?" Hattie indicated a star-shaped, multifaceted purple crystal.

"Amethyst druzy," Yoly stated. "It's one of the most powerful quartz crystals around. It helps balance emotions, enhance spiritual growth, and promote a sense of tranquility."

"I could use all three." Courtney rubbed her palms together.

So could I, I mused.

I removed the display tray and set it on the counter, and Courtney and Hattie began to finger the selections.

"Emma," Yoly said, "a couple of customers walked in. Why don't you tend to these two? I'll see to the newbies." She strode through the shop.

"Can you tell me more about this one?" Hattie pointed to the amethyst. "What's it called again, a druzy?"

"Yep. D-r-u-z-y. Amethyst emits energy to those who interact with it." I thought idly about how the stone would be an excellent choice to offer Frederick because it could help him defeat inebriety. "Amethyst also improves one's metabolism and immune system."

"A miracle crystal," Courtney exclaimed.

"It sounds perfect for me." Hattie hooted softly. "I'll take it. I've been hoping for some serenity. I've been shaken up ever since learning we were in the McKay neighborhood the night Gianna died, and yet we couldn't save her. You must be shattered." She reached for me. "You found the body. I can't imagine. I mean, I can, but I don't want to. I have a very vivid imagination. I'd have nightmares for months if I stumbled upon a crime scene. How are you holding up?"

"I'm doing all right; thanks for asking."

Fiona fluttered to me and did a pirouette. If only she could help me solve the murder.

"You know," I continued, "I often walk around with a tumbled crystal in my pocket so I can finger it throughout the day."

"What an excellent idea," Hattie said.

"So tell me, Hattie, why were you—"

"What kind of crystal beads are those?" Courtney interrupted while indicating my bracelet.

"Black tourmaline and moonstone. Good for emotional healing and anxiety." Which I was feeling in spades.

"Do you have any of those for sale?" she asked.

I slipped a tray of crystal bracelets from the display case, set it on top of the counter, and began again. "Hattie, why were you in the—"

"How's Addison doing, Emma?" Courtney cut in again. "She and her friends have been coming for treatments, right? When they made fairy gardens last week, they were lighthearted. I would imagine her mother's murder has put a pall over the remainder of her nearly divorced festivities."

"She's somber."

Hattie clicked the roof of her mouth with her tongue. "Poor thing."

"Why were you in the neighborhood Tuesday night, Hattie?" I blurted out before anyone could stop me again.

"We have a semiannual neighborhood watch party," Hattie replied. "You should attend next time. Our group covers all the homes to the north of Ocean Avenue."

I regarded Courtney. "Don't you live south of Ocean?"

"I do, but I wasn't the one accompanying Hattie."

"I was with my sister, Hedda," Hattie said.

Both Hedda and Hattie belonged to my grandmother's book club, although neither could attend last Friday's event at the fairy garden shop.

"Do you know Peyton Pelagatti, Emma?" Hattie asked. "She's my Realtor."

"Are you selling your house?"

"No. Heavens. I love it. Peyton's the one who sold it to me. She's so good at real estate. Why, I had no idea how to go about getting all the insurance and such when I first purchased the property. I'd been renting for years. Peyton held my hand through the whole process." For years after her divorce, Hattie hadn't wanted to invest in anything permanent. "Anyway, I mentioned her name because, oddly enough"—she batted the air—"she was in the vicinity when I was."

That detail snagged my attention. Peyton had lied about her alibi on Friday. She hadn't been home knitting.

"In fact, she was outside Gianna's house." Hattie paused.

I didn't speak, hanging on each word.

"Now, I know she was friends with Gianna. Good friends. Business partners at one time. But I've got to say," Hattie continued, "she was acting a tad weird, moving along the perimeter of the house and peering upward."

"The perimeter," I echoed.

"*Mm-hmm.* No windows on the front of the house were open.

No curtains were open, either, so she wasn't trying to listen in on a conversation."

Had she been lurking outside the McKay home to make certain Addison was occupied before she slipped inside and killed Gianna?

"She was wearing a raincoat with the hood up, but I knew it was her," Hattie went on. "She's enamored with her psychedelic slicker. Don't get me wrong, I like colors, but it's *far-out.*" She uttered the term using a Valley Girl accent. "Why wear it? It wasn't drizzling in the least."

"Peyton often comes into my shop to buy fairy figurines for her son in Los Angeles." Courtney used her fingers to describe an object approximately two inches high. "She prefers laughing ones."

Interesting. Perhaps Peyton had hoped to stir her son's sense of comedy with the gifts. Or maybe she was making the fairy gardens at her house in the belief her son would return to the roost and, with a flutter of magic swirling around her property, win Addison's heart. On the other hand, after her spat with Gianna, would Peyton have wanted their two adult children to fall in love?

"Hattie," I said, "did you tell the police you spied Peyton slinking around Tuesday night?"

"I haven't spoken to the police."

"You didn't tell them you were in the neighborhood?"

"Why on earth would I?" Her face pinched with confusion. "I didn't see anything."

"Yes, you did." Courtney aimed a finger at her companion. "You saw Peyton."

"Exactly," I said. "And she's a suspect in Gianna's murder."

"Really?" Hattie gasped. "Heavens. She wasn't running away, and she wasn't carrying a weapon that I could see, although I imagine she could've hidden one under her raincoat."

In fact, a small face pillow could easily be concealed beneath a coat. Unless, of course, the lavender-scented face pillow wasn't the actual weapon. The killer might have used an item of clothing, like a rain slicker.

"About what time did you see her?" I asked.

"Sixish." Hattie checked her watch, as if it could tell her the correct time. "We were pot-lucking it that night. I brought a delicious tortilla casserole."

"Did you hear an alarm go off?"

"Later. Around eight. We were devouring dessert by then. We all heard it. Our hostess went outside, worried it was a fire. She didn't see any smoke and decided an animal must have set the darned thing off, but she was wrong. Apparently, someone was robbed. What is this world coming to?"

Courtney reached for my hand. "Emma . . ."

The way she whispered my name caused goose bumps to pop on my arm.

"Ever since the book club event, I've been meaning to chat with you," she said.

A frisson of dread ran down my spine. "About?"

"I know from experience how reputations can be harmed by gossip."

"Gossip?" I removed my hand from hers.

"You are giving Addison and her friends and family all these treatments at the spa, and with another murder in the midst, people are wondering if the spa is cursed."

"It isn't," I protested.

"But seeing as Addison is your friend, and by extension her mother was, tongues are wagging."

I pictured a murder board I'd seen on a recent TV show, where the persons of interest and the victim were linked by a spiderweb of red yarn. "But Gianna's murder had nothing to do with the spa," I protested.

"All I want to say is," Courtney kept her tone low, "I know how you feel. I suffered the same kind of rumormongering after a man died in my shop. But rest assured, time, as they say, heals not only wounds, it also helps dim the memories. Be of good courage."

After they left, I sank onto the stool behind the counter, deflated yet determined to find out why Peyton had lied about her alibi.

⋆ ⋆ ⋆

At noon, I decided to take Vivi for a walk around town. I needed to clear my head. The air was fresh, the temperature mild. The forecast called for rain later on, but not now. I didn't need a raincoat. Vivi was protected in her carrier.

Ahead of me, a couple of towheaded children clad in grinning pumpkin costumes were skipping along the sidewalk. Two adults strolled behind them, mindful of traffic. On Ocean Avenue, a handful of people were filtering in and out of the various art galleries and shops. A pair of women ahead of us were clad in fairy costumes. The one on the right reminded me of Dewberry, right down to the flower on her head.

Near the library, a group of cyclists whooshed past us, heading toward the beach. Among them, I spied the guy who'd given us the info on Wyatt, and wondered if Sierra had had the courage to ask him out yet.

I turned right on Camino Real to sneak a peek at two neighboring gardens. Each boasted at least ten different varieties of daylilies. As if fate was shining upon me, three doors down I made out the distinctively hunched figure of Peyton Pelagatti. She was conversing with a man and a woman in front of a home marked with a *For Sale* sign. The strap of her briefcase hung over her right shoulder. In her left hand, she held a sheaf of papers. I drew near as the man shook hands with Peyton, then looped his arm around the woman's waist. Moments later, the happy pair climbed into a silver Mercedes EQE with a temporary license plate.

The house they'd viewed was expensive. The new car they were driving had to have cost a pretty penny, as well, and I wondered what the two of them did for a living.

While tucking the papers into her briefcase, Peyton crossed the street to a dark blue Subaru Solterra, a car large enough to accommodate at least six people and ideal for touring properties. She reached for the door handle.

"Peyton!" I hailed her.

To my surprise, she didn't climb into the car and tear off as I approached. On the other hand, staying put didn't mean she was innocent, either. She closed her eyes briefly, as if doing a mindful meditation to keep herself in check, and opened them. "Hello, kitty," she cooed to Vivi while tugging on the hem of her suit jacket. "Aren't you pretty? What kind is she, Emma?"

"Birman."

"I have a calico. Cats are such wonderful companions, aren't they? Offering solace in times of stress. Keeping us on our toes day by day. Reminding us we are human."

I nodded in agreement.

"So, what brings you to this neck of the woods?" she asked.

"I needed to stretch my legs." I drew even with the rear door of the car. "Did you finalize a sale?" I motioned to the clients heading off in their car.

"No, but I have an offer. A very good offer. It always pleases me when I find the right home for a client."

I assessed the house in question, a darling gingerbread with yellow shutters and a half dozen pots of yellow chrysanthemums flanking the front door. In a word, cheery. "Hattie Hopewell was in the Aroma Wellness gift shop earlier and crowed about you as a Realtor."

"Hattie. A dear, dear woman." Her smile warmed.

"She said you go the extra mile."

"I try. Do you own your own place?" she asked.

"I do not. I plan to. But my business comes first."

"Right. I remember now." Peyton pulled a business card from her jacket pocket and offered it to me. "You live in the fourplex your grandmother owns."

"I do. So does my cousin Sierra."

"What a lovely building. I had a client interested in purchasing it at the time, but Lissa was faster on the draw."

"When my grandmother wants something, she acts with alacrity."

"Indeed." Peyton tapped her briefcase. "I must present this contract before someone else jumps on the property. Bye." She made a kissy sound to Vivi.

"Peyton, hold on." I pocketed her card. "I'd like to ask you a question."

Two deep lines formed between her eyebrows. She pressed her lips together. Why? To prevent a sharp retort?

"Hattie mentioned a situation that got me thinking." I raised a finger. "She was near the McKay home on the night of the murder, attending a neighborhood watch party, and she saw you."

"Me?"

"Yes. She was certain it was you. You were slinking around Gianna's home."

"I never slink."

I peeked inside her car. Lying on the rear seat was a psychedelic slicker. "Hattie believed you were wearing your raincoat." I gestured to it. "It's very distinctive. I doubt there's anyone else in town who owns something similar."

"Fine. Yes, I was there," she acknowledged, "but if you're implying I killed my friend, you're wrong."

I waited patiently for her to continue.

She shifted feet. "If you must know, I was upset with Gianna for not returning my phone calls after our set-to at dinner on Monday night. She can be—" She sucked in air. Color drained from her face. "She *could* be stubborn. She always wanted the last word. I went and knocked, but she didn't answer."

"Did you try ringing the doorbell?"

"It doesn't work. It hasn't for years. Gianna refused to get it fixed. She could be cheap that way."

I didn't know if she was lying. On Wednesday morning I hadn't needed to use the doorbell to signal Addison I'd arrived because she'd caught sight of me from the kitchen window.

Peyton continued. "I moved around the property looking for an open window so I might call out to her, but there weren't any."

I pictured the scenario of a suitor strumming his guitar, trying to woo his ladylove.

"I saw Addison sitting in a room with headphones on. I waved, but she didn't see me," Peyton said. "Ultimately, I gave up and decided to try again in the light of day."

"About what time was this?"

"Quarter past six," she replied, confirming Hattie's time frame. "And get this, on the way to my car, a bicyclist almost ran me over. He was pedaling so fast. Like a racer. I can't run. My ailments . . ." She motioned to her body. "They prevent me from living a normal life. I'm not asking for your pity. Merely explaining."

"Did you get a look at the cyclist's face?"

"No, it was past dusk, and he was wearing a dark-colored cycling outfit."

"Did you tell the police?"

She screwed up her mouth. "No. In full disclosure, I didn't want to admit I was in the area. I believed they might suspect me, as you did. Now, if you don't mind, I really do have to run. Duty calls."

"Contact the police," I urged.

She agreed she would, blew another kiss to my cat, and clambered into her car. As she drove off, I considered her response. Was she lying about the cyclist, or was she suggesting it might have been Wyatt in order to throw suspicion on him?

Chapter 17

When I returned to the spa, Riley was perched on a chair in reception, tapping the arms of the chair with both hands. A full glass of water sat on the table to her right. Upon seeing me, she bounded to her feet, and I bit back a laugh. In her black-and-white, skeleton-themed dress, she looked like a cartoon of an X-ray.

"I'm sorry to disturb you at work," she gushed. "Really sorry, but I need to talk to you. Privately."

"Love the dress," I said to slow her down a tad and allow me to catch my breath.

"Addison insisted I buy it. It's not too over-the-top or silly?"

"It's perfect for the season."

Meryl was chatting at warp speed under her breath with Mah at the reception desk, and she appeared to be disturbed, but I couldn't deal with whatever her issue was right now. Riley was my first priority.

"So what's up?" I perched on the other chair, set the carrier by my feet, and motioned for Riley to continue.

She retook her seat and pulled the hem of the dress down to her knees, but the effort was fruitless. It inched up to mid-thigh. She pressed her palms against the material to hold it in place. "Idha." She sighed the name.

"Gianna's sister-in-law."

"She really hated Gianna. I mean, hated with a capital *H*, and I'll tell you why I'm confiding in you. Because Addison really believes in your instinct, and well, she made all of us swear not to talk about the murder with her, and specifically about any family members being a suspect. She's really edgy, you know?"

"Got it. Go on. Idha."

"Her husband, Frederick, um, drinks too much. In fact"—she lowered her voice—"he's an alcoholic, but don't tell Addison I revealed that."

"My lips are sealed," I murmured, though I'd seen with my own eyes.

Riley brushed her luscious red hair over one shoulder. "Poor guy. He's really smart and nice, but he's weak, you know, and Idha—" She heaved another dramatic sigh. "She'll never say it to strangers, but she doesn't think he's a good role model for their son."

And yet Frederick had uttered the same to me, so Idha certainly hadn't kept her opinion from him.

"Not because he drinks but because he's"—she gestured using air quotes—"*ineffectual*. Her word, not mine."

"I don't understand. He's smart. He holds down a good job."

"I think she means he's inept as a husband. As a partner. Do you want my two cents? He's not to blame for his frailties. After all, a person can only take so many personal attacks before his character withers from the taunts, right?"

"I suppose. How old is their boy?"

"Nadal is my age."

How interesting. Both Addison and her uncle had implied Nadal was young. I'd figured he was somewhere between ten and sixteen.

"Nadal and I were . . ." Riley's cheeks tinged pink. "We dated. For a long time. We were serious."

"*Were.*"

She nodded. "His name, which is Indian, means fortunate, but he isn't lucky. In fact, he is . . ." She let the sentence hang.

"He is what?" I prompted.

"He is always getting into trouble. It's why we broke up."

"What kind of trouble can an artist get into? He is an artist, correct?"

"Yes. A graphic artist. But this issue has nothing to do with his talent. He . . ." She tugged on the hem of her dress a second time, to no avail. "He steals things."

"Gee." What else could I say?

"Little things. Petty things. A key chain from a drugstore. A postcard from a spinning rack."

I didn't see how Idha could blame Frederick for their son's behavior, though I wondered whether the adage *The apple doesn't fall far from the tree* had some validity. "Is Nadal an alcoholic, like his father?"

"No. You're missing the point." She sat taller. "Idha thinks it's genetic. She believes Frederick's indecisive, milquetoast nature created a weakness in their child, and she blames Gianna for abusing Frederick and making his disposition worse."

I considered her theory for a long moment. "I could make the same case about Idha if she continually hounds her husband to be more assertive than he is, implying that if he's docile, he isn't worthy of her love."

"Yes, you're right." Riley gnawed on a cuticle. Realizing she was doing so, she dropped her hand to her lap. "Addison would hate it if she knew I was throwing her beloved aunt under the bus, but Addison is grieving so much it breaks my heart, and I thought you . . ." She motioned to me. "I mean, golly, you solved that other murder."

Willow's. To clear myself.

"Being her newest friend," Riley continued, "I thought you might help. She talks about you all the time. She says your treatments are really working at helping her become her better self."

"I'm glad to hear it."

Riley squirmed in her chair. "What if the police suspect Addison again?"

"But they don't."

"How can they not?" She shot her hand at me. "She was there. In the house. How could someone murder her mother without Addison hearing it?"

I tapped my ears. "Headphones."

"You're right." She brightened at the theory but quickly fell into another funk. "What if they do set their sights on her again? What if the police decide the witness who saw her was wrong about the time, or what if they learn Addison ordered another lavender-scented pillow?"

"Did she?"

"No. I'm just speculating, but isn't theorizing what you and the police do?" She flailed both arms, causing the skeleton on her dress to leap to life. "It's all about motive, isn't it? Figuring out why the person killed her? Oh-oh-oh! I almost forgot the most important point." She spanked her thighs. "Have you read Idha's short stories?"

"I haven't. Since opening the spa, it's been hard to find time to read." *Other than the occasional mystery*, I reflected. I couldn't go very long without reading one. "Why?"

"She published an anthology."

"Yes, I heard her talk about it at the dinner."

"I bought it, but I hadn't read any of it until last night. In one story, *Silent Suffocation*, the killer murders his best friend by smothering him with a pillow."

Whoa!

"It's got to count for something, right?" she exclaimed.

I asked why she hadn't opened with that bombshell. She said it was because reading the story had unsettled her so much, she must have blocked it from her mind. Her explanation didn't sound reasonable, but I didn't press. If Idha had indeed written the short story, it was irrefutable evidence that she either knew how to smother someone or had researched it.

Riley leaped from her chair and threw her arms around me. "Thank you. You'll tell the police, right? I can't. I don't have the courage."

And yet she'd found the gumption to come to me? To be fair, I didn't bite, and I was pretty sure Summers might.

I assured her I would.

After she left, I put Vivi in the office and strode to the café. There were two people in line. The tables were full. Sierra beckoned me and excused herself as she cut around the staff.

"Hey, you look in a hurry and . . . windblown." She fluttered her fingers beside her head.

She wasn't mistaken. Because I'd run to the spa to tell her the news about Peyton, my wispy hair had morphed into a very messy bird's nest. Then, after getting waylaid by Riley, I'd forgotten to tame it.

"What's up?" she asked.

"I've got news." I moved out of earshot of customers. "I would've phoned or texted after I bumped into Peyton Pelagatti, but I left my cell in the office so I wouldn't be tempted to use it while enjoying a peaceful walk . . . which was anything but peaceful . . . and then Riley Rhimes came to see me—"

"You bumped into Peyton? Literally?"

"No, you goon. Let me start at the beginning." I laid out Peyton's alibi and quickly followed with Riley's account about Addison's aunt.

Sierra whistled. "Idha? A killer? She seems so normal."

"I know."

"But protecting the ones you love can be a motivating factor."

"And the story she wrote about smothering someone is pretty damning."

"Definitely a strike against her." She glanced at the crowd lining up to get a jump on the lunch hour and refocused on me. "I've got to return to the kitchen. After we close for the night and before our girls' event at Ursula's, let's swing by the theater and check out Idha's alibi."

"I should call Detective Summers."

"And tell him what? Gossip?"

I said, "It's not gossip if Idha really did write the short story."

"True, but I think you should wait." Sierra stabbed the air to make a point. "If you want his respect, you need to get the whole story first. Get the dirt."

"What if there is no dirt? What if Idha is telling the truth about the movie?"

"Then she's sort of off the hook."

Sort of, I thought.

"And we keep looking for someone else to suspect, for Addison's sake."

I thought about what Riley had said, reaffirming Addison had been in the house when it happened. Was it possible she could've missed a killer slipping inside and murdering her mother? Another theory struck me and twisted my insides into knots. What if Addison knew the hours the dog-walking woman passed by and made sure she was in the window at those times, but, in between, she slipped downstairs and did the deed?

Timing. It was all a matter of timing and opportunity.

Mah was typing at the computer when I reentered the spa. The telephone receiver was pressed between her ear and shoulder to free up her hands.

I skirted behind her to peek at the screen and noticed I had a facial at three and a mindful meditation at four.

Mah motioned to tomorrow's schedule. The appointment calendar was full for everyone.

I gave her a thumbs-up. She echoed the gesture and continued responding to whomever was on the other end of the line. *"Mm-hmm."*

I retreated to the office and greeted Vivi. She leaped onto the desk to take a sip of water from her glass before bolting to the floor and hopping onto her pillow. I approached what I was now bleakly considering a murder board and added notes to both Peyton's and Idha's three-by-five cards. I stared at the others and groaned audibly.

Why, why, why was I acting like an amateur sleuth? Why couldn't I let it go and leave it to the police?

Because I liked Addison, I reminded myself, and I wanted to ensure she was innocent. Plus I had to face reality. If Courtney was correct, the spa's reputation could be on the line. The sooner the case was solved, the better for all concerned.

A sign above the doorway leading to the hall read: *Being proactive is the best way to address problems. ~ Nana Lissa*

"Truer words," I whispered.

I went to reception and was surprised to see Meryl holding her mother by her shoulders. They turned to me, startled. Meryl had been crying. Her eyes, which were lined with cobalt blue pencil, gleamed. Remnants of mascara marred her cheeks.

"Everything okay?" I asked. "I'm sorry I didn't approach you earlier, but Riley—"

"I saw you were busy. Everything is fine." When Meryl didn't offer a joke, I knew something was off.

"Is it your son?" I asked, daring to pry.

"Bah." Her mother grunted. "Dante does not know his head from his—"

"Mah!" Meryl chided.

"His foot," her mother finished. "His head from his foot. He treats his mother like garbage. Whatever happened to a child honoring a parent?"

"He honors his father," Meryl said.

"Big whoop." Mah twirled a finger in the air. "His father is worthless. Does Dante not have eyes? Does he not listen to the words his worthless father spews?" She grumbled again. "He does not love Dante. He is using him as leverage."

"To irritate me," Meryl said.

"What will you do when I'm gone?"

I squawked. "Don't talk like that, Mah. You're young. Vibrant."

She eyed me as if I was crazy. "Of course I am, but when I move home to Los Angeles—"

"You're leaving Carmel?"

"Yes, she is." Meryl wiped the last residue of mascara from her face. "She got a full-time gig at a comedy club as the opening act. She'll warm up the crowd three nights a week."

"The comedy scene around here is too hard to navigate." Mah motioned with both hands like the Scarecrow in *The Wizard of Oz*. "Not enough work. And this"—she swooped a hand to encompass the spa—"is lovely, but it is not me. I do not answer the phone well. I do you a disservice. I belong in a comedy club. It is where I thrive. My daughter . . ." She petted Meryl's cheek. "She will survive without me, but she has needed me to listen as she grieves. Who will listen now?"

"I will." I raised a hand in support. "But Mah, are you sure you want to leave?"

"I must." She splayed the fingers of one hand. "I will stay five more days. By then, Dante had better come to his senses or else." She closed the fingers and swooshed the air.

I didn't want to be on the receiving end of her slap.

"By the end of the week?" Meryl gasped. "I thought you started in two weeks."

"I must move and get settled."

The realization I'd have to hire another receptionist loomed large. I texted Yoly to post an ad. In seconds, she replied that she was on the case.

I pocketed my cell phone. "Ladies, I don't see anything on the books for me or Meryl at five this afternoon. Why don't we meet for the mindful meditation I promised you? Mah, you can switch on the answering machine. Deal?"

"What did the card dealer say to the deck of cards?" Meryl asked, an impish smirk brightening her face.

"*Ack!* I can't deal with you," Mah groused.

Meryl swatted her mother. "You're not supposed to say the punch line. Sheesh." She stomped away, but before disappearing down the hallway, she announced, "Five it is. Thanks, Emma."

Five o'clock came in a flash. Meryl and Mah joined me in the meditation room. I advised them to settle on the mat, explained how the session would go, after which I began moving around the room and modulating my tone from sentence to sentence.

"Do not let your minds wander to a previous frustration or past experience. For the moment, do not think of loss." My words were intended for Meryl, but I imagined they would empower Mah, as well. "Instead, focus on your inner light. You are more than the actions of others. You are not defined by someone else's choices. Your power resides in your decision as to how you move forward."

For a half hour, I continued imparting positive energy. "Imagine in your mind's eye you are standing tall. Your feet are firmly planted."

At the end of the session, I strengthened my voice. "You are powerful. You are the creator of your future. You have the ability to shape it, and to walk forward with cool, calm, self-assurance."

I waited a moment before saying, "You're waking up." I toggled the meditation room lights to reach half of their brightness. "You are fully awake, and as we end this session, carry this sense of peace with you into the evening and into the remainder of the week. You are wonderful parents. Formidable women."

Mah and Meryl slowly got to their feet.

"Thank you, Emma." Meryl stretched both arms. "I feel stronger and more centered."

"And I," Mah interjected, "can go to Los Angeles knowing my daughter will find the courage to talk to her son and win his heart."

They group hugged me and traipsed out of the room, Mah first so she could check out customers whose sessions had concluded.

As I emerged into the reception area, Sierra sashayed in, glowing with good vibes.

"What's gotten into you?" I asked.

"The cyclist asked me on a date."

"*Ooh!* Cool. Tonight?"

"No, Friday. End of the work week for him. We're going to dinner at my favorite Italian restaurant. But now, you and I are going to take Vivi home and check out Idha's alibi."

Chapter 18

Cinema Unique's lobby was cozy and eclectic. Vintage movie posters adorned the walls. A variety of comfy-looking, mismatched chairs were clustered in twos and threes around the room. Patrons reading theater newsletters about upcoming releases occupied a few of them. The art deco bar—yes, there was a bar—was set up for wine and personally brewed coffees. The box office was an open area located to the right, in which stood a young woman in a 1930s-style jacket, narrow at the waist, with padded shoulders.

Sierra and I crossed to her, and I asked if we could have a few minutes of her time. She begged off, saying she couldn't step away from her position. People would be coming soon for the seven o'clock showings, but if we so desired, we could speak to the usher. She pointed at a young man in a red-and-black bellboy uniform and a brimless hat with chinstrap.

Sierra and I strolled to him.

"Hi." I offered a wide grin.

"Hello." His voice was reedy, his smile genuine. "What can I do you for?" he asked in the awkward reverse-verb sentence structure that would have driven my mother crazy.

"Did you work on Tuesday?" I asked.

"Sure did. I'm here every night. I usher five evenings in a row, and the other two I watch movies with audiences so I can learn what works and what doesn't. I'm an aspiring filmmaker."

"Good for you," Sierra said.

He inclined his head toward her. "I make dark movies."

Sierra *oohed*. "I love dark movies. *Requiem for a Dream*."

"By Aronofsky."

"Yes, and *Possession*."

"With Isabelle Adjani."

"Haunting."

"Haunting," he echoed.

Sierra addressed me. "*Possession* delved into the themes of marriage and insanity in Cold War Berlin."

How uplifting, I mused. *Not.*

"Yoo-hoo. Tuesday," I said to the usher to redirect the conversation. "A woman I know came to see *The World Dies Wanting*. The six o'clock showing. She's in her fifties and slim and gorgeous. She has lustrous black hair and hazelnut skin."

"Nope, didn't see her," the young man replied.

"You're sure?"

"Yeah. It isn't a popular movie. Four people viewed it Tuesday. The whole idea of a spy agency recruiting normal people for high-stakes missions is ludicrous, and it starred two has-been stars. Rotten Tomatoes gave it forty-four percent."

"The woman in question is a writer," Sierra said, "and she also edits thriller books." She lowered her voice in a conspiratorial fashion. "Maybe she came incognito so she could do psyops research."

"Uh, no. Only guys were here."

A skinny gentleman across the lobby called to the usher, needing help.

"One more question," I added hastily. "How many movies do you screen a night?"

"Three titles, three showings each. We stagger them."

"So, she might have gone to another movie, and her husband got the title wrong."

"Yeah, possibly, but I didn't see her. I'm good with faces, and heh-heh, I never miss a gorgeous face." He winked, as if he was a seasoned heartbreaker. In his dreams. "Sorry, I've got to assist that guy before this crowd exits."

Sierra faced me and folded her arms. "She must have purchased a ticket as a ruse. Therefore, where was she?"

Portofino Ristorante was a happening place located on Fisherman's Wharf in Monterey. It smelled so garlicky and yummy as we entered, I started to salivate. A fish tank filled with neon tetra occupied one wall. The hostess station, adorned with Halloween cobwebs and spiders, stood directly ahead. The chatter between the executive chef and his staff in the wide-open kitchen was lively.

"Good evening." I greeted the hostess, a petite young woman about Sierra's height and build, who was dressed in a witch costume. "Cute decorations."

She frowned. "The boss wouldn't let me do more. He's not a Halloween freak like I am. If I had my way, the entire restaurant would be screaming with spooky décor."

I smiled.

"Table for two?" She pulled menus from a pocket on her station.

"No. Not yet. First, we wanted to ask a question."

Without waiting for one, she answered, "We serve Italian food and fish. The Venetian shrimp with polenta is my favorite, but a lot of patrons like the risotto with mussels and clams."

"Thanks. Those sound delicious, but I need a different question answered. A woman came here for dinner on Tuesday night," I said. "Were you working Tuesday?"

"Yes," she responded.

I described Idha. "Do you remember her?"

"Idha Gibson. Sure. She's a regular. She came in, but she didn't stay. She took a to-go box. She always gets the Ligurian seafood stew. It's to die for."

The idiom made me wince.

Sierra picked up on my unease and took the lead. "Do you remember what time she was here?"

"Let me think." The hostess referred to a maritime clock hanging above the fish tank. "I'd say around seven."

If Idha went to the cinema and purchased a ticket but didn't stay to watch the movie and, instead, went to Gianna's to kill her between five and seven, she could have looped back to Portofino and picked up her dinner to give herself an alibi.

Sierra and I returned to the fourplex. Before we went our separate ways, I said, "May I call Detective Summers now?"

"Do what you will, but you still don't have any proof."

"He told me to keep my eyes and ears open."

She snickered. "And your mouth shut."

"Ha-ha. Very funny. Okay, no texting."

She twirled a hand, said, "See you in a few," and climbed the staircase two steps at a time.

I sped inside, changed clothes, and hurried with Vivi to Ursula's unit. I knocked.

Ursula whipped open the front door seconds later. The sleeves of her tie-dye V-neck caftan wafted with the effort. "You are here! And you brought your kitty. Hello, Vivi," she cooed, and tickled my sweet Birman under her chin. "I have treats." She beckoned me to follow her into the kitchen.

Like mine, the room boasted ceramic tile backsplashes and white quartzite countertops, plus a bistro table for dining, but unlike mine, all the accents were gold-toned. The walls held lots of photographs of a Siamese cat Ursula had once owned, but because she traveled often for work, she hadn't felt it was fair to leave her cat alone and ceded it to her sister. I didn't mention the cat when I visited because I was afraid it would dredge up sad memories.

"Your dress is gorgeous," I said. I'd done nothing more than fix my hair and switch out my apothecary T-shirt for a silk, loose-weave sweater.

"Thank you. It is an online purchase. Do you shop online?"

"Rarely for clothes."

"I find great pleasure in viewing the images. It can calm like meditation."

I found shopping online for clothes nerve-racking. There were too many choices, not to mention I was never certain the piece would fit. Oh sure, I could buy basics like garden soil and batteries and whatnot, but outfits? Forget about it.

"It is okay if I give Vivi a treat?" Ursula asked.

"Yes."

She reached into a gold canister on the counter, pulled out a bag of Temptations, and cooed to Vivi in a babyish voice, "Do you like chicken?" She held a treat out to the cat, who lapped it up. "Yes, you do. And how about a game?" She threw a catnip mouse across the room. Vivi sprinted after it. "Emma, would you like a glass of chardonnay or a cup of tea?"

"After the day I've had, wine sounds perfect."

She poured some into two stemless wineglasses unlike any I'd ever seen, each adorned with a gold honeycomb pattern on the bottom. I complimented her on them.

"Did you buy those online?" I asked.

"No. Like you, sometimes I enjoy feeling things I am purchasing. I found these at a boutique on Dolores near Ninth." She tapped the rim of her glass to mine. "*Živeli.*"

"Cheers."

Someone knocked on the door. Ursula went to the foyer and returned with Sierra and Yoly. She offered them wine, and they gladly accepted.

After doing the honors, Ursula fetched a charcuterie board she'd filled with an array of cheeses, meats, dates, and olives. "Let us retreat to the living room."

Vivi followed us, batting the catnip mouse forward with her paws like a skilled hockey player moving a puck down the ice.

I sat on the curved blue velvet sofa. Yoly and Sierra took the apple-green, channel-back chairs. Colorful pillows abounded. Paintings of shining orbs and winged angels adorned the walls. On a coffee table sat a tooled silver platter similar to one Aunt Sophie owned. Was it a duplicate, or had Sophie gifted it to Ursula? A variety of polished and raw crystals sat on top.

Ursula set the charcuterie board beside the tray, perched on the sofa with me, and repeated her toast. We all sipped our wine and began to chat about life in general, the weather, and the fun Halloween decorations we'd spotted around town.

Ursula mentioned seeing a man in a hideous mask and shuddered. "These I do not care for."

"Me either," I said. "I remember a guy in high school wearing a Ghostface mask to class, and it freaked me out so badly I went to the school nurse. The wide-open ghoulish mouth? Ugh!"

A half hour later, Ursula moved to the ottoman on the far side of the coffee table. "I am nervous, but I am ready to try this. Emma, will you be my first in-person client?"

Yoly wriggled a hand. "I was hoping you'd do my reading."

Sierra remained mute. Her mother had given her crystal readings too many times to count. She refused to do another one. But she was more than willing to be a neutral observer.

"I can do both," Ursula said. "Shall I start with Yoly, Emma? Each reading will take about twenty minutes."

"Sure." I felt a yawn rising and suppressed it. "Is it okay if I make some tea?"

Ursula hooked a thumb toward the kitchen. "You know where it is."

"I'll take a cup, if you don't mind." Sierra wiggled her fingers.

While I heated water on the stove and set caffeine-free chai tea into gold-toned mugs, I listened in on Ursula's spiel to Yoly.

She introduced herself as if she didn't know her. "What brought you in today?"

"I've always been curious about crystals and how they work," Yoly replied.

"What a wonderful place to start. Now, let's center ourselves. Take a few deep breaths. If you like, you may close your eyes. I want you to feel comfortable."

Yoly giggled.

"Do not be nervous," Ursula crooned.

I had to admit I was anxious about what she'd say in my reading. The brief one she'd conducted without me being present had been terse, not insightful. However, because I was now seeking answers about a murder, I wondered whether Ursula might provide a few clues.

Dream on, Emma. That isn't how crystal readings work. Clues are not available in the stratosphere.

"The important thing is, my readings are coming from a soulful viewpoint," Ursula intoned. "For each crystal we discuss, I will provide ideas of how these might affect you. Be advised, the stones will not dictate what you do going forward. Free will is important."

"Um, okay." Yoly sounded hesitant.

"Crystals formed as the earth came into being and are preset with the energy of their creation." Ursula wasn't using the exact same verbiage as Aunt Sophie, but it was pretty close. "They are transmitters of energy to humans. They help us align with our purpose of being."

I brewed the tea and carried the mugs to the living room. I handed one to Sierra, set mine on an end table to cool, and resumed my seat on the sofa. While I was gone, Ursula had placed a square of velvet on the coffee table. On top lay an array of crystals Yoly must have selected.

Throughout the reading, Ursula focused on the changes coming in Yoly's career. She suggested Yoly needed to remain calm and focused and positive about the future.

When Ursula completed the reading, she handed Yoly a tumbled piece of ametrine, which was a muted purple stone with traces of gold weaved into it. "Carry this with you. It will create a feeling of well-being and will connect you to your third eye and crown chakras. The third eye chakra is associated with intuition and spiritual connection. The crown, as it suggests, is at the top of the head and connects with the brain and nervous system. Both of these chakras will need to stay in tune as you proceed."

Looking euphoric, while at the same time uncertain, Yoly folded the stone into her palm. "Thank you. My candle-making venture will be a success."

"Candle-making venture?" Sierra waggled her eyebrows.

"We'll talk." I hadn't informed her of Yoly's wish to become an artisan.

"Emma, it is your turn," Ursula announced.

"Okay. You don't have to introduce yourself to me."

"Thank you."

I watched as she added the stones Yoly hadn't selected from the platter to the ones on the velvet. Among them were a pale blue Angelite, citrine, fluorite, raw apophyllite, and Chevron amethyst, the latter being a unique blend of amethyst and white quartz, usually seen in a *V* or chevron pattern.

"Emma, do you know what the most commonly practiced crystal reading is termed?" Ursula asked.

"Intuitive selection is when I choose the stones that speak to me."

"Very good." She directed me to select nine from the collection.

Though I knew the amethyst could be a helpful stone with clarity and spiritual enlightenment, to be a tad impish, I selected my stones based on color. I wanted to see how Ursula would interpret them. I plucked a black tourmaline from the mix, and then, picturing the three-by-five cards on the board in my office, I selected a blue stone for Wyatt, a pink one for Peyton, a green one for O'Malley, a yellow one for Frederick, a violet one for Idha, and a beige stone for the card with the big fat question mark. I didn't select a color for Addison. I really wanted her to be innocent.

Ursula murmured, "I think you are putting me to the test."

"Of course you chose a black one," Sierra said. "It's your favorite color."

"It is not. Teal blue is, and you know it. Now hush. Don't ruin Ursula's concentration." I'd chosen the tourmaline because it truly had beckoned me.

Ursula scooped up the stones, shook them in her hands, and dropped them gently onto the velvet square. The tourmaline tumbled away to a corner, all on its own, as did the calcite and the raw apophyllite, meaning none of them were significant to the reading.

The Angelite, citrine, fluorite, and pink rose quartz clustered in the center. Two others were touching to the left of those. The remaining two were near one another but not in contact.

"*Hmm,* very interesting." Ursula pursed her lips.

"Why?" I asked.

"The way these three stones are surrounding this one." She indicated the soft green fluorite. "Let us address it first, shall we? Fluorite promotes intuition and understanding. It brings chaos into order. It helps with unbiased reasoning."

Well, I'll be. Was the reading going to help me solve the murder after all?

"You are searching for answers, no?"

A chill ran down my spine. Ursula did not know I was looking into Gianna's murder.

"As I said to Yoly," she went on, "this fluorite links to the third eye chakra. It is very protective. It will battle negative energy and stress."

"And anyone who might be coming after her?" Sierra asked.

I threw her the stink-eye.

She didn't flinch. "Ursula said you need to beware."

A clanging sound resounded outside.

Vivi caterwauled and leaped into my lap.

Within seconds, someone started pounding on a door on the lower level and yelling my name.

"Sheesh. It's my mother." I ran out the front door and peeped over the railing. "What's going on, Kate?"

"The danged ladder attacked me." She shot out a hand at the equipment the painters had neglected to stow in a safe spot.

I rushed down the stairs to help her.

"Look at me." Angrily, she brushed off her skirt using both hands. "I'm a mess. You need exterior lights. Tell your grandmother to spruce up the security here and order the painters to responsibly put away their equipment at the end of day. Honestly."

I apologized and reached for her hand.

She recoiled. "Don't touch me."

"Why not? Do I have cooties?"

"Stop."

I tamped down a giggle. "Why are you here so late?"

"Your father is leaving town again. Tomorrow."

He hadn't mentioned anything to me. "You two are talking?"

"We've been trying to resolve our property settlement issues, to no avail."

They'd been divorced around fifteen years, and Dad hadn't allowed Kate to buy him out of his share of the house, not to mention he hadn't taken all of his things. Kate had relocated them into the guest room, but she hadn't trashed them or donated them to Goodwill. For years, I'd convinced myself Dad was dragging his feet because he planned to return to the States and rejoin the family, at which time he would woo my mother and win over her indignant heart. It had been a silly fantasy, of course, and wouldn't have benefited anyone.

"He's impossible," she stated. "I thought you should know."

"You could've called."

"I wanted to see you."

I glanced upward. Sierra, Yoly, and Ursula were gazing down at us. Ursula, who was holding Vivi in her arms, looked upset. I hoped she wouldn't think it was a bad omen that our crystal reading had been rudely interrupted. In my opinion, it had been going swimmingly.

"Mother, why don't you meet Dad for coffee tomorrow before he leaves?"

"Why on earth would I?"

"Because he likes coffee and so do you, and in a restaurant, you could talk civilly. Bring a list of everything you want him to take."

"I want his name off the mortgage."

"Why? He's paying half without living there." The fact had also fueled my inane illusion about a reunion.

"What if I want to sell? To move?"

My eyes widened. "Do you?"

"No, but if I did, I can't." She moaned dramatically. "Your nana always warned, *Beware how you give your heart.*"

The line was from Jane Austen's *Northanger Abbey*. Kate loved to show off her smarts by citing lines from the classics.

"Why didn't I listen to my mother?" Kate went on. "Why did I fall for him in the first place?"

"Because you were willful?" I teased.

She gave me a scathing look.

"The good news is, you got me out of the bargain."

She shook her head dismissively. "Good night."

"Coffee!" I yelled as she clambered into her car. "He likes coffee."

Chapter 19

I shifted the ladder to a safe spot and went upstairs to Ursula's unit. Sierra, Yoly, and Ursula surrounded me in the living room.

"Are you okay?" Sierra asked.

"Yes, of course." I told them why my mother had come, and I eyed Ursula. "Do you think it was Kate you saw wanting to hurt me?" I winked to make light of the warning. "If so, she didn't. All is well."

"No, Emma, it is not—" Ursula cut herself off, clearly shaken by my mother's arrival.

I rested a hand on her arm to calm her. "I'm fine. Let's call it a night. You don't need to finish my reading. You are more than ready to meet with real clients."

"Do you think so?"

"Yes, you're wonderful!" Yoly exclaimed.

"Almost as good as my mother," Sierra said.

Ursula blushed with pride.

"We will work you into the schedule at the spa soon," I said.

"Thank you. I am happy." She rushed from the room and came back with the fluorite stone in her hand. She placed it in my palm and folded my fingers over it. "Keep it with you."

She didn't add that it would protect me from harm, but I was pretty sure the thought was in her mind.

"I still want to read tarot for my regular clients," she said, "so perhaps I could do crystal readings once or twice a week?"

"Perfect." I would alter our spa menu to reflect her services after we finalized the details.

On Tuesday morning, I awoke super early but felt refreshed and calm. Was the fluorite Ursula had given me working its magic? Were the chaotic thoughts plaguing my mind going to end soon? I dressed in jogging clothes and went to the kitchen to prepare Vivi's breakfast. Like an Olympic vaulter, she leaped onto the counter and began to paw the window. I peeked outside and spied Dewberry in the front yard flitting from bush to bush. She paused in midair, beheld the two of us and, beaming, zipped to the window. She touched the glass where Vivi was pressing her nose, and Vivi mewed.

"Yes, we can go outside. For a minute or two." Why not? I needed to make a mental to-do list of gardening jobs and fertilize the azaleas while they weren't in bloom. "Backyard, Dewberry," I said loudly and pointed.

I threw on a sweater, grabbed an iPad for my notes, and opened the rear door. A waterproof bag of fertilizer stakes stood to the right of the door. I nabbed three and the rubber-headed hammer I used to drive them into the ground and headed for the azaleas. Vivi scampered out and leapt into the air by a daylily to try to bat the fairy with her paw. Dewberry scooted out of reach, giggled, and zipped back. She perched on Vivi's nose.

I laughed. "You are too cute."

"So are you," she said.

I gawked. "I can hear you."

She grinned. "And I can hear you." Her voice was teensy and cheerful.

"Why haven't you spoken to me before?"

"You needed time, I was told."

"By whom?"

"Me!" Merryweather Rose of Song whizzed into view. "Hello, Emma, dear."

I glanced between them. "Why are you here?"

"Your grandmother expressed concern," Merryweather said. "She thinks you have been rattled. She thought you could use some support."

"Meaning you'll help me solve Gianna's murder?" I asked hopefully, though according to Nana Lissa, nurturer fairies could only encourage and guardian fairies could only instruct and inspire. Neither could sleuth.

"No." Merryweather wagged her head. "We do not have such an ability. But we can listen."

Dewberry flew into the air and pirouetted in front of my face. "I'm a very good listener."

Apparently so, seeing as she hadn't spoken a word to me until today.

"Okay, here goes." I recapped everything I knew about the murder. The scents I'd smelled. The murder weapon the police had yet to find. The suspects topping my list. The alibis exonerating Peyton and O'Malley.

"It seems to me," Merryweather said, "you might like the sister-in-law for the crime, but you have set your sights on the ex-husband."

"Soon-to-be ex-husband," I revised. "His alibi is the hardest to prove."

"My advice? Find out more about him." Dewberry clapped her hands, her wings flapping briskly. "Do you feel calmer?"

Honestly, I did. I nodded.

"As for those azaleas," Dewberry added, "you should consider adding Epsom salts."

"Huh?"

She tapped her nose. "It will help me work my magic. One tablespoon for each plant, thank you very much."

"She learned these facts in my plant physiology class," Merryweather said like a proud teacher. "And now we will bid you adieu."

Vivi pranced to me and sat dutifully by my side.

"Good kitty," Dewberry said, and rewarded my Birman with another visit on her nose.

The passionate purr emanating from deep within Vivi's chest astonished me.

"Aw, true love," I murmured.

Wouldn't it be nice to find it for myself? I mused as I continued to fertilize the garden. Not yet, of course. Not while I needed to focus on growing the business. But someday.

An image of Zane popped into my head, but I whisked it away. I didn't need any distractions.

After a quick jog on the beach to open my lungs—though not an exercise buff, lately I'd been enjoying it a bit more—I showered and dressed for work in leggings and a simple black T-shirt. Finishing ten minutes earlier than anticipated, I decided I'd earned a latte from Percolate.

I swung by the coffee shop and was about to step inside when I caught sight of my mother.

Sitting with my father!

He was leaning forward, scrawling on a piece of paper. Kate was smiling, albeit tightly, but a smile was way better than a frown. Was Dad executing the document she had longed for him to sign?

Rather than disturb them, I decided I'd get a cup of coffee at the spa.

I proceeded along San Carlos Street near Ocean Avenue and began to cross the road when the roar of a truck made me wheel around. I spied a person in a Quasimodo latex mask driving straight at me. I knew it was Quasimodo, the hunchback of Notre Dame, because the left eye was black and the right was covered by flesh. The driver was hunched forward, both hands on the wheel, elbows splayed like chicken wings.

I *eeked*.

Someone grabbed my arm and yanked me backward. The truck didn't slow. The driver didn't pause to see if I was okay. Instead, the vehicle veered right at the corner, tires screeching, and disappeared from view.

"Thank you," I rasped to my savior, who turned out to be Brady Cash, the handsome owner of Hideaway Café, one of my favorite restaurants. He and Courtney Kelly were an item.

"You okay?" he asked.

My heart hammered my rib cage. "Yes, thanks to you. What was the guy thinking?"

"If it was a guy."

"You're right. I guess it could've been a woman."

"It's crazy at Halloween time." He grinned. "People get distracted. Do you want me to escort you to the Courtyard of Peace?"

"No, I'm fine."

"My advice? Stay on the sidewalks and keep to the crosswalks, and you should be all right."

I thanked him again, drew in a deep breath, and continued on while wondering if the driver had aimed at me on purpose. If so, who had it been? Did Wyatt own a truck? O'Malley drove an Acura, and Peyton had a Subaru, but any of them could have rented a truck.

Brady could be right about the driver getting distracted. Whoever it was might have been consulting a phone or checking GPS.

But the memory of the truck bearing down on me sent chills up my spine.

"Yoo-hoo." Nana Lissa whistled as I trudged up the steps to the Courtyard of Peace. Little known fact other than to her closest friends and family, my grandmother had won a whistling competition as a teenager. She was seated at a patio table. A cup of tea and a pumpkin oatmeal muffin sat in front of her. "Join me for—" She bounded to her feet and rushed to me. "What's wrong? You look like you've seen a ghost." She gripped my elbow.

"Someone . . ." The emotions I'd been pushing aside until now clogged my throat so fast I could barely breathe. "A truck ran me off the road. Near Percolate. Probably nothing." My words were coming out choppy. "Brady Cash pulled me out of the way. He said . . . he said Halloween brings out the crazies."

I shuddered. Was the driver the person Ursula believed might do me harm?

"What kind of vehicle was it?" Nana asked.

"A Toyota truck. Nondescript."

"Did you see the license plate?"

"No. Too shaken."

"Breathe," Nana Lissa said. "C'mon, a deep breath."

I obeyed and continued, "The Quasimodo mask the driver was wearing made it impossible to tell if the driver was male or female. I don't know if the incident was on purpose. It happened so fast."

"If it was, who would you suspect?"

I recapped my thoughts.

"We should tell Dylan," she said.

"He'll shrug it off. I'm fine."

"Sit," my grandmother commanded, retaking her seat.

I did need to calm my nerves before opening the spa, so I perched on a chair and folded my hands on the table. "Why are you here?"

"I was hungry."

I frowned. "Nah. I don't believe you. You wanted to chat with me about Kate."

"When did you get so smart?" She grinned.

"Did she call or text you?"

"She rang me at ten p.m. last night. She sounded agitated, and she certainly never reaches out to me late at night."

"About my father leaving town without settling things?" I asked.

"Yes, but by the end of our chat, I felt better about her. She would rally."

"I think you can relax. On my way here, I spotted the two of them at Percolate, and no claws were out." Had my mother actually taken my suggestion and initiated the appointment? I couldn't imagine fate had brought them together. "I think Dad was finalizing paperwork to cede his portion of the house to her."

Nana lifted her teacup. "Wonderful news."

"What's so wonderful?" a man asked in a less-than-civil tone.

Summers materialized on Nana's right. Officer Rodriguez trailed him by two strides. By the look on the detective's face, I could see he wasn't happy. With me.

"Good morning, Detective," I began cheerily to take the edge off, but it didn't work.

"I need you to butt out, Ms. Brennan," he warned, sotto voce.

Uh-oh. No more calling me Emma. No more giving me the green light.

"Hold on, Dylan." Nana Lissa aimed a finger. "You may not talk to my granddaughter in that fashion. I'll have you know she was nearly run off the road earlier when she was walking. Where are speed-control police when we need them?"

"Run off the road?" He arched an eyebrow and asked the same questions my grandmother had.

I told him I didn't catch the license plate or have a clue as to the identity of the driver.

"Halloween," he muttered. "It's a nutty time of year."

I frowned, realizing he'd acted exactly as I'd expected—dismissive.

"We'll look into it and check out the video footage," he said, as if picking up on my discontent.

"Carmel doesn't have CCTV," I stated.

"We have our own way of getting the images. The police department has asked local businesses and residents to join the fairly new CAPTURE program, a registry of privately owned security cameras."

"Ahh." Perhaps I should help out and sign up for CAPTURE, seeing as I had a Ring system at home.

"Now, to the matter at hand," he said. "Yes, I may talk to you like I did, and I will continue to do so. You are meddling with my investigation."

"No, she's not," my grandmother inserted.

"I've got this, Nana." I put a hand on her arm to silence her. "How did I interfere?" I asked, and silently cheered. The fluorite I'd tucked into the waistband pocket of my leggings was imbuing me with confidence.

"Did you or did you not speak to Peyton Pelagatti in front of her clients yesterday?" he demanded.

"No, I did not. The clients had driven away."

"But you did speak to her."

"Yes. I bumped into her while I was on my walkabout."

"Your walkabout?" Rodriguez asked. "Like an aborigine does?"

"No. The guru I studied under in Tibet labeled strolls to clear one's head *walkabouts*. They can be short or long. I like the term. I think it's charming." I addressed my grandmother. "Peyton received an offer on a house from her clients and was heading for her car to make the presentation."

"Why did you feel the need to speak with her, Ms. Brennan?" Summers asked.

"Emma," I said cheekily.

"Officer Rodriguez and I have had multiple conversations with her." His glower was scary but not Halloween slasher–film frightening.

Having survived a near-fatal incident, I felt empowered. "Hattie Hopewell was in the gift shop yesterday. She claimed she and her sister were in the McKay neighborhood the night Gianna was killed, and they spied Peyton slinking around, about a quarter past six. Has Hattie contacted you?"

Rodriguez regarded me. "We received a message from her, and we were planning on following up this morning."

"Good. Anyway, I was curious why Peyton would've told you she was home knitting Tuesday night."

"It's our job to find out if she lied," Summers stated.

"Yes, sir, but I was face-to-face with her, by coincidence, when the topic came up."

"You pressed her."

Aha. Now I understood his peeve. Peyton must have complained I'd strong-armed her. "Did she tell you someone on a bicycle nearly ran her over the night of the murder?"

"Yes, and we've got some leads." He chopped the air with a firm hand. "I want you to stop nosing around this instant."

"Dylan," Nana murmured soothingly, "if I recall, you told Emma to keep her eyes and ears open."

"Open. Nothing more. Not to pursue suspects and search for clues. Understood?"

"Yes, sir," I replied. "However—"

"No *however*," he barked, preventing me from sharing what Riley had told me about Idha Gibson's appropriately titled short story. "I've had enough out of both of you."

My grandmother huffed.

"Got me?" He lasered me with a look.

I remained mute. Heaven forbid I tell him I went on a hunt to investigate Idha's alibi.

"Eyes and ears, ladies. Good day." He turned on his heel and, grumbling words that sounded like he had Courtney Kelly to thank for this, he marched down the stairs to the street.

"Officer," I whispered to Rodriguez before she departed, "what's his problem? It's not me and my nana. Does it have something to do with your sister?"

"You're very astute. Yes. She officially broke up with him."

"Because of his temper?"

She peeked over her shoulder as if expecting him to rise like the phoenix. "She won't discuss it with me, but I think he was getting cold feet, so she decided to cut bait. Don't quote me." She dashed after her superior.

I sat down in my chair, the confidence I'd felt for a brief moment completely erased. "I need a smoothie." I kissed my grandmother on the cheek, told her not to worry about me and the truck incident or about my mother, and to enjoy the peacefulness of the courtyard and its fountain.

"I'm going to call Brady," she said. "He might have seen the license plate."

"Good idea. Thanks." I went inside the café.

Many of the tables were occupied. Customers had been streaming in while we'd been going toe-to-toe with the police. Sierra waved from the counter. I held up two fingers signifying I'd like the smoothie of the day. She responded with a thumbs-up gesture. The benefit of owning the place was the ability to butt in line without actually cutting in line.

I scanned the crowd and was surprised to see Idha Gibson at a table by herself. Her laptop computer was open. She was rummaging through a stack of files to her right. Why come here? She didn't have a treatment scheduled.

Choosing to be proactive, I sauntered to her. "Morning."

She squinted at me and tucked a loose hair behind her ear. "Morning."

"You're out and about early."

"I couldn't sleep and couldn't work at home because I've been so wound up in knots. A cup of green tea and one of Sierra's turmeric dark chocolate muffins should help ease the anxiety."

"You've come here before?"

"Often. We live nearby."

I relaxed a tad when Idha didn't launch into a tirade, meaning she probably didn't know about me and my cousin disproving her alibi.

"Care to sit?" She tapped the empty chair at her table.

"Sure."

Her face was as pale as the sweater she was wearing. The lines beneath her eyes were more pronounced than when I'd first met her. Was she finding it hard to sleep or concentrate because she was struggling with a guilty conscience?

Sierra delivered my smoothie to me in a to-go cup. "Here you go, Cuz. A delicious combo of blueberries, bananas, and Greek yogurt." She pecked me on the cheek and whispered in my ear, "Pin her down."

I thanked her and turned to Idha. "Frederick came in for a treatment."

"He told me."

"He looked bereft."

"He hasn't been himself since his sister's passing."

Passing? What a quaint word for murder.

Idha sipped her tea and set down the cup. "In some bizarre way, I think he blames me."

"For?"

"For her death and, well, everything. Like Gianna, I have high expectations, and Frederick . . ." She went silent and peeled the wrapper from her muffin.

"He doesn't feel he can live up to those expectations," I said.

She fixed me with a searing stare.

Why? Because I'd dared to finish her statement? Because her husband trusted me enough to confide in me? Unintimidated, I went on. "Did you blame Gianna for being overbearing, thereby causing his, what should I call them, shortcomings?"

"Is *shortcomings* the word he used?"

"No." I wasn't lying. When she didn't offer more, I gestured to her stack of files. "Are any of those short stories for a new anthology?" I sipped my smoothie, waiting.

A few seconds passed before tears bloomed in her eyes. "No, Idha, do not cry," she chided, and dabbed the moisture with her napkin.

"I'm sorry," I murmured. "Did I upset you?"

"I think Frederick suspects me of killing his sister."

"How could you have? You went to the cinema and out to dinner by yourself, he told me."

"No. I mean, yes, I purchased a dinner to-go." She wadded the napkin and plonked it on the table. "And I went to the theater and bought a ticket, but—"

"You didn't stay, did you?"

She hung her head. "No."

"What did you do?"

"I won't lie."

I leaned forward, waiting for an admission of guilt.

"I never liked Gianna," she said finally. "She stifled Frederick. When I fell in love with him and we became a team, I hoped he would change. But he didn't. He complied with her every wish and command. *Jump, Frederick*, she would order, and he'd say, *How high?* It was infuriating." She lifted her teacup and glanced over the rim at me. A fresh tear trickled down her cheek. She brushed it away.

"What did you do, Idha?" I asked again.

Her eyes widened. "Heavens. If you're thinking I killed Gianna, I didn't, though many times I contemplated it."

I remained silent.

"The night she was murdered"—she set down the teacup, this time with a *clack,* and surveyed the room as if to make sure no one else was listening in—"I did not stay at the theater because I was tailing our child."

"He's in his twenties, right?"

Her eyes widened, surprised I knew about him. "Twenty-eight."

"Riley said she and Nadal dated."

"Riley." She wrinkled her nose. "They were good together, but Nadal got in trouble too many times with the law, and finally, Riley could take no more."

"What kind of trouble?" I asked.

"He steals things. Trivial things. He has been caught, but he has not served time. He has been let off with community service. Alas, punishment does not seem to stifle the impulse. Last Tuesday"—her face pinched with pain—"when I spoke to him on the telephone at five, I felt something was off."

"Off?"

"Like he couldn't control an impulse. He sounded aggressively irritated. So I bought the takeout dinner and purchased a theater ticket and drove to his apartment. And I waited."

I couldn't grasp why she would need a theater ticket.

"Around seven, he proved me right. He went out, and I followed him, and I caught him stealing a bicycle." Tears surfaced again, but this time she didn't stem them. "A racing bicycle! I couldn't believe it. The smaller things he took were ordinary. One could say he swiped them as a lark."

I doubted it was a caper. I'd bet Nadal suffered from kleptomania, a mental disorder causing an irresistible urge to steal items of little value.

"But an expensive bicycle?" she went on. "I confronted my son. He was embarrassed I'd caught him. He begged me not to tell his father."

Aha. Now I understood why she'd gone to the theater. "You went to Cinema Unique and purchased a ticket so Frederick wouldn't know what you were really up to."

She nodded. "Frederick has ordered Nadal to seek treatment, but he is an adult, so Frederick cannot make him. It pains me to say this, but if my son is diagnosed with mental issues, I will be devastated. You see, my father"—she pressed a hand to her heart—"had severe impulse control disorder, which evidenced as intermittent explosive disorder, as well as trichotillomania. Have you heard of it?"

I shook my head.

"He repeatedly pulled out his hair. I have never told Frederick."

Her husband didn't know about her father's illness? Wow! The secrets families will keep, indeed.

"Papa's illness got so bad he wound up in a ward and died there. I do not want our child in an institution. Please, I have not revealed this to anyone, but there is an aspect of you that makes me feel safe to confide to you."

An aspect? Maybe my winning personality was reassuring her. Or perhaps the fluorite in my pocket was emanating trust vibes.

She eyed me. "You're certainly calm with the information I have imparted."

Wrong-o. My insides were roiling.

"Will you keep silent? I need time to figure out what to do." Idha's shoulders rose and fell.

I reached out but didn't touch her, opting to rest my hand on the table instead. "You should tell the police. They're going to find out you didn't go to the movie theater."

"Why would they care about my whereabouts?"

"Because of your short story, *Silent Suffocation*."

Chapter 20

She didn't protest. Didn't respond. She let out a slow breath. If she was dumbfounded by my revelation, she didn't show it. After a long moment, she whispered, "I should get back to work." She motioned to the stack of papers to her right.

"Of course." I rose to my feet.

"I'll talk to the police."

I hoped she would and tossed the remnants of my smoothie into the trash on my way out. It wouldn't keep, and my appetite had waned. If I became hungry later on, I'd come back to the café for a snack.

My grandmother was no longer sitting in the courtyard. Through the shop window, I saw Yoly freshening up the displays. I didn't spy any customers inside yet, even though Yoly had turned the *WELCOME* sign over, but I wasn't worried. It was early in the day for shoppers.

Before heading into the spa, I sauntered to the stairs leading to the street and faced west toward the ocean. I wanted to wash away the negativity and frustration I was feeling, as well as the fear I'd experienced after the truck incident. Because I couldn't see the water over the buildings and gigantic Monterey pines, I closed my eyes to imagine it. I spread my arms and inhaled for three counts, and then I exhaled for three counts. I repeated the exercise three times.

Refreshed, I opened my eyes. I jolted when I caught sight of Wyatt on the sidewalk. He was standing beside a bicycle, casually viewing his watch. Dressed in black, he reminded me of a bad dude in a biker movie. My knees wobbled. My breathing spiked. Why the heck was he here? Idha's presence was a fluke, but Wyatt's? Not on a bet.

Pent up and ready for bear, I dashed down the stairs and marched toward him. I felt safe. There were plenty of people out for a stroll. "Ahem," I said to get his attention.

Surprised, he jerked up his head. "You."

"I happen to own this courtyard and those businesses." In fairness, my grandmother owned the majority, but Sierra and I were her partners.

"Heh, of course." An *Outside* magazine was tucked beneath the waistband of his riding shorts. My father used to subscribe to the publication. It focused on travel, sports, gear, and fitness.

"Do you ever work?" I asked. "Shouldn't you be making a tour of your stores?"

He didn't answer, as stumped by my question as a contestant on a quiz show.

"Why are you here?" I asked pointedly.

"I'm, uh, waiting for Addison."

"Haven't seen her," I replied, wondering if her father should get a restraining order after all.

"She's got an appointment. My friend, Cara's husband, told me she and Cara both have one."

"Not until way later."

"My mistake."

Was it? Or was I in error? Addison might have changed her booking. Studying Wyatt's face, I recalled Peyton saying a cyclist had nearly run her over the night of Gianna's death. Casually, I motioned to his bicycle. "What make?"

"The best high-end performance race bike around. A Specialized Tarmac SL8. It's got a great combination of aerodynamics and ride quality." Addison had told me he was an expert. He didn't disappoint. "Aerodynamics and the weight of a bike don't mean you win races. Speed is what makes the diff. But overall, it's a better bike than the Milan San Remo or the Tourmalet Climb. Are you in the market for one?"

"No," I remarked, "but my cousin might be interested."

"They're not cheap. They run close to ten K."

I whistled. "Can a woman ride it?"

"Heck sure. Creating male or female bikes is passe. FYI, this baby is stiffer at the pedals and more compliant at the handles."

"You sure know a lot about them."

"With my affliction, it helps if I focus on facts and figures. Like really focus."

"Your affliction?"

He combed his dark hair with his fingers. His shirt rose ever so slightly, revealing firm abs. "I've got antisocial personality disorder, or ASPD."

"I've heard of it," I said, not letting on that I'd done a deep dive.

"People like me can have trouble with planning and sustained attention. I'm good with short-term memory, but long-term memory? Not a chance. So for my line of work, I memorize facts and rattle them off like a pro."

"From what I understand, people with ASPD might have trouble with impulse control and driving," I stated. "Do you?"

"Nope."

"Do you own a truck?"

He blinked. "I've got a Chevy Tahoe. Some might call it a truck, but to me, it's just an SUV."

The answer seemed forthright. I didn't detect guile in his gaze. "Does your affliction affect operating a bicycle?"

"Nah. I'm an ace on a bike. Now, don't ask me to operate a conveyor belt or a newspaper press. Those could pose a challenge." He offered a charming smile, and I could see why Addison had fallen for him. But it was also disconcerting that he'd smiled, because one wasn't warranted. Was he trying to put one over on me?

"Do you ride a lot?" I asked.

"Whenever I'm not working or sleeping."

"Peyton Pelagatti insisted a cyclist nearly ran her over the night Addison's mother was killed, and I wondered if it could've been you. She was near the McKay house at the time."

His smile vanished. "How could it have been me? I was watching news at home."

"Business news."

"Yep."

I tilted my head slightly, waiting for more.

"Don't you believe me?" There was an edge in his tone.

"Peyton stated the cyclist was dressed all in black, like you are now." Actually, she'd told me the cyclist was wearing a dark color and, to be fair, she hadn't said *he*.

"Peyton couldn't have seen me. I happen to know she was home Tuesday night, like me."

"Yeah, no. She lied. Someone spied her sneaking around Gianna's house, and when confronted"—by me, as fate would have it—"she admitted she'd hoped to chat with Gianna and clear the air, but Gianna wasn't answering her phone and didn't respond when Peyton knocked on the door."

Because she was dead by then? I wondered. "I'd bet the police are reviewing security footage in the area, trying to decipher if Peyton is telling the truth. What do you think?"

"Carmel doesn't have CCTV."

"They have other means."

Wyatt pulled down the hem of his shirt and pursed his lips, as if trying to decipher some hidden agenda in my words.

"Did you happen to take a breather from watching business news?" I asked. "If you were out riding in the vicinity, you could confirm Peyton's alibi."

"She doesn't like me."

"It doesn't mean she's lying. Were you?"

A pair of women passed by us.

When they were out of earshot, he said, "Listen, I didn't want to own up to this because Addison hates when I ride at night, but yeah, I was out. I've been training for an event."

Addison had taken umbrage with him when he'd barged in on the dinner Monday night.

"I'm obsessed. My training is one of the continual fights of our relationship. When we get back together . . ." His words drifted off.

Did he honestly believe he and Addison would become a couple again? *Earth One to Wyatt.* I dared to point out the obvious. "Um, I doubt you will."

"I hope to win her over."

Okay. He wasn't completely delusional.

"Anyway," he went on, "I didn't see Peyton until the last second because I don't put a light on my helmet. It would throw off my weight distribution."

Whoa. He was confessing to being in the vicinity? Had he killed Gianna? Had he been fleeing the scene? "Why were you riding in the neighborhood if you were afraid of Addison knowing what you were up to?"

"Heh-heh. Good point." His suntanned cheeks blazed with embarrassment. "Training requires lots of laps, and her neighborhood has tons of sharp turns. It's good for dexterity. So I thought I could kill two birds with one stone." He balked. "Wait! That didn't come out right. I mean, I rode through her neighborhood because—"

"Because you were suspicious," I inserted. "You wanted to see if she was really staying at her parents' house and not handing you a line of bull."

He massaged one handlebar with his thumb.

"Did you see anyone enter or leave the McKay house?" I asked.

"No, but each lap took three to four minutes, so I could've missed someone. But I saw Addison in the window every time. She was rocking out like she does whenever she's listening to music. Man, I wanted to yell out and get her to come downstairs and hash things out with me."

Once again, the image of a hapless suitor with a guitar flickered in my mind.

"But she wouldn't have heard me, not with those noise-canceling earphones on."

"Plus you didn't yell because she'd realize you were training."

He nodded sheepishly.

"What time did you almost run over Peyton?"

"Close to seven. She seemed okay. I mean, she didn't, like, faint from fright or anything, so I ducked my head and didn't apologize."

"And you biked home."

"No. I kept riding. Around eight an alarm went off in the neighborhood. I worried if it was a fire alarm, and if the place blew, it might ignite other houses." He scratched the back of his neck. "When I saw a few people running down the street toward the ruckus, I yelled at a woman to get Addison out of the house."

"Do you remember what the woman looked like?"

"She had a Great Dane on a leash. It was taller than my bike. I'd seen her on an earlier lap. Anyway, I didn't stick around because, well, Addison might have been hustling down the stairs to check out what the commotion was and see me." He cast his right leg over the crossbar of his bike and inserted his foot into a toe clip. "You don't have to tell Addison I was hanging around. I'll do it."

"And confess where you were Tuesday night?"

His eyes darkened. "I didn't kill her mom."

As he rode off, I wondered if he'd admitted to almost running over Peyton because I'd supplied the information. On the other hand, a dog-walking neighbor told the police they'd seen Addison often in the window with headphones on. Did the woman own a Great Dane?

Despite my better judgment, before entering the spa, I rang Detective Summers in an effort to obey his eyes-and-ears-open order. I stood beside the fountain at the rear of the courtyard to find some peace.

He answered gruffly. "Ms. Brennan, to what do I owe the honor?"

"Sir, thank you for taking the call." I launched into what Wyatt had revealed and his time frame. "Does the witness who ID'd Addison the night of her mother's death own a Great Dane? Wyatt contended the woman he alerted was hurrying in the direction of the house where the robbery occurred."

"There wasn't a robbery."

"Was it a fire?"

"Nope. False alarm. A pet set off the internal alert. Now, if that's all you have to share, thank you. We will look into Mr. Lacey's claim to be training at night and ask him why he provided an alternate alibi."

False, not alternate, I reflected. "Apparently, his obsession with training irked Addison, so he didn't want her to know because he hopes to win her back."

"Not likely with a happily divorced party planned."

"Between you and me, I'd bet he didn't want her to think he was stalking her."

"A much better reason. Good-bye." He ended the call.

Okay, I hadn't expected him to be warm and fuzzy, but at least he hadn't yelled at me. Progress.

I poked my head into the gift shop and greeted Yoly. She told me she had put an ad in the *Carmel Pine Cone* for the new receptionist position and had posted online, as well. She would review responses daily and weed out those who didn't pass muster. I thanked her and crossed the courtyard to the spa.

Meryl was rounding the reception area with a dry mop to collect dust. Her mouth was downturned. I didn't see her mother anywhere.

"Meryl!" I noticed she was wearing earbuds and drew closer. "Meryl."

She startled. "You're here." Her face was streaked with tears. She swiped at the mess. "I'm listening to a sad song." I knew she was fibbing, because I was able to pick up bits of the comedy sketch she was listening to—Robin Williams and the ridiculousness of the game of golf. My father and I had watched YouTube videos of him doing the sketch a couple of times.

"Where's your mother?"

"Occupied. She'll be out in a few."

I rested a hand on her arm. "Are you sad she's leaving? Is that the real reason you're crying?"

Meryl shook her head. "No. I'm okay with her decision. She needs to live her life. She'll get stale here. It's . . ." She turned off her program using an app on her phone and removed the earbuds. "It's Dante. He called and yelled at me for being an unfit mother. I'm not." She snarled. "His father is poisoning him against me. It's so frustrating. I've talked to my shrink, but she says I've got to rise above it all. To chill. All boys rebel, she says. But this . . . this harassment. It's unfair. I didn't do anything. I love him." She tilted her head to one side and righted it. "Sure, yeah, when he was living with me, I might've verbally bashed his father, but the guy walked out. Poof. I never received the support I was due even though my attorney sent demands." Beads of tears clung to her eyelashes. "Ugh! You do not need to hear all this negativity." She set the mop aside and shook her arms. "Bad juju. Fly away. Bye-bye."

She hadn't learned the chant from me. I hoped it would work.

"Listen"—I patted her arm—"you can talk to me any time you want. I'm all ears." The words *all ears* reminded me of my conversation with Summers and made me want to laugh, but I didn't, lest Meryl take my mirth the wrong way. "I'm here for you."

"Thank you." She rounded the desk and drew up the appointment calendar on the computer. "No facial appointments today. You do have the mask-making class at one thirty. There are a number of attendees. And Addison switched her three o'clock massage to a sound bath. She's bringing her pals."

"Why do a sound bath? They already experienced a mindful meditation."

"Addison said she's feeling brittle, and she wants to try every experience the spa offers. By the way, we need to boost clientele. Some of our masseuses are asking for extra hours. We have the space. Don't be concerned, though," Meryl advised me. "We're good, but we could be good-er." She waggled her eyebrows, knowing she was making up a word. "And don't be concerned about me. I found a book entitled *How to Solve Fifty Percent of Your Problems* . . . so I bought two."

"Ha! Funny." I breathed easier. If she could come up with a corny joke in the midst of her misery, she would recover.

I sauntered to the office thinking about mothers and sons, and specifically about Idha and her son, Nadal. I forgot to ask Summers if she'd confided in him. Would her son, if pressed by the police, admit he had a thievery problem? Would he hold his mother's snooping against her and, like Meryl's son, cut ties with her?

Another thought struck me. What if Idha had lied to me about following her son in order to bolster her alibi? She'd admitted to being angry at Gianna for the way she'd treated Frederick.

I pushed thoughts of her aside when it dawned on me I hadn't heard from the Etsy designer, ChaCha. I opened her Etsy shop page and sent a follow-up message asking if she'd seen my first.

She sent an immediate response.

ChaCha: **Emma, I am red-faced I didn't reply days ago. Not a good business practice. Please accept my apology. As a matter of fact, I did sell a second one to Addison's mother, Gianna.**

I gaped at the message. Really? Gianna had reached out to her directly? I couldn't remember seeing a second one in the master bedroom. Detective Summers hadn't mentioned finding an additional pillow.

Me: **How do you know it was Gianna McKay who purchased it?**

ChaCha: **Because her name is on her Etsy account like yours is, and I sent it to her home address.**

I leaned back in the desk chair. It was conceivable the killer saw a duplicate in Gianna's bedroom and, on the spur of the moment, came up with the idea to use it. It was also possible the killer hacked Gianna's account and ordered the additional pillow, and when it was delivered, he or she pirated it from the porch.

I wrote the note about the second pillow on a white three-by-five card and crossed to the murder board. I secured the card with a pushpin, and it dawned on me I hadn't asked ChaCha when Gianna had purchased the pillow. I supposed it didn't matter. An additional pillow existed, and the killer might have used it and destroyed it, rendering the search for a pillow with a lipstick smear fruitless. Dang.

"Knock-knock." My father stepped into the office. He joined me by the board and his eyes widened. "Is that what I think it is?"

"Can you be more specific?"

His gaze pinched with concern. "I can understand why you did this when your friend was murdered." I'd told him about Willow. "But why now? You're not investigating at will, are you? You haven't become a PI while I've been away, have you?"

"Don't pull a Kate on me, Dad," I chided.

"A Kate?"

"I'm not being reckless." At least I didn't think I was. "I'm trying to help Addison find closure. Besides, I'm worried how the news about the murder might affect my business. After all, Gianna McKay was a regular client here. If we're blamed in any way—"

He held a finger to my lips. "Got it. Tell me what we're looking at." He motioned to the cards.

I recapped what ChaCha had confided.

"You think the killer might have hacked Gianna's account?" He tapped the white clue card I'd pinned up a moment ago.

"Yep. Hey, what if O'Malley ordered it and hid it until he needed to use it?"

"He was in San Francisco at the time of the murder. What about Addison? Or one of her friends?"

Wow. I hadn't considered any of her friends suspects. Didn't Riley say she would do anything to help Addison, even lie for her? What was her alibi? I wrote her name on a beige card and posted it beside the big fat question mark card.

"How did it go with Kate this morning?" I asked.

He tilted his head.

"I spied the two of you at Percolate."

"Ahh." He smiled. "It went well. As Lao Tzu would say, *A strong wind may topple the sturdy oak, but the willow bends and lets the wind pass through.* I bent, which appeased your mother. I arranged to move everything, and I've already rented a storage unit. Movers will come tomorrow to pick it all up. I also signed off on the house. That brought a smile to her face."

"Ha! A rare win."

"She didn't get the nickname Ice Princess from her students for nothing."

I giggled. "Now what? Will you continue to be a rolling stone, or did you take the foundation's offer?"

"I'm mulling it over."

"You like raising funds around the world."

"I do."

"And you enjoy traveling."

"How wise you've become." He reached for my hand. "For now, I'm off to Somalia."

Panic rose in my gut. "But they're fighting there. It's ongoing."

"There is fighting everywhere, baby doll. I've seen my share. My team and I are welcomed by both sides. We're problem solvers. We wear those special badges like the press do. Don't fret."

I wiggled my nose, definitely *fretting*. I pushed the uncomfortable feeling aside. "What about the woman you want to meet up with in San Francisco?"

"She's off on an adventure. We'll get together soon and decide our future."

"Sheesh. How can you manage that if you're never in the same country?"

"Right now we FaceTime." He grinned. "You can get to know a person well by talking. You don't always need to be in the same room holding hands."

"What a romantic," I joked.

He pecked my cheek.

Chapter 21

At one thirty, Nana Lissa, Hedda, and Ursula showed up for the mask-making class. Yoly—she'd closed the shop for the hour—strolled in right behind them. So did Courtney and Brady and, to my surprise, an additional man—Zane Ashford.

Brady said, "Emma, you know my buddy Zane."

"I do. I'm in his tai chi class. You're friends?"

"For years. He came to the restaurant to take a cooking class and we hit it off." Brady elbowed Zane. "Being a lover of learning, I told him he had to check out Aroma Wellness and its classes."

"Lover of learning." Zane grinned. "Now there's a turn of phrase."

Brady guffawed. "I'm not glib. Sue me."

I was enjoying their camaraderie.

"Between you and me, Emma," Zane said, "I think Brady wanted a wingman since Courtney was forcing him to come to this."

"Ahem," Courtney said with mock-offense. "I don't force anyone to do anything ever."

Brady slung an arm around her waist. "Cool it, oh fierce protector of all things fairy."

She slugged his arm in jest.

"Hey, Emma," Brady said, "I'm sorry I didn't catch the truck's license plate. I told your grandmother the incident happened so fast, and I was more concerned about protecting you. How are you doing?"

"I'm okay," I lied. I wasn't fully recovered, but I was calm enough to convince myself someone had not intentionally tried to run me over. It had been an accident.

Brady explained the incident to Courtney and Zane.

"Wow." Zane placed a hand on my arm. "That had to have been scary. Are you sure you're all right?"

The scent of him was heady, his touch warm and reassuring. "Yep."

"Your resilience speaks volumes." He winked, and I nearly swooned.

"Thank you," I managed to say and then, realizing I had a schedule to maintain, added, "Everyone, take a place at one of the stations."

In the meditation room, Meryl and I had set out rectangular tables covered in sea-green plastic covers. On the tops of the tables sat items each participant would need to make their mask: pumpkin puree, honey, natural yogurt, and cinnamon, as well as mixing bowls and utensils, measuring cups, a handheld blender, and a container to store the cream.

I didn't dim the lights. The attendees needed to see well enough to complete their tasks.

My station stood at the head of the room. "Today, I'm going to show you how to make a simple pumpkin mask." I paused and grinned. "Hey, what's a pumpkin's favorite western? *The Gourd, the Bad and the Ugly*."

They laughed.

"Why was the pumpkin afraid to cross the road?" I asked. "Because it had no guts."

More chuckles, followed by a few groans. I would have to thank Meryl for the silly kid-joke material. She swore it was a great way to break the tension, and she was right.

I clapped my hands. "Down to business. Pumpkin is like a miracle fruit."

My grandmother said, "It's a fruit?"

"Yes. According to botanists, it is a product of a seed-bearing configuration of flowering plants." I often found useful tidbits online. "Here's another fact of science. Pumpkin puree infuses the skin with bioflavonoids and helps hydrate and plump the skin."

Yoly raised a hand. "Are we going to be tested on this?"

"Nope. This is a test-free zone," I quipped. "Continuing on. Pumpkin provides antioxidants and age-defying benefits."

Ursula whooped. "My skin could use that."

Heads turned to inspect her face.

"Ha!" Courtney scoffed "Your skin is beautiful. You don't need any mask whatsoever."

Ursula's mouth quirked up on the right. "Thank you for the compliment, but I am wearing makeup."

I said, "Pumpkin contains vitamins A, C, and E, all of which will help the skin glow."

"I want to glow!" Hedda cried.

"Now, please note"—I shot a finger in their direction—"any fresh mask will spoil, so you need to use this one soon after making it. Got me?"

"Uh, Teach"—Zane cleared his throat—"I'm giving classes for the remainder of the day. I don't want to put it on and scare my students."

Teach? Had he actually called me *Teach*? I supposed I could live with the sassy moniker. "It'll keep in the refrigerator for at least forty-eight hours," I said. "Do you instruct classes for forty-eight hours straight?"

"No, I make time for normal life." He met my gaze, and I felt my cheeks warm.

"Then you're set." I pressed on. "One of the benefits of making your own mask is you can be sure there are no preservatives or anything else that might cause you to react adversely." I frowned. "Unless you are allergic to pumpkin. Is anyone?"

They all shook their heads.

"Phew. Good." Though an allergy to pumpkin was rare, I needed to be cautious. A susceptible person could suffer hives, shortness of breath, and even anaphylaxis. Not happening on my watch.

For the next few minutes, I showed the class the amount of ingredients I used for one mask. "Two tablespoons pumpkin puree, one tablespoon honey, one tablespoon Greek yogurt." I measured each and put them in a mixing bowl.

"What's the yogurt for?" Hedda asked.

"It makes the cream smoother. Add a dash of cinnamon . . ." I paused. "Is anyone allergic to any of these items?"

They all wagged their heads.

"Maybe you should consider having students sign waivers before future classes," Nana Lissa suggested.

"Didn't Mah ask each of you to do so?"

"No," Nana said.

Dang. Mah was supposed to have handed them out as the students arrived.

"I waive my rights." Zane flailed a hand.

"Me too." Brady mimicked him.

The rest of the class did the same.

If I had installed a security camera in the room, I'd be covered by the raised hands, but I couldn't and wouldn't. Privacy for our clients mattered. "Can I trust you to keep your word?" I asked. After receiving a resounding *Yes!,* I continued. "For a big batch, I like to whip the pumpkin puree with a blender to make it light and fluffy, but for this small amount, I'll use a whisk." I demonstrated. "When your mask is ready, wash your face with water or a light cleanser and pat dry." I used the water and terry-cloth towels I'd set out prior to the class. "Apply the mask to your face, but not your eyes or eyelids"—I daubed the mask on my face, smoothed it beneath my eyes, and swirled it above my eyebrows. "If desired, apply to your neck." I didn't. "Then lie down and let the mask rest on your face for twenty minutes. When ready, wash off the mask with warm water and moisturize your face." I removed the pumpkin concoction from my face and left the soiled towel in the water.

"Which moisturizer do you use?" Hedda asked.

"I enjoy the one we sell in the spa. I purchase it from a respected company." I held up a jar. "But I also recommend a simple, over-the-counter coconut oil cream."

Ursula visibly shuddered.

"What's wrong?" I asked her. "Are you allergic to coconut?"

"No, I . . ." She motioned with her hands. "I see an aura around you. A red aura."

"Honestly, Ursula," Nana Lissa chided, "now is not the time."

"I cannot leave these realities unmentioned." Ursula looked pained. "This aura signifies Emma feels anxious and not in control."

"I'm in control of this class," I joked, although I was taking Ursula's warning seriously. After all, she read palms, tarot, and now crystals. For all I knew, she was also pursuing psychoneurological studies with my aunt as her tutor.

"I see it, too," Zane said, suddenly somber, "although it's more a deep purple, I think."

I couldn't see auras. I wanted to, and I believed they existed, but the gift remained out of reach.

"What has you worried, Emma?" Ursula asked, unwilling or unable to stop seeing the glow.

Losing Detective Summers's respect maybe, I reasoned, but revised the notion. Perhaps Ursula was picking up on my concern about the spa's reputation being damaged.

The others in the class went silent, awaiting my answer.

"Nothing," I lied. "Everything is fine. No worries."

"Do you fear the driver of the truck will return?" she asked.

What the blazes? I wanted to shout as my father was inclined to do. The thought hadn't occurred to me. "No, no, and no."

"The truck almost hit you, Emma," Zane said gently.

"By accident," I assured them all. "It was unintentional." Yes, I was digging in my heels, but I couldn't give in to fear. Despite my bravado, a shiver skated down my spine as the image of the person in the Quasimodo mask loomed in my mind.

Intent on regaining control of my emotions, I focused on the powerful words Zane had uttered in the tai chi class—*deflect, redirect*—but it didn't help, so I attempted a silent mindful meditation. *I am the best me I can be. I am powerful. I am in control. I do not fear my future.*

Feeling stronger, I lifted my gaze, met the class's concerned stares, and smiled . . . until Ursula repeated her warning.

When the class adjourned, Zane didn't hang around. I didn't take his hasty departure personally. Instead, I pushed Ursula's words from my mind and spent the next hour preparing the meditation room for the upcoming sound bath.

Addison, Riley, Cara, and Tatiana arrived in a cluster, each munching on a treat from the café. They were dressed in Halloween-inspired sweaters, which I quickly learned Tatiana had gifted to the friends. A lot of money was being spent this week, I noted, and reasoned each of Addison's friends might be trying to bolster her, due to the loss of her mother and the impending divorce.

"These sweaters rival ugly Christmas ones, don't you think?" Tatiana pulled on the hem of hers. It featured a patchwork of skeletons, pumpkins, witches, and black cats.

Riley snorted, nearly spewing the muffin she was polishing off. "Mine's the best." She licked crumbs from her lips. "A cardigan Day of the Dead in orange is so not my style." She stuck out her tongue at Tatiana.

I studied the women, and the question my father asked came to me. What had these women been doing on the night of the murder? Had the police checked out their alibis, Riley's in particular?

Get real, Emma. Riley is a children's book illustrator, not a killer.

"All right, ladies"—I dimmed the lights—"as you did for the mindful meditation, take a seat on a chair or on the floor mat and prepare for a relaxing, centering experience."

I moved about the room, stirring the singing bowls with the crystal rod and, as I had with Mah and Meryl, explained that the women were not to say anything themselves.

I focused on finding peace in this stressful time. "With each breath out, release tension and worry. Imagine a leaf floating on a stream." My teacher in Tibet often used nature to paint a picture. "Notice how it moves gently at times and at other times with speed. Like the leaf, your feelings can ebb and flow. Don't hold on. Let them drift . . . drift."

I went silent and allowed the melodic tones of the crystals to encompass the room.

Forty-five minutes later, I said, "As you breathe out, let go of any lingering sadness. Reflect on what closure looks like to you. It does not mean you must forget the past, but hopefully find peace with it. Your journey proceeds, one step at a time." I raised the lights to normal level.

The women stretched their arms. Riley yawned. So did Cara.

"Emma, amazing." Addison got to her feet and trailed me as I replaced the crystal wand on its holder. "Utterly amazing. I think I fell asleep."

"It's highly possible."

"By the way, ChaCha reached out to me. She told me you asked about an extra pillow my mother ordered. I had no idea she had. I don't know where it is. You don't think there's an extra pillow floating around that the killer—" She covered her mouth with her hand.

"Used?" Riley finished for her pal.

Addison blanched. "Perhaps Mother gave it as a gift to a friend. Or she . . . she . . ." Tears brimmed in her eyes. She growled softly.

"Or she what?" Riley prompted.

"I'd hoped today's session would help me find the peace Emma talks about, but to this day I'm holding on to so many bitter memories. I did say I hated my mother to Wyatt."

Riley slung an arm around her friend's back. "Don't judge yourself. You and Gianna were at odds like all mothers and daughters."

Tears bloomed in Addison's eyes. "I miss her so much."

Riley eyed me. "Hey, what if Addison's dad ordered the pillow?"

"Uh-uh." Addison rejected her friend's theory with a wave. "He did not kill my mother. He was in San Francisco at the time."

"Sure, but remember him saying, like you and me, he'd browsed some of your aunt Idha's short stories?" Riley widened her eyes purposefully. "I told you to check out the one about suffocation. What if he read it, too?"

Addison knew of it? Yikes.

"No!" Addison was adamant. "My father is not a killer."

"But he loves you more than life itself," Riley argued. "He would do anything to protect you."

Like Idha would for her son and my father would for me.

"I didn't need protection from my mother. She wasn't an ogre. She was stern." Addison shook her head adamantly. "No. Not possible." She headed toward the door. Her friends followed.

"Riley, what were you doing Tuesday night?" I asked nonchalantly.

"Not saving my pal from heartache, like I should've been," she wisecracked, and had the decency to blush. "Sorry, how inconsiderate of me. I was babysitting for Cara and her husband. They were celebrating their tenth anniversary."

Cara patted Riley on the shoulder. "She is the best babysitter. She gets the kids involved in all sorts of art projects."

Each alibi corroborated the other.

Riley said, "Cara asked Tatiana to sit because her kids love soccer, but Tat was giving a private lesson."

"To high schoolers"—Tatiana pulled a face—"whose parents want their kids to go pro."

"Wyatt killed Mother." Addison opened the door and exited down the hall toward reception. "He did it."

"He couldn't have," I countered. "He has a solid alibi."

She drew to a stop. "What?" Her voice skated upward. "How is watching the news verifiable?"

"He lied," I whispered, hoping the soundproofing on the spa rooms was as reliable as the builder had claimed and the patrons hadn't heard her frantic pitch. "As it turns out, he was riding his bike in your neighborhood."

A second *What?* exploded out of her, and she marched to reception.

"Shh, Adds," Riley warned. "Emma, do you know what he was doing there?"

"Spying on me, of course," Addison snapped. "Why else? Man, he's toast. He crossed the line. He's going to hear from my lawyer."

She stormed out of the spa, her friends trailing her. At the same time, Nana Lissa entered carrying a café to-go bag.

"What was that about?" She frowned.

I explained. "You know, Riley got me thinking. What if Addison's father is guilty?" I told my grandmother how speedily he'd dialed the hotel manager when my father and I bumped into him at the restaurant Sunday. "He acted as if one phone call would exonerate him from all possibility of being a murderer. But what if it was a ruse? What if he paid the hotel manager a tidy sum to lie for him and say he'd fallen ill in order to give himself an alibi?"

Chapter 22

My grandmother turned to Meryl, who was manning the desk. "Does Emma have any more appointments this afternoon?"

"No, ma'am. She is as free as a bird. In fact, so am I, but I'm covering for my mother. She had a doctor's appointment."

"Is everything okay?" I asked.

"Of course. She's stressed about leaving me in the lurch." Meryl batted the air. "Nothing a glass of wine won't fix." She grinned. "Like I say to my mom, wine improves with age. We improve with wine."

Nana clasped my elbow. "Let's go."

"Where?"

"To the Hilltop Hotel in San Francisco. You drive."

I didn't argue. My grandmother could be commanding when on a mission.

* * *

Nestled in the heart of San Francisco, the Hilltop Hotel boasted an inviting façade featuring elegant Victorian architecture with intricate cornices and charming bay windows. Lush greenery and blooming flowers created a welcoming atmosphere.

A twentysomething valet greeted us promptly when we arrived and asked if he could help with our luggage. We replied that we weren't staying. Just visiting. He handed me a claim ticket, wished us well, and advised us where we might find the bar and lounge if we'd like a beverage.

Boy, would I, but I'd have to wait.

Inside, the décor was a combination of classic sophistication mixed with modern touches. The iconic view of the sunset beyond the Golden Gate Bridge through the huge window at the far end of the lobby was exquisite.

I turned in a circle to admire the curving staircase that led to a second-floor open area above the lobby. When I caught sight of the valet again, an idea came to me. "Nana, come with me."

"Where—"

I didn't wait. I strode outside and tapped the attendant on the shoulder. "Hi. Have you got a sec?"

"Sure." He had a compelling smile.

"Do you know O'Malley McKay?"

"Sure do. The dude is one of our regulars. He does a lot of business in the City."

"May I ask, were you working a week ago today?"

His forehead wrinkled as he processed the question. "Yep. Tuesday to Saturday without fail. I take Sundays and Mondays off so I can go hiking."

"I like to hike," I said, trying to make a connection.

"I know every trail in a thirty-mile radius."

"Wow."

"There's a book mapping them all out."

"Cool. Say, could you tell me if Mr. McKay left the hotel Tuesday afternoon, around three or so?"

He scratched the nape of his neck, somewhat bewildered. "I don't think he was staying here."

"He said he was."

"If so, he didn't use valet, and I can't recall seeing him go through the front door."

My grandmother and I exchanged a look. She muttered under her breath, "You heard his brother-in-law taunting him at dinner Monday, chiding him for always using valet."

"Maybe he wasn't staying here after all."

Nana Lissa wagged her head. "The manager confirmed he walked into the bar around eight thirty, right?"

"True."

I thanked the valet, gave him a couple of bucks for his trouble, and we returned inside. My grandmother lingered in the foyer to admire an orange-themed silk flower arrangement in the foyer. It was adorned with pumpkins, bats, and spiders on skewers. I crossed to reception, where a female clerk with a brown bob and a pert nose was crossing items off a list.

"I'd like to see the manager, first name Robert."

The clerk grinned, displaying a set of teeth any dentist would be proud of. "Mr. Smith is in a meeting and unavailable."

"When might he break free?"

She checked a schedule on her computer monitor. "An hour or so. It's the end-of-day wrap-up. All available staff members are attending. Will you still be here then?"

"I might be. I'll check in with you." I offered my winningest help-me expression. "Is it possible to tell me which room O'Malley McKay stayed in on his visit last Tuesday?"

"No."

"But he did stay here?"

"Revealing a guest's room number is against company policy," she replied, not exactly answering the question. She looked to her left. An impatient-looking couple stood farther along the counter. "I'm sorry. I have to attend to those guests."

I rejoined my grandmother. "She was cagey, but I'm pretty sure she confirmed he was staying here."

"All right. What next?"

"I have a theory. What if he didn't phone the manager from his room but, instead, from his car? What if he didn't utilize the valet service, and he slipped out a side entrance sometime in the afternoon to avoid being seen?"

"Go on."

"He fetched his Acura from a public lot—"

"A premeditative choice."

"And he drove to Carmel. He killed his wife before six fifteen, when Peyton started sneaking around, and he made it back to the hotel in time to show his face in the bar just after eight."

"Driving such a long distance in two hours would be difficult in evening traffic," Nana said.

"He'd have been going against traffic on the return trip."

"True."

I tapped a finger to my chin. "The Acura."

"What about it?"

"It's silver. Remember how Frederick asked O'Malley about his flashy red Corvette? Do you think he sold it so he could purchase a car similar to other nondescript vehicles in Carmel?"

"A distinct possibility." She grinned. "You should tell Dylan Summers what we've discovered. While you're at it, ask him whether anyone noticed someone driving an Acura in Gianna McKay's neighborhood Tuesday night."

I frowned. "He's going to be ticked off at me."

"Do it."

I obeyed and dialed him.

Summers answered with a grunt. "What surprising detail are you going to grace me with now, Emma?"

I didn't appreciate his flippancy, but I understood it. "I presume you have viewed all the footage from private security cameras for the night of the murder by now."

"We have."

"Did anyone notice a silver Acura in the McKay neighborhood?"

"I don't recall. Why?"

"O'Malley McKay drives one."

Summers cleared his throat. "You seem to have forgotten he was in the City that night. He has a solid alibi."

"Does he?" I summed up what we'd learned at the hotel.

He bellowed, "Dang it, Ms. Brennan, I've warned you to steer clear of this. Why are you—"

"Dylan." My grandmother snatched the cell phone out of my hand. "It's Lissa. Before you read my granddaughter the riot act, I'll have you know I was the one who suggested we come to the hotel to learn more."

Summers responded snappily. Nana Lissa cupped her mouth and the phone's microphone and rasped words I couldn't make out, but I heard Summers curse.

"Well, I never." Nana Lissa held the phone in front of her face and scowled at the dark screen. *Call ended.* "He's not pleased."

"No, really?" I grinned.

"He's worried we're poking a hornet's nest."

"O'Malley won't guess we came to the hotel unless he's here conducting business and sees us. We haven't given our names to anyone. I doubt the valet or clerk at reception will be able to describe us." I was dressed in dark clothing. My grandmother was in gray trousers and a gray silk blouse. We weren't clad in any garish Halloween garb that might make us particularly memorable. I glimpsed to my left. "Where do you think the restrooms are?"

Nana pointed to a sign. I hurried in that direction. I needed to relieve myself before driving back to Carmel.

I passed a housekeeping cart on the way to the facilities. The housekeeper, a woman in her thirties with dark hair and thick eyebrows, was consulting a chart clipped to the cart's handle.

"Hi." I smiled.

"Hello." She had a faint Eastern European accent, reminiscent of Ursula's.

I entered the restroom and paused when it dawned on me that I'd caught a familiar scent in the hall. I stepped out and inhaled. The scent had vanished. I spied the housekeeping cart farther down the way, but I didn't see the woman. There were no guest rooms on the first floor, but there were meeting rooms. I presumed she was tidying up one of them. I raced to the cart and drew in another breath.

Yes! The scent I'd detected was the same one I'd smelled at the murder scene. Sweet and fresh and similar to white musk, like the perfume on Gianna's bathroom counter.

I bent closer to the cart, searching for the source.

"What are you doing?" The housekeeper emerged from a room. She held a feather duster in one hand.

I wasn't intimidated. She couldn't clobber me with it. "Do you smell the sweet and fresh scent?" I waved a hand toward my nose, encouraging her to do the same. "It's coming from an item on your cart." I spotted Lysol and other cleansers and ruled them out.

"Do you mean this?" She pulled a box of dryer sheets from the lower shelf and held it out to me.

I lifted the box to my nose. Bingo! "Why do you carry these with you? You don't do the hotel laundry, too, do you?"

"No. My sister does. These I use for the baseboards." She took the box from me. "They are good dusters and excellent for warding off bugs."

I remembered reading somewhere that dryer sheets contained the ingredient linalool, which could be found in plants like coriander and basil, plants that naturally repelled garden pests.

"My cousin puts one in his pocket when he goes fishing," she added. "Voilà. No pests. No gnats." She withdrew a sheet from the box and handed it to me. "Try. You'll see."

A notion came to me as I remembered the Monday night dinner and O'Malley saying he was immune to mosquitos, while Frederick was a bug buffet. O'Malley had claimed to have a secret weapon he employed to repel bugs when on the golf course. Could it possibly be dryer sheets? Did he, like the housekeeper's cousin, put them in his pocket? He'd been surveying golf courses Tuesday. Had he stuffed one into his trousers? Had he killed his wife and used the sheet to wipe incriminating fingerprints from doorknobs and keys, the action leaving a telltale scent?

I thanked the housekeeper, rejoined my grandmother, and reported what I'd discovered.

"Think about each detail." I counted them off on my fingertips. "Around four, O'Malley rang his friend the manager and told him he was under the weather, which established the first step of his alibi. In reality, he was in his car on his way to Carmel. No one would guess. It wasn't like he needed to prove he was in his room. Let's say he put a DO NOT DISTURB hanger on the door. He stole down the rear stairs and proceeded to a public parking lot. He might have worn a disguise so no one could identify him. He drove for two hours and parked around the corner from his home. He hoofed it from there, keeping to the shadows. He slipped into his house and, knowing his daughter's habits and confident she was listening to loud music with headphones on, he used the key to open the door to the bedroom he shared with Gianna. He found her in bed." I paused.

"How did he drug her with Rohypnol?" Nana asked.

I stared straight ahead until the scenario came to me. "He grabbed a tumbler from the kitchen and poured her a drink. Maybe an early toast to their upcoming anniversary. Once she drank, she drifted off to sleep . . . and he smothered her. No fuss, no muss. He washed the glass—not as pristinely as Gianna would have—and replaced it in the cupboard."

A pair of young boys in Batman and Robin costumes zoomed by us, quickly followed by anxious parents. "Stop, you two, or no trick-or-treating!" one yelled.

Hilarious giggling from the children ensued.

"Why kill her?" Nana Lissa asked. "What was his motive?"

"You heard them Monday night, constantly bickering."

"Married couples bicker. Papa and I did. Out of earshot."

"Case in point: O'Malley and Gianna didn't take their arguments to another room. They made a spectacle in front of others."

"They'd been married decades," she stated.

"Couples divorce after lengthy marriages. When Addison asked why they'd stayed together, he said, *Because your mother and I hate each other fifty percent of the time and tolerate each other the other fifty. True love.* Think about the way Gianna treated Addison at the dinner, ridiculing her and nitpicking about her weight and more. It angered her father. No, it incensed him."

A raucous knot of teens wearing matching black-and-orange T-shirts paraded past us. Each was carrying a gift bag. From the names on the bags, I guessed they'd visited Pier 39, the popular mall at the wharf where sea lions were a big draw.

"O'Malley adores his daughter like my dad adores me," I added when the noise subsided. "A Papa Bear can be very protective."

"It's a theory. Let's run it by Dylan."

"Not now. He's hot under the collar. Let's wait until we can provide him with facts."

"How do you propose to do so?" She arched an eyebrow. "You can't confront O'Malley."

"No, but I can return home, go online, and research all the parking facilities around this hotel. I'll put out feelers to see if anyone remembers him and his Acura. If he charged the parking fees, it would certainly call into question why he'd parked there and give the police evidence to run on. Agreed?"

She grinned. "I like the way your mind is attentive to details."

When we were driving along the 101 freeway somewhere near San José, Yoly rang me. I answered hands-free.

"What's up?"

"My sister needs me," she said, sounding out of breath. "I have to close early."

"Is she okay?" Her sister was one of the women who ran the

bakery and café located in the same courtyard as Open Your Imagination.

"It's our grandmother. She fainted. She's fine, but my sister is taking her to the hospital. I have to watch my niece." Yoly's sister recently had a baby. Her first. "I have to fetch her from the hospital."

"Go. Give them my love."

"One more thing. I'm so sorry to ask this of you. We were swamped this afternoon, so I wasn't able to put together the basket Dottie Summers ordered, and the specialty plant-based soy candles she requested won't arrive until nine tonight. The deliveryman's truck broke down. All the other items are sitting by the cash register ready to go. Could you accept the order and finalize the gift? Dottie is coming at eight a.m. to pick it up."

"Sure. Speaking of candles, when do I get to view some of your creations?"

"Soon. Next week. Good night."

I heard a familiar beeping in the background. She was setting the alarm.

"Night," I replied, and ended the call.

"Candles?" my grandmother asked.

I told her about Yoly's plan to become an artisan candlemaker.

"And give up a career as a massage therapist?"

"Yep. She didn't feel it was a good fit for her. I'm sad, because I thought she'd have been great, but a person has to do what feels right. I'm not worried. We have plenty of talented masseuses. At least Yoly is staying on at the shop in the meantime. When she has enough product, we'll sell some of them, and if her business soars—and I bet it will—we'll find a new salesperson."

"Have you replaced the receptionist yet?"

"No, but the ad has only been in the *Pine Cone* and online a nanosecond."

My cell phone rang. Again I answered hands-free.

"Hey, where are you?" Sierra asked, her voice crackly because of an iffy connection. "I just finished up the batter for tomorrow's muffins and thought I'd invite you and Nana over for a glass of wine."

"Nana is with me in the car. We're driving home from the City." I recapped our mission and findings in San Francisco.

"You really think Addison's father is guilty?" Sierra asked.

"It's a good possibility." I told her about the gift basket I needed to throw together. "I'll drop Nana by your place, go to the shop—it shouldn't take more than fifteen minutes tops—I'll return, feed Vivi, and come right up. All three of us should be able to track down the information we need for Detective Summers, don't you think?"

"Nana and I will get a jump-start on it."

Chapter 23

The exterior lights were illuminated at Courtyard of Peace, as they always were. We wanted it to be inviting to passersby. The pale green neon signs in the café, the gift shop, and the spa were on, as well, so people who weren't familiar with the business would become aware of it.

I parked on the street and hurried up the stairs to the gift shop. I zipped inside and strode to the alarm to disarm it. As promised, the items for Dottie's basket sat on the counter beside the cash register. When would the candles arrive? I checked my watch. It was already five after nine.

I moved to the laptop computer, pulled up the internet, and retrieved the link to track the package. The driver was *on the way*, last updated twenty minutes ago. Swell. I sure hoped Yoly was right about the estimated arrival and I didn't have to wait until midnight.

Assembling the items would be a cinch. Yoly had set out a vibrant, five-inch green agate geode on a stand, a green malachite energy stone, a small bottle of tea tree oil, two tea tree aromatherapy shower steamers, and a mint-green aventurine crystal bracelet—aventurine being a crystal meant to aid in the manifestation of wealth and prosperity.

I gathered white crinkled paper to line the basket Yoly had adorned with green ribbon.

The fairy-themed cuckoo clock hanging above the register—I'd purchased it on a whim a month ago at Courtney's fairy garden shop—chimed nine times and then, *boing*, the front door sprang open and out popped a wooden fairy. Even though I'd expected the darling creature to emerge, I flinched. I'd reacted the same way to jack-in-the-boxes as a girl.

Seconds later, I heard a creak. I peeked in the starburst mirror to the right of the clock, hoping to see the delivery guy entering. Wrong. It was O'Malley McKay. My breath snagged. Why was he here? Had someone at the hotel alerted him about Nana's and my inquiry? And why, why, why hadn't I locked the danged door? Ursula's premonition about a person wanting to do me harm suddenly felt probable.

I mustered an expression of nonchalance and turned to greet him. "Gee, hi, sorry, but we're closed. Come back tomorrow."

"I think not." His voice was strained. His face was etched with anger. He locked the door and strode with purpose between display tables. "You and I have business to discuss."

The delivery guy will arrive soon, I assured myself. *He'll see something is amiss.*

"You're mistaken. Our business is concluded," I said. "The check Gianna wrote me covered all expenses down to the penny."

"You know that's not what I'm talking about."

"You're not?"

Emma, you sound like a little girl. Find your voice.

But how could I, when my mouth was as dry as toast? I recalled a quote I'd stumbled upon last week and planned to post at the spa from Bryant McGill, an innovative thought leader who was seeking inspiration, health, freedom, and truth around the world. *Your calm mind is the ultimate weapon against your challenges. So relax.*

"Is it Addison?" I asked smoothly.

Good. Keep your cool.

It dawned on me that I could trigger the security alarm. Not the self-monitored kind. The real kind.

Slowly, so as not to alert O'Malley, I inched to the cash register and reached behind myself. Blindly, I felt under the counter and came upon the Panic button. I pressed it. How long it would take the security company to send a guard to investigate was anyone's guess.

"Really, you'll have to leave." I moistened my mouth with my tongue. "I don't allow employees to be in the shop alone after closing."

"With me here, you're not alone."

"You know what I mean. It's inappropriate."

"I'm not here to sexually assault you. I came to talk business. I waited outside your fourplex," he said, "but you were quick about dropping off your grandmother, so I followed you."

What kind of dolt was I? Why hadn't I noticed him tailing me?

I moved to the main sales counter and placed my palms on the glass. "What business do you want to discuss?"

When he grinned, he reminded me of a Doberman pinscher with its teeth bared. "Addison informed me that you consider me a suspect in my wife's murder."

OMG. The hotel hadn't reached out. Meaning he didn't know what I knew.

"No, I don't." I forced a chuckle. "She must have misunderstood me."

"She was distraught about it. " He slipped his hand into his pocket and rummaged around. Was he trying to grip a gun?

I gulped and proceeded. "Here's the story. See, we—Addison, her pals, and I—were chatting after their sound bath, and Addison said she learned her mother ordered an additional scented pillow, and the bunch of us were ruminating about why Gianna would've wanted a second one. Perhaps to give to a friend, Addison suggested. But Riley theorized you might have ordered it."

"Why would I purchase a pillow?"

"Exactly. But Riley wondered aloud if you'd used it as the murder weapon. Of course Addison protested. As did I."

"Enough with the lies. No more chitchat. The manager at the Hilltop Hotel reached out to me an hour ago."

Crud! He was clued in.

"Apparently, the receptionist told him a young woman fitting your description was asking about me earlier. The same woman was also seen chatting up the valet."

"It wasn't me." My denial sounded lame.

"I should have realized you were up to no good, Emma, the way you grilled Peyton, Wyatt, and Idha."

How did he know who I'd questioned? Perhaps he'd gone to the police, acting like a poor innocent, grieving husband, overwrought that his wife's murder hadn't been solved, and they'd spilled the beans.

"But given Addison's presumption," he went on, "I put two and two together."

Even from this distance, I could smell his garlicky breath and musky body odor. Ugh.

"Has anyone told you your curiosity will be the death of you?" he added.

"Actually, my father praises my curiosity, though my mother despises it."

"Can it!" He withdrew a gun from his pocket.

I recoiled. The pistol was small, compact. O'Malley glimpsed it as if surprised to see it in his hand and lowered his arm to his side.

The fact that he was mentally debating whether or not to shoot me was a good sign. So why was my heart pummeling my rib cage like angry waves slapping the sand?

"If Brady Cash hadn't saved you, we wouldn't be having this conversation," he said.

"You were the one in the Toyota truck wearing the Quasimodo mask?"

"The same. He is one of my favorite antiheros, often taking unconventional actions to achieve his purpose."

"Where did you get the truck?" I asked.

"I lived a misspent youth when I was a teen. Hot-wiring hot rods was my specialty. How I loved the rev of a V8 engine." He lifted the gun ever so slightly. No more than an inch. "This is a Sig Sauer P938, in case you were wondering."

"I wasn't." My tone was steady. A super spy couldn't have acted cooler.

"It's a solid weapon. Simple to conceal. Accurate. Reliable. Have you ever stared down the barrel of one?" He elevated it to shoulder height.

"Sir, you don't want to shoot me." My voice trembled, meaning my super-spy persona had turned tail. Swell.

"Don't I?"

"No. You're not a killer. What happened to your wife . . ." I began but stopped.

I couldn't say it was an accident. As my grandmother and I had determined, the murder had to have been premeditated. O'Malley had sold his red car so he could drive a commonplace silver sedan. He purposely did not use valet at the hotel in order to have a way to drive to Carmel without anyone seeing him leave. He purchased an additional pillow. He established a phony alibi.

"You've put it together, haven't you?" He smirked. "The timing of everything."

Why hadn't the delivery guy arrived yet? Or, at the very least, a security guard?

Forget about them, Emma. You're on your own.

Ducking down would do me no good. A bullet would blast through the sales counter, and if it didn't kill me, the resulting shards of glass might. I scanned the area for an object I could wield and spied a three-volume collection of crystal bibles on the counter to my right. The books were hefty but too cumbersome to wield as a weapon. A six-inch-long chakra wand lay inside the case directly in front of me, but it wouldn't be good, either, unless I was standing within arm's reach of O'Malley. In the grouping of decorative geodes on the counter to my left stood a silver-aqua Labradorite crystal obelisk about twelve inches tall. Of course if I hurled it, it wouldn't beat a speeding bullet, but if I acted first, I might make my accoster sidestep, giving me a chance to flee. I sidled toward it.

"What first put you on the track?" O'Malley asked. "My call to the hotel manager when you, your father, and I were chatting?"

I nodded. "I felt the urge to confirm you hadn't stayed at the hotel."

"Except I had."

"Correct. However, when I found out you didn't use valet as you were prone to do, I knew I was on to something. I dug deeper. If you didn't know, I've got a good nose. In my profession, I have to."

"Your point?"

"I was passing a housekeeping cart at the hotel when I picked up a scent I'd detected at the crime scene. I couldn't pin it down at the time."

"The pillows smelled like lavender."

"No, it was an additional scent. Sweet but fresh. I asked the housekeeper about the aroma. She pulled out a dryer sheet, and a light bulb went off in my head." I clicked my tongue. "Isn't it amazing how an item as unassuming as a dryer sheet could prove to be your undoing?"

"I'm not following," he said, but I could tell he was.

"The housekeeper shared a tidbit with me about dryer sheets and how they repel bugs. I recalled you saying you used to get bitten by bugs until you discovered a secret weapon. You carry dryer sheets with you when you golf, don't you?"

He didn't answer.

"I believe you had one in your pocket the night you murdered your wife, and you used it to wipe your fingerprints from whatever you touched. The bedroom key, the doorknob. It left a scent."

He grunted.

"When I learned about Gianna ordering an additional scented pillow, that was the kicker. You ordered it, not her. I think, after you read your sister-in-law's story, *Silent Suffocation,* you came up with the brilliant idea to smother your wife."

He stepped toward me.

I edged left. "My guess? You started planning when Addison showed you the party favor pillows she was going to give her happily divorced party guests. You set up a meeting in San Francisco to discuss the golf course plans to give yourself an alibi. On a previous occasion, you scouted out parking lots near the hotel and calculated the exact hotel exit door you could escape through without being seen."

He frowned.

"How'd you keep it from closing completely? A wad of gum? A clump of paper? It doesn't matter." I fanned the air. "What I can't figure out is how you could slink through the neighborhood by your house without anyone seeing you. After all, Peyton was lurking about, eager to make amends with Gianna, and Wyatt was doing laps on his bike, checking on Addison."

He looked puzzled.

"Yeah, they both lied about their alibis."

"If you must know, I parked my car in a neighbor's driveway—he and his wife always go leaf-peeping in the northeast in October—and I cut through a few backyards. I'm fit. In my high school days, in addition to being a golfer, I was a hurdler."

"Clever." I felt my cell phone buzz in my pocket. It was probably Sierra, wondering what was keeping me. "Tell me, why did you want Gianna dead? I mean, sure, you two argued, but weren't you used to it after all these years?"

He ran his free hand along the side of his hair and down his neck, as if relieved to finally reveal his motive. "Addison agreed to do everything Gianna asked her to do—leave her husband and make a living on her own. Even so, Gianna was vile to her. She yelled at her. She debased her. When I learned she was going to cut off Addison's trust fund out of spite, it was the last straw."

I inched closer to the obelisk. "You wanted to protect your daughter. You had to rescue her from the monster."

"Yes." He let out a soft mewl of pain.

If I didn't know he was a killer, I'd have felt sorry for him. Girding myself for battle, I lifted my chin. "I phoned Gianna Tuesday night. She was crying. She sounded distraught. I asked her why, but she wouldn't tell me. Did you tell her you were coming for her?"

"Hardly," he scoffed, his abject demeanor receding and his bravado returning. "I rang her as I was driving home and told her I wanted a divorce."

"*Ahh.* But she didn't want one, did she? She loved you."

"She said she treasured me." He coughed out a laugh. "Life was always about her. No one else mattered. Not me. Not Addison."

"You drugged her, didn't you?"

He arched an eyebrow. "Why would you presume I did?"

"She didn't struggle when you smothered her. She looked peaceful, her hands and arms at her sides. I mentioned those observations to the police. As it so happens, they found out Gianna was dosed with the generic for Rohypnol, the date rape drug."

He didn't deny it.

"You came home and fixed her a cocktail. I noticed a pair of crystal tumblers in the cupboard, one with remnants of lipstick on it. I mentioned it to Addison and Detective Summers. Addison found it strange. She said her mother was adamant about clean glassware." Something puzzled me. If O'Malley had told her he'd wanted a divorce, she wouldn't have had a drink to toast their happiness. Then the explanation came to me. "*Aha.*"

"*Aha* what?"

"You apologized to your wife for saying you wanted a divorce, and you begged her forgiveness. To celebrate, you asked her to join you in a toast to your future years of bliss. Eager to make up, delighted to believe everything would be better between you two, she drank the drug willingly. You smothered her, and when you were certain she was dead, you arranged her hair."

His shoulders sagged. "She had such lustrous locks. When we first started dating, I couldn't wait to run my hands through them." He sounded wistful. "I wanted her to look beautiful in death."

"If that were the case, why didn't you fix her lipstick after you smothered her?"

"Yes, it was sloppy of me, but I was out of time. I didn't want to get caught. Not by my daughter, of course. Once she gets into work mode, she doesn't budge for hours. But by someone else. A neighbor. A dog walker. People are always on the move in the neighborhood. I fled the way I came and was on the road by ten past six."

Before Peyton arrived.

"You drove to the hotel and dumped the pillow in a public trash bin."

"Good guess."

I doubted the police would be able to retrieve it a week later.

"At eight thirty, you went to the hotel bar looking wan. I imagine that wasn't hard to do after murdering your wife. You ordered a ginger ale and went to your room to wait for the phone call that was to come. But it didn't. Not Tuesday night. Because Addison didn't discover her mother was dead until Wednesday morning." I tilted my head. "Did you ever stop to think, thanks to all your machinations, you would implicate your daughter?"

"I didn't mean to. Lord knows I didn't. I figured someone would see her sitting at her desk and give her an alibi. When the police considered her a person of interest, I was beside myself, but after they released her, I knew she was in the clear, as was I."

We both fell silent. The *tick-tock* of the cuckoo clock was the only sound disturbing the hush.

Finally, O'Malley said, "I can't admit what I did, Emma."

"I know."

"I have to guard my daughter against losers like Wyatt. If he wheedles his way back into her life . . ." Tears filled his eyes. "If he does, I have to be there for her. I can't leave her to fend for herself. Which means, my dear girl, I can't let you live. You would feel obligated to reveal everything to the police." He thrust the gun forward, finger poised on the trigger.

"Wait, O'Malley." I raised both hands, as if they might stop a bullet. "I'm not going to tell anyone."

He guffawed. "Emma, of course you will. You're exactly like your grandmother, full of righteousness and grit."

What a good description of her, and yes, of me, as well.

"No, I can't let you live." He narrowed his gaze. "You wouldn't be able to bear seeing me or Addison day in and day out, knowing I got away with murder."

"You could move to another state," I said. "Both of you. Change your names. Forge new identities. I won't search for you." I lowered my hands and slid my fingers along the counter. As if to remove dust from it. To distract him from realizing I was edging to the left. Toward the obelisk. "You can get a fresh start. Addison can work anywhere. So can you."

"Not in the golf world. My career would be over."

"Addison will receive the trust fund after all. You'll be flush." Unless she wouldn't be allowed to tap into it because she was on the run with a fugitive. Pushing the thought aside, I wrapped my fingers around the base of the obelisk. "You could reinvent yourself. How about writing a novel? Or why don't you become a painter?"

"I can't draw stick figures." He chuckled sadly at his wry humor.

At the same time, I hoisted the obelisk and hurled it at him. He dodged right and teetered, but he didn't go down. Drat! Given his size, I couldn't run past him to the exit.

"Bad move," he warned.

Banking on the element of surprise—what idiot would attempt to assault her enemy twice in a matter of seconds?—I grabbed a celestite geode hefty enough to be a bookend and raced around the sales counter.

Deflect. Redirect.

He fired, missing wide.

On impulse, I disregarded Zane's advice and confronted with

power. I rammed into O'Malley with the geode. He stumbled, flailed for balance, and lost hold of the gun. It fell to the floor.

I sprinted toward the exit, unlocked the front door, whipped it open, and ran headlong into a guy in a brown uniform carrying a large package. We both wheezed. I reeled backward.

"Sorry, ma'am," he said. "Delivery for Aroma Wellness."

On his heels appeared Officer Rodriguez. "Emma, your grandmother touched base. She's concerned. You aren't answering your—"

"Officer, O'Malley McKay is reaching for his gun!" I screamed.

She pulled hers from her holster and peered past me and the deliveryman. "Don't move, sir." She aimed at O'Malley, who was scrambling on the floor. "I said, hold it. Do not touch the weapon." She eyed me. "What's going on?"

"He murdered his wife."

Chapter 24

"Don't move, Mr. McKay," Rodriguez repeated. She rounded the deliveryman and me and strode farther into the shop, gun aimed at O'Malley.

He didn't budge.

Seconds later, a security guard hurried into the shop and scooted to a halt. "Sorry for the delay, Ms. Brennan." I recognized him. He was one of the guys who'd installed the alarm system. "Trouble with my car battery. What's the—" He took in Rodriguez and her drawn weapon and quickly apologized while hooking his thumb over his shoulder. "I'll stand outside, Officer, if you need any assistance."

"Thank you," she said. "Go on, Emma. Explain."

My knees felt wobbly, but I wrapped my arms around my torso to steady myself and stammered through my summary—O'Malley swapping out his red car for a silver one, parking in an off-site lot, the dryer sheet clue, the motive to protect his one and only daughter, the timeline.

O'Malley tried to interrupt twice, but Rodriguez shut him down both times.

The receiver affixed by Velcro to Rodriguez's shoulder crackled. Keeping her eye on O'Malley, she pulled it off and gave the department dispatcher an update as to her whereabouts.

Soon after, a siren whooped outside. Detective Summers strode in, followed by a lanky redheaded male officer. While Rodriguez provided Summers with a recap of my theory, the other officer retrieved the gun.

When Rodriguez concluded, Summers made a beeline for O'Malley and launched into a recitation of his rights.

"Detective," I said, when he finished, "can you trace where Mr. McKay used his phone in the past week?"

"Why?"

"I think it will show he was in his car when he contacted the hotel manager to tell him that he was sick in his room. It will be one more piece of evidence establishing he was already on his way to Carmel."

"We'll get a warrant," Summers said. "On your feet, Mr. McKay."

O'Malley didn't resist. The redheaded officer cuffed him and guided him outside.

Summers approached me. "Well, well, Ms. Brennan. I suppose this is another feather in your investigating cap."

I stiffened. "It's Emma, please, sir."

"Relax. I'm not going to chastise you. You did good, despite my warnings to steer clear."

"I kept my distance after your last one."

"Did you?" Summers arched an eyebrow.

Officer Rodriguez, who'd remained in the shop, watched us like a referee at a tennis match.

"No"—I shifted feet—"come to think of it, I didn't. I meant to, but when I was on my way to the hotel restroom, I caught the scent of the dryer-sheet fragrance, which led to a slew of suppositions.

Nana Lissa told me to call you a second time, but I didn't think we had enough. I wanted to confirm the parking lot hypothesis."

"At least own up to how foolish you've been," he said. "Sticking your nose into things and stirring up a hornet's nest."

Again with the analogy? I bridled. "I wasn't foolish, sir. I'm not reckless. I caught the scent of something familiar. I acted. Time was of the essence."

"*Essence*?" He regarded me slyly. "Are you attempting a pun?"

"Unintentional."

"A double entendre then?"

"No, sir, I—" I halted. Judging by his smirk, he was baiting me. "Anyway, after learning about the dryer sheets, I didn't pursue Mr. McKay. I didn't call him. Didn't accuse him. I didn't act rashly. I drove directly to Carmel, and I was intending on contacting you the moment I figured out if the parking lot factor could be used as evidence."

"Why wait so long? You've reached out immediately in the past." He cocked his head.

"Because you barked at my grandmother."

"I didn't bark," he muttered.

Officer Rodriguez stifled a snicker.

Summers scowled. "Give Officer Rodriguez your statement, Emma, and then go home. I'll deal with you tomorrow."

"Yes, sir. Oh, and Detective, I hope things work out between you and your fiancée."

"How do you know—" He cut a sharp look at Rodriguez.

"I didn't say a word," she said without guile. If I didn't know better, I'd have believed her.

As he marched out, my cousin and my grandmother rushed in.

A week later, at the happily divorced party, which we'd set up on the courtyard patio, I eyed Addison and her friends standing beside the burbling fountain beneath a banner *Congratulations, Addison, on your brave decision!* On a nearby table sat a number of wrapped gifts.

The ladies, clad in the same witch hats they'd worn on the first day of their treatments, were sipping champagne. Though Addison was shocked by her father's admission and understood the passion behind his motive, she accepted the end result—prison. However, she confided to me that she didn't blame him as much as she held her mother accountable for her ruinous behavior.

Sierra circled the patio, offering appetizers. Nana Lissa, Meryl, and Yoly were attending to the beverage table. Knowing I wasn't needed, I joined Addison and her pals.

"Open it, Adds!" Riley waved to a box packaged in orange gift wrap.

Addison tore off the wrapping. Inside was a small cast-iron cauldron. She burst out laughing.

"What's that for?" I asked her.

"A small and very legal fire," Riley said. "I checked with the fire department. Addison, where's the magic wand I gave you earlier?"

Addison pulled a barbecue-type lighter from her tote bag.

Riley said, "Everyone, put in your spell papers one at a time."

"Spell papers?" I didn't have a clue what she was talking about.

Addison said, "You'll see. Riley"—she playfully flicked her friend on the shoulder—"you start."

Riley pulled a scrolled white sheet of paper from her purse. She held it overhead and incanted, "May your ex-husband vanish from your life like my mother's cooking skills—poof!" She plopped it into the cauldron.

The others laughed.

"Tatiana, you're next," Addison commanded.

Tatiana pulled a scrolled sheet of white paper and scissors from her purse. "Let's turn *happily ever after* into *happily never after*—with a sprinkle of confetti!" She shredded the paper and dumped it into the cauldron.

"Cara, your turn." Addison waved the lighter.

Cara couldn't stop giggling as she removed her scroll of paper from her purse. "With this charm, we bid adieu to Wyatt. May he find a new partner, preferably someone who will appreciate his ASPD personality. Not." She plunked the paper on top of the others.

"Now, you." Riley pointed at Addison.

Gleefully, she produced her scroll and unfurled it. Reading like a preacher at a revival meeting, she intoned, "I conjure this spell to bring about my freedom—like a cat escaping bathtime!" She tossed hers into the cauldron.

Raucous laughter ensued.

"Ignite it, witch!" Riley ordered. She set down her champagne glass, clasped my hand, and told the others to link up.

The four of us formed a circle around Addison and the table. Addison clicked on her lighter and ignited the paper. A stream of fire rose from the cauldron and quickly subsided. As it did, she rummaged in her purse, retrieved her wedding band, and tossed it into the cauldron.

"What are you doing?" I gasped.

She grinned. "When the ring melts down, I can sell the gold. No more memories. No more chains binding me to the past. A fresh start."

After the flame safely destroyed the spell papers, we released hands.

"How is Wyatt?" I asked Addison.

"He's fine. He's entering therapy. Serious therapy."

"Shock therapy, I hope," Riley gibed.

"No," Addison said. "It won't help with ASPD. He's going for mentalization-based treatment in San Francisco. He's moving there. He says everyone rides bikes in the City. It will help expand his business."

"You spoke to him?" I asked.

"Briefly, at Mother's funeral. He accepted that our marriage was over and filled me in on the rest. Now, I am truly free to become a better version of myself."

I felt equally free. I planned to focus on growing my business and bringing peace and harmony to my clientele . . . as well as to myself.

So far, Aroma Wellness hadn't suffered any loss of business due to the murder or the face-off between me and O'Malley in the gift shop. If anything, customers and clients were arriving in droves to get the scoop.

"My aunt and uncle are going for therapy, too," Addison went on. "My uncle says he wants to find his backbone. I joked he might have to consult an orthopedist for that."

Riley smacked her friend on the arm. "Good one."

"Aunt Idha told me Nadal is going to see a psychiatrist, too," Addison said. "He may be a kleptomaniac, but supposedly it's a fixable disease as long as he stays on board with the program."

"Speaking of sons," I said, "my grandmother told me Peyton is moving to Los Angeles to be near hers."

"Brilliant." Addison applauded. "She's always wanted Reginald to return home to Carmel, but his life isn't here. He really did want to become a comedian. He wasn't bad. Maybe with her support, he can give up the assistant agent gig and try again. Sure, she might stifle him at first, but ultimately, I think she'll get so busy as a Realtor she won't have enough time to smother him. In fact, she might enjoy selling multimillion-dollar mansions in Beverly Hills, and he might discover lots of funny mom-related material."

"Mother!" Kate appeared at the top of the stairs.

My father trailed her, which stunned me. Had she convinced him to stay in town and work things out? *No. Not possible. Do not dream, Emma.*

A split second later, an elegant Asian woman came into view. In her snug-fitting blue sarong-style dress, she did not strike me as an eco-scientist. Of course that was narrow-minded of me. Brainy women could be beauties. Was she the reason Dad was sticking around? For how long?

I observed Kate again and realized she hadn't noticed they were behind her. She made a beeline for my grandmother at the beverage table.

My father ambled to me. "Baby doll, I'd like you to meet—"

"Dad, would you stop calling me that?" I pulled a face. "I'm a grown woman." Sure, I liked the term when it was just the two of us, but not in a crowd.

He grinned. "I wondered when the time would come. May I call you *sweetheart*?"

I nodded.

"Sweetheart, I'd like you to meet Hana."

She nodded demurely and clasped my hand. "It's lovely to meet you."

Her Midwestern accent surprised me. Given her appearance, I'd thought she'd been born and raised in Asia. Bad me, again. *Do not presume.*

"Where are you from originally?" I asked.

"Chicago, but after attending Stanford, I opted to stay in California."

The three of us chatted about the charm of living on the West Coast for a few minutes until I begged off, eager to wrap up the celebration, but not before I made my father agree to have coffee with me so he could bring me up to speed.

"Emma!" a man called.

I turned and spied Detective Summers and Teresa Rodriguez's sister. Her hand was clasping his elbow. Had they reunited?

"Tell her," the woman prompted.

I eyed the detective, waiting.

"I'm happy you're safe," he murmured.

"Ditto." I grinned.

"As am I," Kate interjected, sidling to my side with a glass of champagne in hand. "But this has got to stop, Emma."

"This?"

"Investigating."

"I thought you were going to say my business." I brandished a hand to encompass the scope of it.

"Well, yes, of course. It's implied." Kate rubbed the underside of her nose. "I don't know any professors who are receiving death threats and hurling obelisks at killers. All of it is your grandmother's fault. She prodded you into this."

"Aunt Kate, stop." Sierra joined our circle. "Nana doesn't goad either of us into doing anything."

"Who made Emma drive to San Francisco and visit the hotel, *hmm*?" Kate demanded.

"Cut it out, Kate." Nana Lissa joined our group. "Your daughter has a good head on her shoulders. She doesn't take chances. She thinks things through. Why, did you see how organized the board—" She stopped short, her cheeks flaming red.

"Not again," Kate moaned. "Don't tell me you have another murder board in your office!"

Apparently, she hadn't considered the company we were keeping before blurting out her reproach. *Thanks, Mom.*

Summers cut me a stern glance. "Murder board?"

"Look, Detective Summers, I promise going forward—"

He held up a hand. "Save it. Don't make promises you can't keep, Emma."

"I can keep this one. What are the odds I'll stumble across another dead body in my lifetime?"

"You never know," Nana Lissa said.

Her grim tone made me uneasy.

Eager to end this conversation, I spun around and ran headlong into Jason Sampson, the wiry twenty-one-year-old who had wrestled in high school and served as our former receptionist.

"Hiya, Emma." He braced me and held me at arm's length.

Meryl raced to him. "You're here!"

"What do you mean, *You're here*?" I echoed.

"For the job. The position." Meryl flapped both hands. "He saw the ad."

Jason raked his shoulder-length hair with his fingers. "The writing job didn't pan out." He'd quit to write a true-crime story of a murderer in a town near San José. "It turned out the guy didn't do it, a woman did, so the people paying me decided to go with a female writer to get that perspective. It didn't matter that I'm gay and have a similar slant." He guffawed. "It's cool. I like it better in Carmel. So . . . will you hire me?" He slung an arm around Meryl. "I miss your corny jokes."

"They're not corny," she mock-frowned.

"They're not good," he taunted.

She punched him.

"Yes!" I cheered softly. "Yes. Thank you. Hired. When can you start?"

RECIPES

Banana Protein Muffins, Regular and Gluten-free

Blueberry Banana Acai Smoothie

Double-Chocolate Chip Cookies, Regular and Gluten-free

Kale Leek Mushroom Quiche

Pumpkin Delight Smoothie

Pumpkin Oatmeal Muffins, Regular and Gluten-free

Banana Protein Muffins

From Sierra:

This recipe does not require any oil or butter. It binds because of the eggs, honey, and other essential ingredients. They are delicious and moist. The protein powder gives them an extra plus of being "good for you." They do not freeze well, though. Eat soon.

(Yield: 10–12 muffins)

2 bananas, mashed
2 eggs
¼ cup honey
2 tablespoons water
1 teaspoon vanilla extract
1 cup all-purpose flour
½ cup protein powder, vanilla flavored
2 teaspoons baking powder
½ teaspoon cinnamon
¼ teaspoon salt
½ cup chocolate or carob chips

Preheat the oven to 350 degrees F. Line a muffin tin with 12 liners and set aside. I like to spray the liners with oil because the protein powder (or any gluten-free batter) can stick to the liners.

In a large bowl, whisk together the mashed bananas, eggs, honey, water, and vanilla extract.

Add in the all-purpose flour, protein powder, baking powder, cinnamon, and salt. Mix well.

Stir in the chocolate chips or carob chips.

Scoop the batter into the liners. If desired, add a few extra chocolate chips to the tops.

Bake 18–22 minutes until a toothpick comes out clean. Remove from the oven and cool on a rack for at least 20 minutes.

Banana Protein Muffins

(Gluten-free version)

(Yield: 10–12 muffins)

2 bananas, mashed
2 eggs
¼ cup honey
2 tablespoons water
1 teaspoon vanilla extract
½ cup almond flour
½ cup sweet rice flour
½ cup protein powder, vanilla flavored
2 teaspoons baking powder
1 tablespoon whey powder
½ teaspoon cinnamon
¼ teaspoon salt
½ cup chocolate or carob chips

Preheat the oven to 350 degrees F. Line a muffin tin with 12 liners and set aside. I like to spray the liners with oil because the protein powder (or any gluten-free batter) can stick to the liners.

In a large bowl, whisk together the mashed bananas, eggs, honey, water, and vanilla extract.

Add in the almond flour, sweet rice flour, protein powder, baking powder, whey powder, cinnamon, and salt. Mix well.

Stir in the chocolate chips or carob chips.

Scoop the batter into the liners. If desired, add a few extra chocolate chips to the tops.

Bake 18–22 minutes until a toothpick comes out clean. Remove from the oven and cool on a rack for at least 20 minutes.

Blueberry Banana Acai Smoothie

From Sierra:

Here's a tip. To freeze a banana, you need to remove it from its peel. So cover it tightly in plastic wrap and then freeze. Why use frozen fruit? Because it helps create a chillier smoothie. Why have this smoothie? Because the acai is super food and the protein powder is power food. A double whammy. Enjoy.

(Yield: 2 8-ounce smoothies)

8 ounces acai juice
1 banana, frozen and diced *Note: remove from peel before freezing
½ cup blueberries
¼ cup milk, your choice
2 tablespoons protein powder, vanilla flavored
1 cup crushed ice cubes

Place all ingredients in a powerful blender and process until smooth.

Double-Chocolate Chip Cookies

From Emma:

These aren't exactly wholesome *because of the sugar, but honestly, who can pass up a good chocolate cookie? So I convinced Sierra to offer them at Aroma Café. We want our customers healthy but also satisfied. The occasional splurge is okay. This recipe looks complicated, but it's not. If you're a new baker, divide the recipe into halves—the first half liquid ingredients (up to the vanilla extract) and the second half dry ingredients, starting with the flour, and not including the chocolate chips. The goodness of having double the chocolate will make you salivate. Look for the gluten-free version below.*

(Yield: 18–20)

½ cup unsalted butter, room temperature
½ cup granulated sugar
½ cup dark brown sugar, packed
1 large egg, room temperature
2 tablespoons milk
1 teaspoon vanilla extract
1 cup flour
½ cup + 2 tablespoons dark cocoa powder
1 teaspoon baking soda
¼ teaspoon salt
1½ cups semisweet chocolate chips

In a large bowl, combine the butter and sugars. Beat together on medium-high speed until light and fluffy, 2–3 minutes. Blend in the egg, milk, and vanilla, and scrape down the bowl if needed.

In a separate bowl, whisk together the flour, cocoa powder—remember the extra 2 tablespoons—baking soda, and salt.

Add the dry ingredients to the wet ingredients and mix until incorporated. Fold in the chocolate chips.

Refrigerate the mixture for 2 hours.

When ready, preheat oven to 350 degrees F. Line 2 baking sheets with parchment paper. Roll about 2 tablespoons of dough into a ball and place on the baking sheet. Flatten slightly. They should be far apart. They will spread.

Bake at 350° F for 10–11 minutes. Remove from oven. Let cookies cool on the baking sheets for about 5 minutes, then transfer to a wire rack to cool completely.

Keep in a tightly sealed container. Individual cookies may be frozen if covered in plastic wrap and sealed well.

Double-Chocolate Chip Cookies

(Gluten-free version)

(Yield: 18–20)

½ cup unsalted butter, room temperature
½ cup granulated sugar
½ cup dark brown sugar, packed
1 large egg, room temperature
2 tablespoons milk
1 teaspoon vanilla extract
1 cup gluten-free flour
1 tablespoon whey powder
¼ teaspoon xanthan gum
½ cup + 2 tablespoons dark cocoa powder
1 teaspoon baking soda
¼ teaspoon salt
1½ cups semisweet chocolate chips

In a large bowl, combine the butter and sugars. Beat together on medium-high speed until light and fluffy, 2–3 minutes. Blend in the egg, milk, and vanilla, and scrape down the bowl if needed.

In a separate bowl, whisk together the gluten-free flour, whey powder, xanthan gum, dark cocoa powder—remember the extra 2 tablespoons—baking soda, and salt.

Add the dry ingredients to the wet ingredients and mix until incorporated. Fold in the chocolate chips.

Refrigerate the mixture for 2 hours.

When ready, preheat oven to 350 degrees F. Line 2 baking sheets with parchment paper. Roll about 2 tablespoons of dough into a ball and place on the baking sheet. Flatten slightly. They should be far apart. They will spread.

Bake at 350° F for 10–11 minutes. Remove from oven. Let cookies cool on the baking sheets for about 5 minutes, then transfer to a wire rack to cool completely.

Keep in a tightly sealed container. Individual cookies may be frozen if covered in plastic wrap and sealed well.

Kale Leek Mushroom Quiche

From Sierra:

There's almost nothing more soothing than a slice of quiche. I love the savory blend of vegetables and cheese, and the creamy texture is delicious. Kale, as many of you might know, contains antioxidants that can help reduce inflammation and may lower the risk of heart disease, Alzheimer's, and some cancers. It's also high in fiber.

(Yield: 1 quiche, 6 servings)

2 large leeks, whites only
2 cups chopped kale
¼ cup portobella or shitake mushrooms, rinsed and diced
2 tablespoons olive oil
5 eggs
⅓ cup milk
½ teaspoon salt
½ teaspoon white pepper
½ teaspoon cayenne pepper
2 teaspoons prepared mustard
1 cup grated Gruyère cheese
9-inch pie crust (regular or gluten-free; store bought is fine)

Rinse leeks and slice off the green ends. Discard and use only the whites. Chop the whites. Place the leeks and olive oil in a sauté pan and cook over medium heat about 3 minutes.

Add the chopped kale and diced shitake mushrooms, and sauté about 2–3 minutes more. Remove sauté pan from heat and allow the vegetables to cool slightly.

In a medium bowl, whisk the eggs, milk, and spices. Mix in the grated Gruyère cheese.

Place cooked kale, leeks, and shitake mushrooms in pie crust. Pour egg-cheese mixture over.

Bake in a 375 degree oven for 35–45 minutes.

Pumpkin Delight Smoothie

From Sierra:

'Tis the season to enjoy lots of pumpkin treats. This smoothie does not disappoint. The maple syrup is such a delicious addition. While not truly a health food, because of its sugar content, maple syrup contains beneficial minerals, making it slightly better for you than refined sugar. All things in moderation, right?

(Yield: 1 smoothie)

1 cup crushed ice
⅓ cup pumpkin puree (not pumpkin pie mix)
1 banana, diced
⅓ cup plain, full-fat Greek yogurt
½ tablespoon maple syrup
½ cup milk (may be regular, almond, or oat milk)
¾ teaspoon pumpkin pie spice or a mixture of cinnamon, ginger, and clove spices
½ tablespoon natural almond butter
1 tablespoon vanilla-flavored protein powder

Add all of the ingredients to a blender and whisk until smooth.

Pumpkin Oatmeal Muffins

From Nana Lissa:

I remember when Sierra and Emma were girls and I taught them to bake. Flour was everywhere. Giggles abounded. One of their favorites things to make were muffins. They enjoyed putting the paper liners into the tins. The texture of these muffins is what makes them special. Pumpkin mixes well with oatmeal.

(Yield: 12 muffins)

⅓ cup melted coconut oil
½ cup maple syrup
2 eggs, room temperature
1 cup pumpkin puree (not pumpkin pie mix)
¼ cup milk (may use almond or oat milk)
1 teaspoon ground cinnamon
½ teaspoon ground ginger
¼ teaspoon ground nutmeg
¼ teaspoon ground allspice
1 teaspoon baking soda
1 teaspoon vanilla extract
½ teaspoon salt
1¾ cup flour
1 teaspoon baking powder
⅓ cup quick-cooking oats
½ cup regular or golden raisins, if desired
2 teaspoons raw sugar

Preheat oven to 325 degrees F. Grease a 12-muffin pan with non-stick cooking spray and fill with liners.

In a large bowl, beat the coconut oil and maple syrup. Add the eggs and beat well. Add the pumpkin puree, milk, spices, baking soda, vanilla extract, and salt and beat again.

In a separate bowl mix the flour, baking powder, and oats.

Add the flour mixture to the pumpkin mixture and blend. It will look a tad lumpy. If desired, add raisins and stir well.

Divide the batter between the muffin liners. Sprinkle the tops with the raw sugar.

Bake for 22–25 minutes or until a toothpick comes out clean.

Cool the muffins completely.

They'll keep for 2–3 days at room temp. Otherwise, refrigerate. They may be frozen if individually covered with plastic wrap.

Pumpkin Oatmeal Muffins

(Gluten-free version)

(Yield: 12 muffins)

⅓ cup melted coconut oil
½ cup maple syrup
2 eggs, room temperature
1 cup pumpkin puree (not pumpkin pie mix)
¼ cup milk (may use almond or oat milk)
1 teaspoon ground cinnamon
½ teaspoon ground ginger
¼ teaspoon ground nutmeg
¼ teaspoon ground allspice
1 teaspoon baking soda
1 teaspoon vanilla extract
½ teaspoon salt
1¾ cup gluten-free flour (I like a sweet rice flour/tapioca starch blend)
1 tablespoon whey powder
1 teaspoon baking powder
1 tablespoon psyllium husk (if you have it)
½ teaspoon xanthan gum
⅓ cup gluten-free quick-cooking oats
½ cup regular or golden raisins, if desired
2 teaspoons raw sugar

Preheat oven to 325 degrees F. Grease a 12-muffin pan with nonstick cooking spray and fill with liners. Note: For gluten-free muffins, it helps to spray the inside of the muffin liner, too. The batter tends to stick.

In a large bowl, beat the coconut oil and maple syrup. Add the eggs and beat well. Add the pumpkin puree, milk, spices, baking soda, vanilla extract, and salt and beat again.

In a separate bowl mix the gluten-free flour, whey powder, baking powder, psyllium husk, xanthan gum, and oats.

Add the flour mixture to the pumpkin mixture and blend. It will look a tad lumpy. If desired, add raisins and stir well.

Divide the batter between the muffin liners. Sprinkle the tops with the raw sugar.

Bake for 22–25 minutes or until a toothpick comes out clean.

Cool the muffins completely.

They'll keep for 2–3 days at room temp. Otherwise, refrigerate. They may be frozen if individually covered with plastic wrap.

Acknowledgments

Whenever I write the acknowledgments, it's daunting, because so many have helped me on this journey, and I don't want to forget one name. But I will. I just hope it's not *you*.

Thank you to my family and friends for all your encouragement. You have cheered me on and helped me face the ups and downs of the publishing business. What a roller-coaster ride, right?

Thank you to my talented author friend, Hannah Dennison, for your words of wisdom and encouragement. Thank you to my PlotHatcher pals: Krista Davis, Janet Bolin (Ginger Bolton), Kaye George (Janet Cantrell), Marilyn Levinson (Allison Brook), Peg Cochran (Margaret Loudon), and Janet Koch (Laura Alden, Laurie Cass). I adore you.

Thanks to those who have helped make the second book in the Aroma Wellness mysteries come to fruition: my publisher, Kensington Books; my editor, Elizabeth Trout; my copy editor, Randy Ladenheim-Gil; my agent, Jill Marsal; and my cover artist, Michele Grant. Thank you to my clever map artist, Melinda Nash. And many thanks to my stalwart supporter and sister, Kimberley Greene.

Last but not least, thank you to my early readers and reviewers. Thank you to all the bloggers who enjoy reviewing cozies. Thanks to Dru Ann Love and Lori Caswell for leading the charge with blogs for readers. You are the best. Thank you, librarians, teachers, and bookstore owners. I hope you enjoy the fragrant world of an enlightened entrepreneur in Carmel-by-the-Sea. And may you encounter a fairy at least once in your lifetime.